The Two Sams

Men of the West

by
F. M. Worden

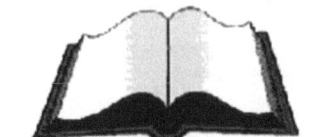

CCB Publishing
British Columbia, Canada

The Two Sams: Men of the West

Copyright ©2009 by F. M. Worden
ISBN-13   978-1-926585-16-1
First Edition

Library and Archives Canada Cataloguing in Publication

Worden, F. M., 1930-
The two Sams: men of the west / written by F. M. Worden – 3rd ed.
ISBN 978-1-926585-16-1
I. Title.
PS3623.O74 T96 2009   813.6   C2009-900632-4

Publisher: CCB Publishing
              British Columbia, Canada
              www.ccbpublishing.com

An American story of a father and son in the 1800's, making their way in the American West.

Contents

Chapter 1

Sam the Father

Jess Duncan, was born in the colony of Virginia in the year 1758 to an Irish and Scottish family. He was the third son of a religious father and mother, he had five brothers and one sister.

At seventeen, Jess joined the Army of northern Virginia and went to war with General George Washington. When the Revolutionary War ended in 1783, upon returning home, he married his boyhood sweetheart, a Pennsylvania born, Dutch girl named, Greta Miller.

Jess took his new bride and moved to the Tennessee Valley to claim the land, one hundred and sixty acres, he received as a bonus for fighting in the war. On the claim, the two built a farm with their own bare hands and a mule. The work was hard. It was not easy for Greta to conceive or bear children. Jess couldn't understand it, he wanted a big family. Finally a son was born in the year of 1788, he was named David, after David in the bible who became a king. It took four more years before another son was born, he was named Samuel, after the man who had God's ear in the bible.

In the years that followed, the farming was hard and they didn't prosper too well. Jess took to drinking. When he had too much, he was mean and bad tempered, he took the bad times out on David and David in turn took it out on Sam.

At fourteen young Sam had enough of his brother's bad

treatment. He told his Ma, "I'm gonna go west, I want-a be my own man." His Ma understood how he felt. She told him, if that's what he really wanted, he should go. He told his Ma how much he loved her and his Pa too but he had to go on his own. He was a big strapping boy. Almost six feet tall and weighing a hundred and sixty pounds. He told his Ma, "Don't be a fret-en. I can take care of myself." She wanted to stop him but she knew in her heart it would be best for him to go find what he was looking for.

After midnight, on a spring morning, Sam took his leave. With only a burlap sack of food his Ma had fixed, a blanket, a knife and the clothes on his back, he started walking west. By walking and hitching rides, he reached the town of Memphis, a port town on the Mississippi River.

There he found a job on the docks as a roustabout. He met lots of people that travel the river. He heard of places up north and of men going west to find their fortunes. He soon had an itch to see the places he was hearing about. Somehow the feeling he had, had to be answered. He quit the docks and got a job on a flat boat going north up the Mississippi River.

At the town of St. Louis, he looked for work and found a job with Hawkin the gun maker. Jake Hawkin was a man who had just started to make flint fired rifles, the first gun makers in St. Louis. The Hawkin gun shop was less then a year old when Sam went to work. Jake Hawkin found that Sam had a good way with wood. He was so good he was put to work making gun stocks, he was given a bed in a room in back of the shop. He was also the night watchman of the shop.

Sam made friends easily, the trappers and mountain men that purchased guns talked of the wonders of the western mountains and how trapping was a great way to make money. Sam got the itch to go take a look.

After a year of stock making Sam told Jake he just had to

go and see the mountains. Jake Hawkin knew how he felt. He told Sam, "Boy, if I was younger, I'd go with you, I hate to lose you but I understand. As a bonus I'm giving you the best rifle that we have ever made."

It was a Hawkin fifty caliber Kentucky long rifle. With it, he was given a patch box, a ball pouch, extra flints and a powder horn. Sam was told a man by the name of Daniels, a packer who traveled west as a freighter with a pack mule train, needed help. He was in Franklin, Missouri a small town by the Missouri River west of St. Louis.

Sam packed his belongings in a sack and he walked the miles to Franklin. There he found the packer Daniels. He hired on as a pack saddle packer of mules. Daniels was known as the mule man, a rather cantankerous individual who got his disposition from his mules.

When there were enough customers for supplies to make a trip, the outfit would be on the trail for Taos, in the New Mexico Territory. In less than a month a train was made up and ready to go west.

Sam was on his way to Taos with his plans to go on to the town of Santa Fe the jumping off place for mountain men.

On the way to Taos, Sam's duty was to saddle, pack, feed and take care of 10 mules. He had to unpack and unsaddle every night, gather wood for the camp fires and tend the same. Some times he was asked to cook and help the other drovers. All the time he had to walk and see that his charges stayed in line with the train. Not a very easy job most of the time.

Sam and the train reached Taos after weeks on the trail. He was so tired and worn out it took several days for him to be feeling himself again. He had packed and unpacked 10 mules every morning and every evening for almost two months.

As soon as the train arrived at Taos, he went to the mule man and asked for his pay. He was told, "As soon as I'm paid, you'll gets yours." The man seemed angry that this boy wanted to be paid. It took several days of asking before Sam was paid. One hundred and ten dollars in gold coins.

The mule man told him, "We start for Franklin in two days, be ready." Sam tells him, "I'm gonna quit. I ain't gonna go back with you." "Ha" says the mule man, "You kin't stays here. These Mex's ain't gonna like you's stay-n here. You best come back with us. I'll give you's a mule to ride all the way back to Franklin."

Sam told him, "As soon as I get rested, I Gotta go west, I want-a be a trapper and mountain man." The mule man started laughing and tells him that all he's gonna get is his hair lifted by some young Indian buck. "He'll hang your scalp on his belt. The young ones have to kill to become a warrior. You's is just the ticket for one of them bucks to make himself a big warrior." Sam said he had to try. "If that's the way it's gonna be, so be it."

His mind was made up. He camped out in the hills north of Taos and rested until he felt strong enough to go on. Then he started asking people if they knew where he could find some mountain men. Finally a friendly Mexican told him in his broken English, "Go see Kit Carson. He's a mountain man, he would know."

Sam was shown the house where Kit Carson lived. He knocked on the door early on a Sunday morning. A very handsome young lady answered and asked, "Can I help you young man?"

"I'm looking fer Mr. Kit Carson. I understand he lives here?"

"Kit isn't here. He's back east at this time. Can I help? I'm his wife."

"Ma'am." As he spoke to her, he removed his hat. "I'm looking, fer some mountain men. I'd shore like to join with some going west. Would you know where I can find some?"

"Young man, do you know the Mexican Government don't want you people here. Now you be careful who you talk to. You talk to the wrong people, you might end up in jail. I understand there's some mountain men down Santa Fe way. That's where you will find them. If you go, go quietly and be careful who you talk to." Sam thanked her for her information and concern. He started within the hour walking down the trail toward Santa Fe. It was sixty miles to the southwest, A very long walk by any ones standard.

Sam walked steady for ten hours. He stopped well after midnight and slept four hours then back on the trail. On the second night he stopped on a high hill and in the distance he could see lights. Thinking it was Santa Fe, he took time to sleep again.

Early the next morning he met some Mexican sheep herders who told him the lights were from the town of Santa Fe. Walking hard, he entered the town just before noon. After securing some food from a friendly Mexican vendor, he asked a friendly Padre if he knew where he could find some mountain men. The Padre informed him a group was camping a few miles southwest of town. Sam headed that way as fast as he could walk. Soon he smelled burning oak wood. In a few minutes he could make out a group of men by a camp fire.

He called, "Can I come in?" They returned an invitation. Walking in, he saw ten men dressed in buckskin clothing with coon skin caps setting and laying around a fire. Most had a jug of whisky in hand and were trying to kill it.

A tall older man got up and asked his name and what he wanted. "I'm Sam Duncan and I wanta be a mountain man and trapper. I would like to join men on the way west to trap. Are you people trappers?"

The tall man told him his name was John Colter. "You

might say I'm the head man of this here outfit. We call our selves trappers." He laughs, "Or any thing else you's might want to call us." He slapped his leg and laughed harder. "How come ya think you's is good enough to be a trapper and be one of us? You's is just a little shaver."

All this time the other men there were laughing and making fun of this young boy. Sam told him he had looked at the hind end of ten mules all the way from Franklin and after watching their back side, "I can do anything."

John Colter looked this boy over damn good and said "That's a mighty fine rifle you're a tote-n. Can you's shoot her?"

"I'm a fair shot" Sam tried not to be a bragger. John told Sam as he walked away "Come with me."

They walked about a hundred yards. John pinned a playing card on a tree. "Now let's go back and see if-n you's can hit her."

Back by the fire, Sam took his rifle, primed the pan and cocked the Hawkins. "Wait boy." John said. "I believe the boys are gonna make a few wagers." It took a few minutes. The bets were on. "Go ahead, hit her if-n you's can."

Sam leveled the rifle, set the trigger and let her fly. A dead center hit. John slapped Sam on the back and said, "Good as any man can do in this outfit, you're on boy."

John introduced the men. "That there feller by the fire is named Tom Fitzpatrick. The big black man beside him is Jim Beckworth. Them men you want on your side in a fight. The man with a full beard is Hugh Glass, another man you shore can count on. Jebediah Smith is the feller sucking on the jug, he'll back your play any time, if-n he's your friend. We're waiting for the Sublette brothers and their friends. Soon as they get here, we're on the way to the Gila river country."

The next day the Sublette brothers and seven of their

friends arrived. A day later the group packed up and headed for the Gila wilderness country in the Mexico territory. Sam was on his way to be a trapper.

John gave Sam a job. Hunt camp meat, help gather fire wood and keep eyes pealed for Indians. He told Sam they would help make him some buckskin clothes when they got enough hides to do it. "Then you's be a real mountain man." Sam was very successful hunting game. He had deer meat in camp every night. All the men praised him for it.

He was away from camp hunting when he spotted a large buck moving thru the timber. He followed it intently. He got a clean shot and brought it down. He approached it carefully. Seeing his shot had hit its mark he started dressing the buck.

He never knew what hit him. When he gained consciousness, darkness was falling on the forest. He tried to move. His hands were tied at the wrists, his feet tied together at the ankles. Hands and arms over his head. He could see he was stretched between two small sapling pines. His head was bursting. The taste of blood in his mouth. His body was sore all over. He could hardly move. The smell of pine wood burning, flooded into his nostrils. His eyes burned. He could, by bending his neck, see Indian figures moving around the fires. The moon cast shafts of light thru the trees.

"Captured! Is this to be my end? Am I to die by the hand of a savage?" The first time in his life he prayed to God. "If I am to die here, please God, make it fast."

The long night seemed to never end. A minute seemed an hour, an hour seemed forever. The moon went down. Total darkness. It rained for what seemed like hours. No way he could sleep, he couldn't turn or roll, his body just got sorer and sorer.

Morning light came thru the trees. The Indians woke from their sleep. Fires were being made. Sam could see most of the people were squaws moving around. One old one came to look at him. She gave him a hard kick in the side. She said something he didn't understand and went away. Several more squaws came to look and all had something to give him, a hard kick in the side.

When the sun was high, a small girl, barely walking, came and stood over him and smiled. He smiled back and licked his lips. She went away and returned with a gourd filled with water. She let it run slowly into his mouth. It was so good. He tried to tell her with his eyes and smile. She left and returned with an older girl of maybe twelve or early teens. She, from a gourd, with her fingers, put a dried ground wet meat in his mouth. He ate and smiled between mouth fulls. She talked to him, not in Indian but in Mexican. When they finished, they both left.

Later that day a tall painted Indian came to see him. He checked to see if he was still tied. Several other young men came to look. One pulled his knife across his throat as if cutting and pointed his finger at Sam.

Night fell again, a long miserable night. The morning light brought a surprise. Two, what looked to Sam as black men, stood over him. The tall painted Indian was with them. One of the blacks cut the bounds holding his hands and feet. Told him to set up. Sam did not speak, just looked at them wide eyed.

One of the blacks said "Boy we own you, we just paid a pound of coffee beans for you and a bottle of whisky... Don't utter a word until we're free of this camp. These people are Mesculero Apaches, the toughest and meanest of all the Apache tribes."

Sam followed their instructions as the best he could. A pony was brought up and Sam was loaded on. He was told, "Hang on, we're a leaving."

Somehow Sam managed to stay on, although weak. In a

few miles they stopped to make camp. He was lifted off and set against a tree.

His wounds were attended to. His wrists were bleeding from the rawhide ties. The back of his head cut deep and bleeding. At least he was alive and thankful to the Lord. He thanked the Lord out loud.

The men asked his name and told him who they were, Charles and William Bent.

"We've been in these mountains for years now," they told Sam. "You're a lucky boy, that tall painted Apache is Victorio the war chief of the Mescalero tribe. He'd soon kill as look at you, why he didn't, we don't know."

Sam told of the little girls that helped him. "Who are they?" he asked.

"The older one is Mexican, was captured years ago. She's Victorious woman, the little one is their daughter."

Sam asked about his rifle. Had they seen it? Did they get it? Charles told him that the war chief took the gun for his own. He kept saying, "You must be a good shot and warrior to have such a fine rifle. We think that's why he didn't kill you."

Sam felt better each passing day. The three traveled southwest. In four days they came to John Colters camp. Such a surprise. "Sam," he said, "We shore figured you's a goner. We saw where a kill was made, with all the blood, we could see where them savages' drug something off with their pony's. Shore glad you made it back. I'll tell you Bents, this is one hell of man."

Charles told John, "He's had a bad time. Been plumb to hell and back. He needs some time to get over it."

John asked if the Bents would go with em to the Gila? "We sure will" answered William, "We been gonna go down in that country for sometime. Looks like it's a good time to go now."

John told them "We pull out in first thing in the morn-n."

In two days of travel the party hit the head waters of the Gila. The river was teeming with beaver and muskrat. All the men gave a big war hoop as they had hit the biggest pot of gold they could ever have dreamed of. All the country they were in was New Mexico Territory. It would be death to gringos if caught by the Mexican army.

The party stayed on the Gila for most of two years. They never saw any sign of the Mexican Army. Sam learned to trap and cure the pelts. His biggest job was hunting and cooking for the men.

They sent pack trains north and east with mules loaded with as much as they could carry. On each return trip, more mules were purchased, more pelts were sent.

In the spring of the second year the group felt they must move to more lucrative country, the trapping became slow on the Gila.

The party headed north. Sam and three others were to scout ahead and leave signs so the others could follow. In two days they came to a dark deep black canyon. On the other side they moved thru heavy forest of pine trees. No sign of the Indians. Moving north by northwest a large plains was encountered. Moving into the plain a large party of painted savages came out of the trees to the west. Their Horses were painted white and red .They looked menacing. The trappers moved into a small clump of aspen trees and hurriedly threw up breast works of pack saddles and logs.

Soon the warriors came from the trees and started to attack. War hoops filled the mountain meadow. The trappers with two rifles apiece and a pistol stopped the attackers in their tracks. The rifles with their long range, dropped eight braves. The warriors returned to the trees. Soon the Indians tried again. With only bows and arrows and a few lances. Eight more braves were sent to the happy hunting grounds. The warriors again retreated back to the trees. Soon the Indians came on foot too pickup the dead. The trappers held their fire and watched as the Braves carried their dead back into the trees.

Darkness fell. Back in the trees the trappers could see fires were started and could hear the Indians singing, dancing and beating on drums. They sang death songs and yelled war chants late into the night.

As the morning light came, the Warriors massed for a big attack, just as the rest of the trapper party came into the meadow. They saw what was going on and set up on the flank of the attackers and sent a hail of lead into the massed Indian warriors. The four in the aspen trees sent their volley of lead at the mounted braves, the Indians again retreated back into the trees. The party joined the four in the aspens. Tom Fitzpatrick told them, "The warriors are Tanto Apaches. A different tribe from Victoria's in the south. His tribe is Mescalero Apaches. These are said to be mountain Apaches. Few if any had ever seen a white man. I hope they'll give in and let us alone."

Darkness fell there was no sign of the Indians. Next morning Sam and Tom crossed the plain to check on the warriors. None were there. They had vanished into the forest. They had taken they're dead with them.

The party loaded the mules and horses and turned to the northwest. Sam and the three again were sent out to scout the trail ahead. Late the next day the four came upon the biggest canyon Sam had ever seen. A river ran in the bottom. They stood at a point where the canyon made a turn to the west from the north. The men were in awe of such a sight. It was absolutely magnificent. No one had any idea of such a place. It must be a mile across. They all agreed the main party must turn in a north east direction.

Sam was sent back to tell of their find. All agreed to go have a look see. The entire party camped on the edge of this canyon. They stayed for two days just to marvel at such a sight.

They turned away from the canyon and headed northeast across a vast open country. Another tribe of Indians scouted, watched and followed the trappers. Never moved to stop or interfere with their travel. Tom said these Indians were Navajos.

The party after days of travel found them in the high rocky mountains. Streams were teeming with beaver. The trappers stayed the summer and into the fall. When the snow came, they moved to a valley location and prepared for the winter. They built log cabins and smoked all the meat they could. The snow stayed on the ground until late spring.

The Bent brothers talked all winter of starting a trading post. They took their leave and went east to find a proper location.

Charles and William had asked Sam, "Come with us, we like your company. You're free to do your own mind."

Sam thanked them and said, "I owe my life to you, I'll always be in your debt, I would like to stay and trap in these mountains."

Sam and the others heard later the brothers had settled on the Santa Fe Trail along the Arkansas River and married Indian women.

A new trapper joined the party, a man most of the older men knew. All the men seemed to be happy to have the new comer with them. John introduced him to Sam. "Jim Bridger, most call him Old Gabe. You'll soon know why he's called that."

Sam soon found Old Gabe was a tall tale teller and a run away talker. Sam found the man to be friendly and a desirable companion. Fact is Sam and Old Gabe became fast friends. Old Gabe had just come from St Lu. Jake Hawkin had sent Sam a new rifle as the word had drifted back of his ordeal, this rifle was the new type cap lock. All the men had to look her over. Some didn't like it, until Old Gabe showed how it worked. Didn't need a primer pan or flint? With the caps the gun was always ready to fire. "Just hammer her back and let her go." Everyone said it was just a great idea.

Old Gabe had been in these mountains for some time before and knew the Indian tribes well, he had lived with some. "We can get along with all except the Blackfeet. They're the ornery, meanest, doggone fighten-est bunch he ever ran into. They fight all the other tribes. I don't think they like themselves. Be on guard for them all the time." He told Sam and the others.

John Colter bids the men goodbye and decides to go farming in the Missouri country. He dies before Sam can see him again. People and things change rapidly even in the mountains.

The American fur company is established and Mexico gets its independence from Spain and opens its streams and rivers to American trappers.

General Ashley sets up the first rendezvous on the Green river for all the trappers. Sam and his party attend and it's fun and games. Business is conducted and the General buys all the furs the trappers have. The General sets up the next rendezvous for the following year. Sam had made more than five hundred dollars for his share for the entire year.

All the next years, the party Sam is with having the best trapping there ever could be, it's the high mark of the fur trade. Most of the Indian tribes trade with the trappers, many trappers take Indian Squaws for wife's. By now Sam is feeling he should return home to see his Ma and Pa and at the rendezvous he tells Old Gabe his plans to go home.

"How long you's was gone from home?"

Sam tells him, "Best part of ten years."

Gabe tries to tell him, "Nutt-n gon-a be the same. Some times it's best not to get your hopes up, it ain't gonn-a be like it was when you's left."

"I hope it will be better," Sam said with hope in his voice. Sam's mind is made up to go home.

Chapter 2

The Farmer

Sam sold his extra ponies. Kept the two best, one to ride, the other to pack. Sold his traps and rigging's he wouldn't need any longer. After selling his pelts and skins, he pocketed one thousand dollars in gold Coin.

Sam said goodbye to Old Gabe. "I'm gonna miss you Gabe. You have been a good friend. I'll always remember you, the rest of my life." Old Gabe tried to hide the tear in his eye. He brushed it away with his left hand.

Sam had never seen him with a tear before. They gave a big hug to each other. Gabe slapped him on the back. "Get the hell on the trail, you's a loosen daylight."

Sam mounted and with the pack horse in tow, turned his face east. It was a long ride out of the mountains. Out on the plains he could make better time. Small villages, houses, and farms began to appear where there hadn't been anything before. "Looks like farmers are taken over the whole prairie," he said to himself. At one farm he stopped to talk. He was told emigrants were coming by the thousands from Europe to take the land the government was making available for home-steading.

Most of the homes were made from the prairie sod. Cut into square blocks and stacked like brick. The roofs were covered with prairie grass. Some had dug into the ground like a prairie dog. He saw men digging water wells and some were putting up wind mills. It all looked strange to Sam. The whole country had changed.

When he rode into St Louis, the town had grown to be a city. It truly had become the gate way to the west. He never thought it would look this way. The whole town had changed.

He rode thru the town and to the rear of the Hawkin gun shop. Knocking on the back door, it was answered by Jake Hawkin who recognized him right away. Anyone would have thought Sam was his son, the way he carried on. All the men in the shop came to welcome him. Jake had become one of Sam's best friends. He thanked Jake for sending a new rifle by Old Gabe. He told him it saved his life too many times to count. "I'll keep the rifle until my dying days."

Jake asked all about the mountains and trapping. "I've seen places I never thought existed." He told of the New Mexico country, the Apache Indians and his capture by them, How he was saved. "The rifle you gave me saved my life. The Apache chief liked it so much he let me live. He said I must be a great warrior to have such a fine piece." Jake smiled and told Sam, "I hoped it would do good by you's."

Then Sam told him of the Gila wilderness. "It's a great place. Hot as hades in the summer but nice and warm all winter." He had to tell of the big canyon he had seen. "It's miles across and it's so deep, if you throw a rock in it you will never hear it hit. A river runs in the bottom. The colors in that canyon, I ain't never seen before. Jake I tell ya, it's worth the trip just to look at it."

He then talked about his time in the Rocky Mountains. "There's forest that it takes days to ride thru. Valleys with clear cold streams are every where. It is a wonderful place to be."

He told of the men he had worked and lived with for so long . "I'll never have such fine men around me again. They're true friends. I'll always remember them."

Sam told Jake he was going home to see his folks. Jake tried to tell him, his home won't be the same. "Time waits for no man. Nothing will be the same."

Sam stayed in town a few more days while he sold his horses, tack and camp gear. He would never part with his Hawkin rifle. With his war bag in hand, he paid for a ticket on a paddle wheeler going south down the Mississippi and got off at Memphis. Then he walked and hitched rides all the way back to the Tennessee Valley. Along the way he stayed in several towns at night. Cross roads that became towns while he was away. It was great to get a hot bath, a hair cut and shave.

Arriving home he found his Pa and Ma had passed on to their reward several years ago. His older brother David had married and had sole possession of the farm. Not being welcomed with open arms, Sam was hesitant to stay, but his brother talked him into spending the winter.

His brother's wife didn't cotton to him at all. She made it plain he was not welcome every time she spoke to him alone. His stories had his brother hanging on every word. She may have been afraid her husband was getting the itch to go see the west.

In the spring Sam said his goodbyes and went back to Memphis. There he got a job as roustabout again, loading river boats on the docks.

During this time he had the good fortune to meet a beautiful southern belle, Elizabeth Moore. Her Pa owned the dock Sam worked on. He fell head over heels in love with her. She being only 16, her Pa didn't approve of any relationship with a man so much older. Sam was twenty-six years old.

Sam and Liz as he called her, became lovers. They would meet down on a path by the river. Liz fell for Sam and against her parent's wishes she wanted to get hitched, but the only way was to elope with him .They did in the late summer. They went west into Arkansas, were married by a justice of the peace in a small town.

They moved on to Fort Smith. Sam found a job in a livery stable. Not satisfied with this work, Liz and he decided they wanted to try to buy a farm. Having heard farms were selling cheap down south in Louisiana, Sam and Liz traveled south into the Red River country south of Shreveport. They found just what they were looking for.

With 1,000 dollars in a gold coin from his trapping. He made a deal for a farm that had been abandoned by two brothers, whose Pa had died. Wanting no part of farming the brothers were more than willing to sell the farm cheaply.

The property was in bad repair. Sam and Liz were delighted with what they had purchased. The house was a two story structure, half rock half wood. From a back porch that covered the back of the house a large kitchen was entered. It consisted of a large fire place and a stair way to the upper rooms. An open door way led to the parlor. Off the parlor to the right was a large bedroom. Up stairs was a long room having been used as bedrooms. The house was well furnished.

The place suited Liz just fine. Left of the porch and a few feet out, an old well still had water. Under the porch a cistern could be seen through the cracks in the floor. Back from the house a few hundred feet stood the best structure on the place. A large half rocks, half wood beautiful built barn. There were well-built wood pens on both sides of the barn. On behind the barn a few hundred feet nestled in a group of trees was a small cabin built of logs in bad need of repair.

East of the house, a small orchard with peaches and pear trees. On beyond the orchard, a cow pasture of about thirty acres, well fenced and showing new grass growth.

The whole place couldn't have suited them more. A

happier couple could not be found in the entire country. Fix up and rebuilding started immediately. The south field was plowed and prepared for planting sugar cane. The southeast field plowed and planted in sugar beets. All together it took several months to get organized and to make plans.

During this time they met their neighbor to the east. One Bill O'Reilly. A man of some advanced age, who became a very dear and trusted friend. A man who took this couple under his wing. He fell in love with Liz and made no beans about it. He admired Sam and wanted to help the couple all he could.

His farm was the show place of the whole county. He had untold acres, a beautiful home and many slaves. He had lost his wife to some unknown sickness and had never totally recovered. Liz and Sam gave him a new lease on life. He often sent his darkies over to help, even before he was asked. Sam got a long find with them. Sam tried to hire help, but the only ones he could find and uses were poor white trash or scallywags. They would steal and lay around and get nothing done. He had to try to do something. The farm was starting to do well and it was too much work for just the two of them. What to do was a dilemma .He asked Mr. O'Reilly what they should do. He suggested they should buy some slave help.

A slave auction was held in Shreveport the first Saturday of every month. Sam objected. He didn't want to own another person, but O'Reilly convinced him. "It's not bad if you treat em right."

Sam and Liz gave it a lot of talk and finally decided they must buy a man slave. With only five hundred dollars, Sam was gonna try to buy a helper the next auction day.

Sam and Liz lay awake a long time that night talking about the buying of a slave. Liz asked Sam to try to get a kind and gentle man. "I don't want no darkie we can't trust and have to be chasing after all the time."

The first Saturday in March, Sam hooked his mules to the spring wagon and drove to Shreveport. A three-hour trip.

Entering the town of about six thousand people, he passed a feed store, blacksmith shop, hardware store, a tavern and many other small stores. Then he saw the slave auctions big signs that read SLAVES FOR SALE - CHEAP SLAVES - BEST PRICES WEST OF THE MISSISSIPPI.

Sam drove onto a wagon yard not far from the auction house. He asked, "How much to care for my rig while I go to the auction?"

"Fifty cents," yelled the owner. Sam paid the man. Then walked the board sidewalk that lead to the auction house.

Walking along the board sidewalk, he watched the traffic and the people going about. Saying all the time to himself, what am I doing here? When he entered the auction house, he could see a long empty room, with just a counter off to the left side. On thru the building he could see a large door opening into a large walled open area. He walked on in. There was a platform facing about twenty wood benches. A crowd of mostly men filled the benches. Sam moved on down half way and sat on the end of one of the benches. The man next to him spoke up right quick.

"My name is Henry Stone. Are ya here to get some of them young bucks?"

"No," replied Sam, "I'm looking for help for my farm."

"These bucks ain't no good. They're from some big plantation over in Mississippi. Problem bucks, most have whip marks on em. You'll be out chasing- em most of the time, if-n you get one. The old ones are all wore out, ain't a good one in the whole bunch."

Sam was looking over at a wire pen that held male slaves, most had chains on their legs and wrists, with a rope around their neck. Stone poked Sam. "Look at them Nigger women.

They're young, real young. Wish I had the money to buy one. A fat chance I'd have, there's river men here. They'll pay big bucks for them young gals." Stone went on and on.

"How come, they want black girls so bad?"

"Them river boys, take em up river make whores out of em."

"They're too young for such goings on, why they can't be more than twelve or thirteen year's old." Sam was uncomfortable with Stones words.

"Where you been man? Them boys up north love that black meat, they'll pay big money to sleep with a black gal, the younger the better." Sam was visibly up set.

"I've seen Indians take slaves, but they sure as hell don't make whores out of them. Some things dead wrong with that. There should be a law against it."

"Ever man to his own poison I say." Stone was talk-n and look-n. "Wish I had the money, them gals will go for thousand dollars each, sure wish I had the money."

Sam watching the women said, "There's a few older ones, wonder what they'll go for?"

"Them old ones done wore out. A man get a mammy pretty damn cheap, if that's what you want." Stone kept on talk-n.

Sam turned his attention to the men. Got up and moved over to get a closer look. An old looking fella setting up against the fence turned his head. He looked right into Sam's eyes. He seemed to be pleading. Not a word was passed between them. The look penetrated Sam's soul. Why would he buy this man? Sam asked himself. He returned to the bench.

The auction started. "Who'll start this auction, who'll give a thousand for this fine young buck?" Screamed the auctioneer. Someone in the rear yelled, "He ain't worth that, look at all them whip marks."

"He's learned his lessons, I guarantee he'll give you no

trouble," returned the auctioneer. "Most these boys are fresh off the boat, you'll never find a better bunch than this. Look at the muscles on this buck, you'll never find better. Who'll give a thousand?" Up came the thousand. He sold for two thousand dollars to a man in a white linen suit.

Sam said softly to himself, "My five hundred ain't gonna buy much here today."

As the auction continued most of the prices stayed the same. More than sixty men were sold before the older ones came up. The first sold for five hundred.

Then the one he had looked at was on the block. First bid. One hundred, second, one fifty, then two hundred. Sam blurted out two fifty. The auctioneer cried for more. "This old buck has many more years in his old body. He knows more about cotton and animals than all the others put together." He couldn't get any more bids. "Going, going, gone to man in the black hat." Sam had made a purchase of a slave. He felt total remorse about buying another human.

A short skinny man came and poked Sam. "Come with me you gotta pay for your old nigger." Sam followed him to the counter inside the building. The man behind the counter said, "So you got an old one, good luck."

Just then a rope was given Sam. In a gruff voice the man handing Sam the rope said, "Good luck! I'm a bet-en this old bastard dies before you get him home." Sam's temper got the best of him. "Get that rope off his neck and take the chains off him, do it NOW!"

"What! Hell he'll run the first chance he gets." The gruff one said.

"Hell, he's so weak he can hardly lift his head. A fine bunch of ass-holes you people are. I wouldn't treat a dog this way!" Sam was mad. Every blood vessel stood out on his face and neck.

"These ain't people you son of a bitch," the man said in a sneer. "They're just niggers." Sam in a fit of rage, drew back his right fist, it hit the loud mouth square on the nose. The blood fairly flew.

With blood freely flowing, "You broke my nose you dirty son-of-a-bitch," the man cried. Sam drew his fist back again. Before he could let go, someone grabbed the bloody one and rushed him out the door to a water trough.

The man behind the counter handed Sam a bill of sale. "Get this old bastard out of here now. We don't want no trouble," he said in a loud voice.

Sam turned to the black man and said, "Follow me." Out of the building, down the wood sidewalk to the wagon yard. There he told the old one, "Get in the wagon."

Now the old one as he climbed in the wagon, spoke for the first time. "Master," he said, "I knows you's a good man, I can see's it. I works this old body to the bone. I'z a never run a way, if-n you's help me!"

"Help you, what do you want?"

"Master, did you see the woman in the grey dress?" The old one was trembling, as he spoke.

"I did. Why?"

"She's my woman. We... we be together long time, can's you's buy her? She's a good field hand, picks more cotton than any them young bucks and she's with chill-en." The old mans eyes were red and tears began to fill them. He was begging Sam.

"How do you know she's with child, she don't look that way to me." Sam was looking for some assurance. "She knows, she told me so. We'ze done had two chill-en together."

"Where are they now?"

"Kin't rightly say, they was sold for house chill-en." The old one said as he wiped his nose with the back of his hand.

"White folk like little nigger chill-en . They keep- em to play with their chill-en. They been gone a long time. I needs this woman-I needs this woman," he was begging. "Please Master can you's see's to get her? She won't sell for much."

Sam thought for a moment. I have some money left he said to himself.

"Please wont's you's try?" the old man was pleading again.

"Get in the wagon and stay put, I'll go try. I can't promise but I'll try."

Sam once more entered the building and on to the sale yard. He got some bad looks from some of the auction men. He didn't see the one he had hit.

The young girls were on the block. The bidding was going crazy. Sam was amazed the kind of money being paid for these young black girls. They were bringing thousands of dollars.

He sat on the same bench. Stone was still there. He said with a smile, "Heard you got some trouble, at the counter."

"Not much."

The last of the young girls went up on the block and were sold. Stone got up and left. Now the one Sam came for was on the block. No bids. She looked terrible. In a dirty grey dress, more of a rag than a dress. She was bare footed, stood with her head down, never looking up. Blood streamed down her hands from her tied wrists. There was no reason for anyone to buy this woman.

The auctioneer was screaming for a bid. Sam let him scream. Still, no bids. Sam watched the crowd. It had thinned out quite a bit, still no bids and then Sam bid. "One hundred dollars."

"Sold to the man in the black hat." Sam was surprised he got her so cheap. He headed to the counter, paid the money, got his bill of sale. He was handed the neck rope. This time the gruff one backed away saying, "No trouble, I don't want no trouble."

Sam lifted the rope off her neck, tossed it to the man and said to the black woman, "Follow me."

A man standing in the door said, "Watch her she'll run off."

Sam gave him a dirty look and showed him a clinched fist. Sam was uncomfortable with this whole business of buying slaves. To have some white numbskull say something made him mad. The man backed away. No more was said, any way not to this man. Sam had the look of a man of fixed conviction.

At the wagon yard, no words were passed between the two blacks but their looks told Sam all he needed to know. For the first time a smile broke the two black faces.

"We better hurry, it'll be dark soon and we have a long way to go." He hitched up the mules and turned them toward the front gate. He was looking down below the seat. He said, "There should be three sacks here, I see only two."

He turned to the black man and asked, "Did you see two or three sacks?"

"Only two," the black said as he showed two fingers.

Sam stopped the wagon, hopped down and entered the livery stable. "You the owner?" he spoke in a harsh tone to the man standing there. "Yeah, what's the trouble?" The man seemed unconcerned.

"I have a sack missing from my wagon. I want it back, right now!" Any blind man could see he was mad.

"Okay, okay, if it's here, we'll find it. If it ain't, too damn bad." The man said and shrugged his shoulders.

"Too damn bad for you," Sam said and opened his coat to show the handle of his pistol.

"OKAY, OKAY. Hey boy," he yelled to a little black boy standing in the door of the tack room. "You seen this mans sack?"

"I ain't see'd nutt-n'. I ain't see-d no sack," the little boy called back.

Just then another older black boy came from the harness room, holding a sack and asked, "Is this it?"

"That's it." He took the sack and returned to the wagon.

The three started the trip home. Sam Duncan had purchased two black slaves. A man and a woman.

Chapter 3

Slave Owner

Sam and his blacks drove on thru town to the south road. They drove for over an hour. No words were passed between Sam and his newly purchased blacks. The sun was starting to set.

Sam announced, "We must stop and fix something to eat. I'm hungry, I ain't had nothing since this morning."

Finding an open spot in the trees, he pulled the mules off the road. Getting down he tied the mules to a nearby tree, retrieved two nose bags and slipped them on the mules. During this time the black ones were picking up leaves and twigs to start a fire. As they finished Sam handed the woman his flint and steel. She struck a fire immediately. Sam took down a water jug and from a sack of tin utensils, a coffee pot and filled it with water. Set the pot by the fire. We'll have coffee as soon as the water boils.

All three sat silently staring into the fire. Soon the water boiled. Sam from a small sack, took a hand full of ground coffee and dropped it into the boiling water. From a food sack he took a chunk of meat wrapped in oil cloth.

"Possum killed and cooked yesterday," he told them.

"I shore like's possum meat," the black man said licking his lips.

Sam brought forth tin cups and plates, from the utensils

sack. He cut three chunks of meat and put them in a skillet by the fire to let them heat. Cold biscuits and a baked potato finished the meal.

"Go ahead, eat, eat." He set three tin cups on the ground and filled them with coffee. He motioned for them to pick up and drink. "Careful, it's hot," he advised. They both cupped the cups in their hands and sipped slowly looking at Sam as they did. It burned the man's mouth.

"Blow on it," Sam kinda laughed. "Never had hot coffee before?"

"No sur, never has. I'z a wonders why our white folk always had to have coffee in the morning."

Sam laughed, "Now you know."

"It's good."

They built the fire up. Now they could see each other as the darkness came on, the fire danced in their eyes. Sam could see hunger had taken them over as he handed plates to eager hands. They pushed the food into their mouths with their fingers as fast as they could.

"Take it easy you wanta to choke. When was last time you had some food?"

"Kin't rightly say. Been some time...ni-on two- three days."

"What-ya drink if you drank no coffee?" asked Sam.

"Well water mostly, had apple cider one time when the foreman ain't looking. We squeeze pear juices when they was ripe, if we could steal some pears." The man hung his head as to be ashamed of stealing.

"I ain't been told your names, what do I call you?"

"My name is Joe," the man replied.

"What's your name?" he asked the woman.

She replied, "I ain't never had a named."

"What would you be called?" Sam asked.

The man spoke up. "I calls her sweets."

"I can't be call-en her sweet's." Sam laughed. "How come you think she's with child?"

The woman stood up, pulled her dress up and showed him her little round belly. "I believe you're right," Sam said. "She sure looks like she is." He had no more questions.

After eating they put out the fire, loaded the wagon, untied the mules, climbed aboard and drove on toward home.

When they turned into the farm it was well after dark. Light from the kitchen thru a dim light on the wagon and mules.

Liz called out. "What took so long, you been gone all day, did you buy one?"

Sam yelled back, "Come see for your self."

The two blacks climbed down and stood on the ground by the wagon. The dim light hardly showed how they looked as she appeared in the door way.

"My, you got two?"

"Why sure," Sam said with some pride. "And ones a woman."

"Good lord, ones a woman?" She came closer to see them. "I can't believe it," she responded. "How in the world did you manage to do that?"

"Just lucky I guess."

Liz motioned for the woman to come into the house.

"Joe and I will put the mules away," Sam called

The two women entered the kitchen. The black one looked all around. Liz asked, "Can you talk?"

"Yes-m I shore can."

Liz told her to come over by the fire. "Are you hungry?"

"Yes-m, we done ate on da road, I'z a still starved. I needs a drink of water."

"You can have all you can drink," Liz told her. She set a pitcher and a cup on the table. The women took two... three... four cups full. "My, my, you had a terrible thirst. When the men get back we'll set some food on the table. I've cooked a chicken, baked some fresh bread and made a peach cobbler. What do I call you? What's your name?"

"I ain't never been named," she said with a frown on her face.

"You never had a name? Good lord how come?"

"Don't know and don't rightly care. The foreman don't give a rip, if you's got's a name or not. I-za always works as a field hand."

"Well!" Liz said. "I had a Mammy growing up, her name was Maude. I loved her like my own Momma, my Ma was sickly all the time while I was growing up. Maude was like my Ma, when Ma died I cried for days. My Maude died a few days later. I never knew if I was a crying for my Ma or for Maude. I was twelve years old then. Will you be my new Maude? I'll call you Maude, okay?"

"Good with me," the black woman seemed please to have a name. "My name is Maude? Maude, Maude. I like's the sound of Maude. Was your Maude a slave?" the woman asked.

"I didn't know. She was always living at our house. She was always there." Liz then asked the woman, "How old are you?"

"I don't rightly know, Maybe..." she stopped. "Maybe, maybe thirty years." She covered her face with her hands as she spoke, she looked to be much older. Liz could see the cuts around her wrists.

"Good lord what has they did to you? Your wrists are bleeding. What-a they do to you?"

"They tied us with wire, our legs too. We all stayed tied til we was sold. We rode a wagon from our home place. The man was afraid we'd run off." All the time she spoke she rubbed her arms and legs.

"I'll fix your cuts." Liz went out of the room and returned

with a jar of salve and treated Maude's cuts. Liz asked again if she knew how old she was.

"I'za don't rightly know."

"Did you know your Momma?"

"No ma'am, I don't think I had a Momma."

"You had to have a Momma. What's the first thing you remember?"

"I'za on a big boat. We niggers was all down inside the boat. All kind of us blacks, more men, just a few women and us chill-en." The woman seemed unconcerned.

"Who raised you?" Liz asked.

"No one's. I hung around the plantations slave cabins. Someone would take time to feed us chill-en. All the white folk call us pick- a- ninnies. I guess we was." Her voice trembled, her eyes were red and blood shot.

As she spoke she wiped tears away with her dirty grey dress. "I'za chopped and picked cotton as soon as I'za big nuff."

"When did you and Joe? You know get together?"

"I knowed Joe a long time. He crawled into my bed one night when I was young. We been together all the time. I had two chill-en with Joe. The master wants me to have chill-en, so's they can sell em."

The men returned from the barn and came into the kitchen. "We've washed up and ready for some food," Sam said.

"Set, I'll put it on the table," Liz told them. The two blacks pulled back, looked in astonishment. Sam demanded, "Set, yore in our house now." They did but very uneasy. They never had set at a white man's table before. They both looked at each other, not believing what was happening to them.

Liz spoke as she set food down. "I've named this woman Maude, how you like it?"

"Okay," said Sam.

"Okay with me. How you like it Maude?"

"Fine."

"You know what? Liz" Sam said. "This woman is with child, how you like that Liz?"

"Lord e lord," Liz said. "I've got news for you, I'm with child too."

Sam couldn't believe it! How long they had tried and now, could it be true? He questioned her. "How do you know?"

"We women know that something has changed."

Sam was overjoyed, could it be true. A baby on the way! Sam asked again,"How do you know, are you sure Liz?"

"You can be sure I know." Liz smiled as she spoke.

Sam asked, "When will it happen?"

"Some time in December," Liz replied.

"When you gonna have yours Maude?" Sam asked

"When it's ready to come" was her answer.

"Looks like about the same time," reported Liz. "Maybe hers will be a little earlier."

No more was said about babies that night.

Sam said, "These folks need some clothes. There's men and women things in a trunk in the upstairs. Come Maude, let's go take a look." Sam started for the stairs.

Liz stopped him and took the lamp saying, "Maude and I will look." Up the stairs the two women went.

Sam moved to and sat in a chair by the fire. Took his pipe, filled, and lit it with a stick lit from the fireplace. He asked Joe, "Do you smoke?"

"No sur. Tried a grape vine once, didn't like it."

Sam laughed, "So did I when I was young boy, burns the heck out-a your tongue, don't it?"

"Yes sur never tried again."

Liz and Maude came down the stairs, both had arms loaded with clothes, shirts, trousers, a coat and hat. "These things are yours," she said as she laid the clothes on Joe's arms. "There's some boots up there too, we'll get them in the morning."

She turned to Maude saying, "I have a dress or two you can have. Come with me." Liz took the lamp and went into the bedroom. Maude followed.

Joe asked, "Can I go to the barn now?"

"Sure, I know you must be tired. Wait, I'll get you a quilt."

Joe was so loaded down. He could hardly get off the porch. Sam could hear him saying, "Some day we-z had," as he headed for the barn.

Liz and Maude returned to the kitchen. Maude dressed in a blue dress falling right down to her ankles. "Now all you need is shoes," said Liz.

"No shoes for me," Maude replied. "Ain't ever had none no how."

Liz told her, "You'll have some now."

Sam interjected with his idea. "I'll make her some Indian shoes out of some buckskin. We have plenty in the barn. I used to wear em all the time."

Liz stretched and yawned and said, "It's late, we must get to bed, it's past my bed time. I'll make a pallet for Maude by the fire. You go onto bed Sam."

"Yes Ma'am." He headed to the bed room, undressed got in bed and went to sleep.

Something woke him up. He wiped the sleep from his eyes and there standing in the moonlight by the window was a naked Liz, with her un-braided blonde hair hanging down over her shoulders, covering her full rounded beautiful breasts. She was more beautiful than he had ever seen her.

"I love you Liz, come to bed," he called.

"I love you too Sam. We better do it now, it'll be some time before we can do it again." She literally melted into his waiting arms.

The sun was streaming into the bed room as Sam came alive. "It must be late?" he said as he stretched and jumped from the bed. "I've slept too long." He could hear Liz's voice coming from the kitchen. He dressed as fast as he could and went to the kitchen.

Liz asked him, "How's ham and eggs sound Sam?"

"I need all the energy I can get after last night, sounds good to me."

"SAM, SAM!" Liz had anger in her voice. "Shut your mouth Sam."

Sam laughed. Maude looked up from her work at the stove, she was smiling. "Maude knows what married folks do," Sam said.

Liz frowned and came back with, "I understand Maude and Joe ain't married, did you know that Sam?"

"I didn't think about it." Sam asked, "Does it make any difference?"

"On our place, there'll be nobody living in adultery. Sam's we must take them with us to church Sunday and get em hitched. I'm sure our preacher will do it, okay with you?" Liz by the tone of her voice, wouldn't be denied.

Sam came back, "Okay by me. Yer gonna make the white folks mad, taking our blacks there. They ain't gonna like it."

"I don't care if they don't." Liz was positive in her voice.

Sam asked, "Has Joe had his breakfast?"

"Yes," Liz replied. "I fixed them a table out on the porch, that's what they wanted."

"I'm gonna eat and go on down to the barn, see what's going on," He told Liz.

He finished and walked to the barn. Inside he saw the stalls were cleaned, fresh straw in place, the whole barn raked cleaned.

"Joe, where are you?" he called.

"I-za out here in tis pen."

Sam pushed the gate open, went on into the pen. He could see the mules were groomed and eating. Joe was working on the horses.

"Them's da littlest mules I done see. Where da come from?" Joe asked.

"They're Spanish mules, smaller than Arkansas mules," Sam told him.

"Kinda mean ain't da?"

"No not really, you gotta work slow around em. They're the best traveling animals you can have. Go all day at a trot, outlast any horse or big mule you've ever seen."

"I see-d they travel really well when we were on da roads. Sure air little ones. They shore fussily. I believe you's when you's say go slow. One shore did its best to kick on me."

Sam laughed. "My wife wants you and Maude to get hitched next Sunday at our church. Okay with you Joe?"

"It shore is." Joe said with a big grin showing his white teeth.

Sunday morning found the two couples in the spring wagon on the road to church. Half mile from the church Mr. O'Reilly passed them in his buggy, driving his black pacer. Sam could hear Joe remark, "Da- at's some horse."

Sam leaned over to Liz and said, "That man has got an eye for horses." She nodded her approval.

The congregation was gathering as they drove up. All in their Sunday best. Liz could hear one lady saying, "What did they bring them Niggers for? This is white Folks church."

Liz heard it plain as could be. Her Irish blood boiled over. She turned on the crowd and the lady with fire in her eyes and voiced, "These people are here with me to get married in God's House, you can like it or lump it, I don't give a rip whether you give a sh-t or not."

Liz never cussed before in her whole life. At least where someone could hear her. This was a time she wasn't ashamed to let her feelings go.

"There'll be no unmarried couples living on our place, ever. I don't care if they're white, black, green or whatever, they have to be married and if your Niggers isn't, you're in just as much sin as they are." She threw up her head, shoulders back and marched into the church.

O'Reilly could be heard saying, "What a woman! I love that woman."

After the church service, Liz apologized to the preacher for using bad language. The black couple sat on a bench under an open church window and sang along with the congregation. Songs they had heard from their past, coming from the white peoples' church on the plantation, they had come from.

After the church service the black couple was married by the preacher man, under a large oak tree. Some of the white people from the church stayed for the joining of the couple. Later at home a few people from the neighboring farms came. Mr. O'Reilly had passed the word. He brought all his blacks for the celebration. Fried chicken and watermelons were had all round. A few black people brought their music instruments. Dancing broke out. It was a merry bunch that Sunday afternoon on the Duncan farm.

The next few months were spent rebuilding the cabin. New roof shingles were cut and nailed in place. A new door was built. New glass windows were installed and last the fire place was rebuilt. Liz and Maude made a new feather bed for the cabin. The black couple moved in.

The rest of the summer, the living was easy, the catfish were biting in the creek, the fruit orchard outdid itself, the grass grew tall, the cows gave lots of milk and cream. Butter was churned. The chickens laid so much, Liz and Maude took eggs and sold them in the little village on the east road.

Liz had her companion and helper. Sam had good help and the summer turned to fall. The crops came in and were harvested. The fall turned to winter. The babies came due. Maude's came first, then Liz had hers. Both women had boys, nice healthy boys. Maude and Joe named theirs Little Joe. Liz and Sam followed with Little Sam. It was joy to the world that winter on the Duncan farm.

Bill O'Reilly had set up a church meeting place on his farm for his blacks and blacks on the adjoining farms. He also found a black fire preaching, preacher for the flock. He had talked most of the farms into letting their blacks attend and the people came. There was a lot of singing. Hal-la-lu-ya's and a-mens could be heard coming from those meetings. Even the little ones were getting some schooling. Liz had made a difference in the community of the blacks.

Time passed, one year, two years. In the third year both Liz and Maude gave birth to boys again. The blacks named theirs Josh. Liz and Sam named theirs Jackson and called him Jack.

The times had been too good. It just couldn't last. Sam had borrowed money to keep the farm going. It was getting close to pay back time. A drought had hit and a depression was covering the whole country in the late 1830's. Sam had to tighten things up. Three more years and he had to go for money to pay on his last loan. It kept building up. He showed a happy face but inside he was hurting really badly. He knew it would come to a head soon and it did.

He drove over to see Bill O'Reilly to ask advice. A mammy ushered Sam into Bill's bedroom. She said he was feeling poorly. O'Reilly sat up and greeted Sam with a smile. "Not feeling so good," explained Bill. "Probably don't look so good, been down for a couple weeks now."

"What seems to be the trouble?"

"Have a lot of chest pain, and can't seem to get my breath. I'll get over it soon. Had it before and it always went away."

"That's too bad." Sam was concerned. "Hope you're up and better soon."

"What-ja want-a to see me about?" asked Bill.

"My troubles aren't yours, I don't want to bother you."

"Be my guest, what's friends for?"

"I'm in trouble with my loan, can't seem to get enough money together to pay it back."

"Don't feel bad Sam, I'm in the same boat, borrowed way more than I should have, can't get my money together either."

"You?" Sam said surprised. "I thought you were all set for life."

"Not hardly, this depression and prices set us all back. I'm in bad shape. I have the whole dang place mortgaged to the hilt, all but my blacks. If the worst comes I'll free the blacks and to hell with the rest of the world. Sam, some times you have to cut and run."

"I hate to bother you more," Sam told him. "I just have my land mortgaged. The tools and stock are free. I'll do the same with my blacks. This old farming is a hell of a life. Get well Bill. I'll send Liz over to cheer you up."

With that Bill smiled. Sam bid him goodbye gave a hug to Mammy on the way out and drove home.

He told Liz about Bill. "He shore don't look too good. His lips are purple."

"I'll go over in the morning and cheer him up, if it's okay with you?" Liz said.

"You bet, he'd like seeing you. I think he's been in love with you since the day he met you," Sam said proudly.

"Sam, I got a letter from my sister, Jane. She married Walter Johnson. Do you remember him ? He did the books for my papa at the docks."

"I seem to recollect, he was a tall lanky fellow? He never had much to say, at least not to me. He was always well dressed." Sam was scratching his head as he spoke.

"That's him. Seems he's got a job with the government running a Indian reservation over in the nations. He needs help. Jane wants to know if we can come help them run their agency. She says they need help bad. He bit off a lot more than he can chew. We could go over and help if things don't work out here." Liz was trying to make Sam feel better. Sam told her he would go in the morning and ask the banker if he would extend his loan.

Morning came, with it bad news. Bill had passed in the night. All who knew this fine man were heart sick. Liz broke down and cried all that day.

The service was short and very sad. All who were there had nothing but good words to say about Bill, his blacks were heart broken, many cried and wailed all during the service.

Bill was a man of his word. He had papers made, that gave freedom to all his blacks. There would no mistake, they were all set free. Most packed their belongings and started walking as a group, north the next day.

Some of Bill's blacks wanted to stay. The foreman Jon Henry who was Bill's oldest black, gave a talk to the remaining people saying, "You have to move on, some whites won't honor Master O'Reilly's paper. Y-all must go while the getting's good." All the rest of the blacks packed and headed north walking to the free states.

Sam rose early. Hardly had anything to eat for breakfast. He rode one of the mules to town to see the banker.

The meeting turned sour almost immediately. Sam could feel the hostility in the room, as soon as he entered. He had known and heard talk that some people had desires on his place. The banker turned on him in a belligerent voice saying,

"Duncan, your loan is past due. You got no more time. Get out now or I'll send the law to put you out."

The man's manners and harsh words had Sam boiling mad. If it wasn't for Liz, he would give this son of a gun a bad beating but he just shook his head in disgust. As he started to leave, he turned back and said to the banker, "We'll leave, I only have the land mortgaged, not our tools or stock. We'll be out in a few days. You keep away until we're gone or so help me I'll be back and it won't be very damn pleasant for you, you low down money grubber."

He turned on his heels and stormed out. On the way home he cussed the banker and said to himself how people with money think they own the whole damn world, he never said cuss words where Liz would hear him.

At home he came in, dropped into his rocking chair, put his face in his hands and said, "Liz I've made a bad mess of things. They won't give us more time. We have to get out. I'm sorry Liz, I know how you loved this place."

She could see he was hurting. "It's not so bad." She was very sympathetic. "It's not the end of the world, lots of folks have had to let their places go. I hear folks are going west to homestead all the time."

Sam looked up, tears in his eyes. She tried her best to soothe him saying, "We have each other and the boys. No one could have done better." Sam just shook his head. Liz said "Let's go on over to the nations. Maybe it'll be just the thing for us."

Sam couldn't say anything. He was sick at heart. He just shook his head.

Liz told him, "Let's get a good nights sleep, you'll see things better in the morning."

Next morning Sam sent for Joe, "We've got to move on. I've lost this place to the bank. You go hitch up the big wagon.

We'll take our stock and tools over on the east road and sell what we can."

They sold all the things they took. People like bargains.

On the way home Sam told Joe to load his belongs in the spring wagon in the morning. "Come help us to load the big wagon, as soon as you're done."

At the farm each went to their own house. Sam was more sick at heart than ever to have lost his farm.

Next morning the wagons were loaded. With one cow in tow, a few chickens and some farm tools, the two families were on the road by noon, on their way north. The third day found them outside Ft. Smith, Arkansas. They camped for a few days. Sam went to town several times.

Early one morning Sam and Liz told Joe and Maude they're free and handed them their papers of freedom. Joe and Maude both threw up their hands and cried. "We-z don't know where to go, what to do, we want's to go with you's."

Sam is stern. "We're going into the nations, there's still slavery there, you won't be safe. Joe, you and Maude have earned your freedom, go north until you reach a free state. Joe, you're the best hand I ever saw, you can do anything, shoe horses, farm as good as any man. The man who hires you will get a real helper. Take the spring wagon and the mules. You can have my shot gun, I have a few dollars for you. You can hunt and fish on the way, keep going north till you find a place you like."

Joe and Maude could see his mind was made up. With misgivings they agreed, many tears were shed by both families.

The next morning, with heavy hearts, Joe and Maude hitched the mules to the spring wagon. With their two boys, they headed the little wagon on the road north. Sam and Liz watched until they were out of sight. With broken hearts they turned their wagon west and a new life.

Chapter 4

Death Comes Early

It took several days to reach the Choctaw Indian Agency. Jane and Walter welcomed them with open arms. Walter showed them a house they could have to live in, it was pretty run down. No one had lived in it for quite a few years. Liz told Sam they could have it in shape in no time. In the mean time Walter said they could bed down in a room in the house with them.

Sam and Liz had the house in good shape in a few days and moved in. The two boys soon had Indian children as play mates. Sam began his duties as a farm instructor to the Choctaws. The Indians were more than willing to learn the white mans ways.

Liz spent her time teaching the women cooking on a stove and sewing on a peddle machine. Most had never seen a stove, let alone cook on one and most of the women had never seen a sewing machine. Liz found the squaws ready and willing to learn, she also found they were smart and fun.

Sam's help was teaching his charges ways of handling horses and mules and general farm duties. The farm work and harnessing of horses and mules was new to the Indians, farm work was not a natural thing for the men, most had always hunted, fished and play games with their horses, it took time. Most of the men finally took to farming, when the crops began to grow, the Indian farmers became proud of their labors.

The government gave each family livestock and farm equipment. Soon the white man started to trade the Indians out of this stock and equipment for just a few jugs of whiskey.

Walter and Sam had to devise a way to stop this practice. There was no law on the Choctaw at the time. Sam gave it all the attention he could. Liz told him she had the idea to brand, "I Don't Trade" on the stock and all the wagons and farm equipment. If a white man had an IDT brand in his possession, it would have to be given back. This stopped the whites and their trading.

Whisky runners became a big problem. Sam and Walter punished the Indians who used the drink by keeping them locked up in the agency jail until they promised to quit.

As his two boys grew, Sam used them to help school the Indians in their way of working with horses, gentle and kind. Both Jack and young Sam became good hands with the horses and mules. Sam was proud of them both.

Young Sam made friends with many of the Indian children and became a fast friend of Charlie Bird. Charlie's family lived near the agency. He had two brothers and two sisters. He was the youngest boy and wanted to live as the white men did. He was too young to know the old Choctaw's ways. He taught young Sam his native tongue and Indian sign language. Sam would use this knowledge later many times in his future life.

Young Sam and Charlie helped Sam with the horses and mules. Both these boys became good hands for Sam. Jack preferred to work with Walter and the cattle. A mule had kicked him and he refused to work around them any longer.

Charlie Bird had two sisters. One was ten or so, the other older, maybe eighteen or nineteen, her name was Blue Bird a very handsome Indian Girl. She liked to come with Charlie to help with the horses. She was a good rider and took a liking too young Sam right away. Many times the three rode the wagon roads and trails of the Choctaw together.

One afternoon on the road above a creek the three stopped to watch a young Indian man and girl down in the bushes by the creek. Sam asked if they were fighting. Charlie and Blue both laughed and rode on.

Back at the corrals Sam asked again about the two they had seen by the creek. Blue told him they were making a papoose. "I'll show you how it's done if you want?" Sam didn't know what to say. He let it pass. It was never mentioned again for a long time.

A fever came on the people of the Choctaw. Many people began to die of high temperatures. No doctor could break the fever or stop the dying. There seemed to be no cure.

Liz was the first to come down with it, then Sam. Both lay in an unconscious state for some time. Young Sam prayed to God to save his Ma and Pa. All to no avail, they both passed on the same night. Sam was heart broken. He loved them both so much. It was almost more than he could endure.

He cussed God for death of his folks. "I'll never ask for any thing from God again," he vowed. He came down with the fever a few days after his folks were buried. He lay unconscious for days, his body was burning with fever, he was expected to die at any time.

An old medicine man came to the agency. He said he was curing the people of the Choctaw, he could save this boy. Walter told him to try. The medicine man filled a horse trough with cold water and lifted Sam gently into the water, only his head remained above the surface. He then shook gourds and danced around the trough singing a chant. This went on for three days and three nights.

Sam slowly gained consciousness. Soon he picked himself out of the trough, the fever was broken. The medicine man said he had many people lay in the creeks in the cold water, he had saved them with his chants and dancing.

"The great sprit came and told me what I should do." The old Indian believed he had cured the people.

The Choctaw returned to normal. The fever had lifted thru out the nation.

It took several weeks for Sam to regain his strength completely.

As the next years passed, Sam and Charlie trained many horses together. One afternoon Blue Bird came to the horse pens and asked to go with Sam for a ride along the creek trails. She asked Charlie not to go. "You stay at the pens," she insisted.

Blue and Sam rode the trail by the creek. She asked if he was ready to see how to make a papoose? He laughed and told her he was ready for her to show him. She turned her horse into some willows along the creek bank, dismounted and began to disrobe. Her beautiful naked bronzed body lit a fire in Sam he had never encountered. She lay on the leaves and beckoned him to come to her. The sight of her slim bronzed naked body, her long black hair, braided in two strands pulled across her full rounded breasts, would invite the natural instinct in any young man. Sam slipped down beside her and kissed her full waiting lips. The two enjoyed each other for some time that afternoon. This was only the first of several afternoons they spent together down by the creek.

The word got around the agency like wild fire and soon Walter asked Sam about the rumor. "Was it true, was Blue Bird and you having girl boy relations by the creek?"

Sam told him that it was true. Walter was devastated and mad as a hornet. "You'll have to leave the agency. The council and Chiefs are mad that you would take advantage of one of their young girls."

Jane came in and said, "The Chief wants Sam whipped as no white boy can violate their women. Sam you will have to leave the agency." She started to cry.

Walter told him he would have to leave. "Don't you know Blue is a blabber mouth? She has told everyone on the Choctaw about your relations. You're so dumb."

That night Walter told Sam he must leave the very next morning. "I can't promise your safety. I know your Pa and Ma would want you to go and make good at something. He talked of a gun maker in St Louis he had worked for. A Jake Hawkin. "He made the rifle your Pa treasured so much. You like guns, you might like to make them, I'll have a letter for you to give him when you get there, we'll give you twenty dollars and your Pa's pistol, we'll keep his rifle here, if you or Jack ever want it, it'll be here."

Sam packed his few belongings in a feed sack. Jane fixed a food sack and next morning, along with many tears, Jack, Jane and Walter bid young Sam goodbye. Sam started his journey to St Louis and into manhood, he would be sixteen years old his next birthday, in December. He would never see Jack his brother again who was killed at the battle of Shiloh, fighting for the Southern cause, nor would see his Aunt Jane or Uncle Walter again. They would both die at the agency.

He walked and hitched a few rides on freight wagons all the way to Ft Smith. There he got a job with a freight company hauling cotton bales to the Mississippi River for shipment north. His main job was to yoke the oxen team each morning and unyoke and tend to them as they grazed in the evening. There were seven teams he had to take care of.

At the Mississippi River they crossed on a ferry boat. The teamster paid him a five-dollar gold coin for his labor.

In Memphis Sam looked for his Grandpa Moore. He found him working on the docks. His Grandpa was delighted to see him. He knew both his daughter and Sam were gone. Jane had sent word the year before. The girl's mother had also died and Grandpa Moore had remarried a lady twenty years his junior. Grandpa was sorry the way he had treated Sam's Pa. "I wish I had that time to do over," he told him. "Things might have turned out different. I want you to live with me and my wife."

Sam's Step Grandma didn't cotton to him at all and she let him know in no uncertain terms. He wasn't welcome to stay. She told him in private, "I don't want any young-ns around. I ain't gonna do for you." She asks him not to tell his Grandpa her feelings. His staying might interfere with the relations with her and the old man. Sam told her he would leave.

"I'll cause you no trouble," he told her.

Sam told his Grandpa he would like to go on to St Louis. "I want-a learn about gun making like my Pa did." He said nothing of his Grandpa's wife's feelings toward him.

His Grandpa saw it was no use trying to get him to stay. He told him he knew all the captains of river boats and could get him passage in a few days to go upriver, he did. On a livestock boat going north the next day captained by a Captain Black. Sam signed on to work as a stock feeder, A job he could do well.

Sam was on his way to St Louis. He had trouble with thieves on the boat and had to show them his pistol several times to keep them away from his sack of belongings.

When the docks of St Louis came in sight, Sam was ready to quit the river. He bid Captain Black goodbye and walked from the boat down the gang-plank to solid ground and up the street.

He was in awe of such a town, there were more people than he had ever seen before. Memphis was big but nothing like St Louis. There were carriages and buggies going ever where, wagons pulled by oxen teams moved thru the streets. Men on horse back seemed to be going in all directions. Sam was impressed with this gate way to the west. Now all he needed was to find the Hawkin gun shop.

He stopped the first man he met to ask for directions. Before he said anything, the man turned on him. "Get the hell away from me boy, I don't give money to bums."

This made Sam mad. "You son-of-a- bitch, I wouldn't ask you for the time of day."

The man shrugged his shoulders and walked away. The next person he met was a lady and before he could say a word she said, "Get away boy."

He said to her, "Nice friendly town you got here." He gave her a high sign and went on his way looking for the Hawkin gun shop.

Sam the Son

Chapter 5

On His Own

Sam walked to the first street that paralleled the river and turned right, passed a blacksmith shop, a dry goods store, a well lit café, several small shops. He stopped at a sign that read "JAKE HAWKIN GUN MAKER." He opened the door. A bell on the door announced his arrival.

A man who looked to be in his thirties asked, "What can I do for you boy?"

"You Jake Hawkin?"

"Yes, what can I do for you boy?"

"Sir," Sam said, "I have this here letter fer you." He handed him the letter.

As the man read the letter, ever once in a while he would look over his eyeglasses at Sam as he read. Then he asked, "You Sam Duncan's boy?"

"Yes sir, I am."

"How is your Pa?"

"My Pa passed some years ago." Sam looked down so as not to show his feelings.

"I'm sorry to hear that," Jake said as he wiped his nose with the back of his hand. "Your Pa was one fine fella. I thought as much of him as one of my own. So you's want a job with us? Just like your Pa. Well son if -n you're as good as him, you'll be a good one."

"My Pa told me he worked stocks. I'd like to try that."

"We can always use another stock man. You's can start now, if-n you's a want-n to. Come meet my brother. His name is Sam too. I want you to meet the rest of our workers."

All the men were corrigible to Sam. Jake showed him a small room in the back of the shop. "Your Pa had this room when he was here. It was a long time ago." He wiped his nose as he spoke. Sam thought he saw a tear in this mans eyes. "You can stay here now in the same room that your Pa had." Sam was pleased to be in a place where his Pa had been.

Sam settled in and was shown how to rough out wood stocks. After work, everyone had gone home, he investigated the area behind the shop. A dirt road or more like an alley passed by the rear of the building. Across the way was a stable where Jake and Sam kept their buggies and horses while at the shop.

To the north of the stables was a gun range. Farther back ran a levy that kept the Mississippi in her banks. Most evenings Sam walked or sat on the levy and watched the river boats pass. It was his only entertainment.

A most enjoyable year passed. He was a good student of rifle manufacturing and repair. Sam would soon be eighteen. Jake let Sam test fire the new rifles as they were finished. Sam liked that duty the best and it showed. He became a crack shot.

Jake told everyone Sam was one of the best shots he had ever seen. "His Pa was good but this boy is the best. I believe I ain't never saw a better shot than this boy."

Sam had been fixing his own meals and was getting tired of eating his own cook-en. On a warm summer Sunday evening walk, he passed the café that was a few doors south of the gun shop and decided to stop in. The smell was just too inviting. He knocked on the back door. A black man opened an asked, "What do you want? We don't let bums in here."

"I ain't no bum, I got money. I work at the gun shop down the street. I'm in need of a good meal. Can I come in and get one here?"

"I done see-d you walking the levy many times. Come on in and set at our kitchen table. I-za fix you some-um right's now."

Sam had almost finished his meal, when a door at the top of some stairs that came down to the kitchen, opened and a pretty lady came out and came slowly down the stairs. Her long blond hair fell over her left shoulder all the way to her waist. Her long silver dress fit tight and exposed an hour glass body. She was a big full breasted lady, it looked like the two were fighting to get out of that tight dress. She appeared to be in her twenties. When she reached the bottom of the stairs she said to the black man, "Who let this bum in our kitchen? George, what's this bum doing in our kitchen?"

"He ain't no bum Miss Sarah. He's a paying man."

She sidled over to the table. Sam stood up. He was a head taller than this pretty lady. "Where you from?" She asked in a sexy voice and a big smile.

"I work at the Hawkin gun shop down the street."

George chimed in, "He's, he's the one been walking the levy, you know Miss Sarah the one you's been a watch-en."

"Shut up George, I'm a talking to this man." She asked Sam to turn around. He did in a complete circle. When he turned back around, she looked up at his face and said, "My, my, you are a good-looking man. How old are you?"

Sam lied, "I'll be nineteen soon."

"George he'll have dessert up in my apartment. She motioned to Sam and said, "You come with me mister gun maker."

She turned and went up the stairs, Sam followed. Her hips swung from side to side as she climbed the stairs. He enjoyed watching the way she moved and looked. An old feeling swelled up inside of him, the one that Blue Bird gave him back on the Choctaw.

At the top stairs, he turned to look down at the men in the kitchen. All were looking up at him. They all gave him a high sign with their thumbs.

He followed her into the room, the most beautiful place he had ever seen. An eating table and chairs was just in side the door, a candle chandelier hung from the ceiling, a setting parlor was at the other end of the room. Thru a door toward the front he could see the largest four poster bed he had ever seen. All the walls were covered with colorful flowered paper, a most pleasing and exciting place to be.

Soon a knock on the door, she called for George to come in. He set a large plate of apple pie on the table with a pot of coffee and went back out, not saying a word.

The lady came over and said, "Eat your pie." She bent over to pour a cup of coffee. Her big beautiful bosoms exposed themselves to him. He had to take a peek. Never had he seen such a sight in his life.

She smiled and said, "You are one handsome young man, finish your pie and come set with me on the settee."

She went and sat down. He went over and stood before her. For the first time she asked his name.

"Sam Duncan."

"My name is Sarah Mackay," she said with a smile. "Please Sam, unbutton and take my shoes off."

He lifted her feet one at a time and did as she asked.

Then she asked him, "Come set beside me."

She told him again as she put a arm around him, "You are a very good looking young man. Tell me true, have you ever had a woman?"

Sam looked away and said "Yes I have." He had a sheepish

grin on his face.

"I don't want to hear about it, I'm lonely and full of love, would you like to make love to me?" she asked in a little girls way.

Sam hesitated, then said, "Yes, you are one very handsome lady. I'd shore be pleased to make love to you anytime."

She got up and took his hand and led him into the bed room and unbuttoned her dress and let it drop to the floor. Next came her bloomers, then her top. She stood before him a beautiful fully naked adult woman. He pulled her to him and kissed her on the lips.

"You are one good-looking woman," he whispered. He undressed and they both got into her bed, for a night of sexual satisfaction to both parties.

Morning came. Sam opened his eyes. It was getting light. Sarah had a leg on him, he pushed it off and jumped up. Told her, "I gotta get to work." He hurried and dressed.

Sarah sat up in the bed asked, "Where you going?"

"To work, I have a job to do."

"You don't have to work any more, stay with me." She seemed to be begging.

"Sarah," he said, "I have to work, I can't lay around here." He sat down on the bed, pulled her to him, kissed and thanked her. "See you later. You beautiful hunk of woman." And left.

At the shop he unlocked the back door and built fires in all the stoves, then went about his usual chores. Soon Jake and brother Sam came thru the door. "Slept late did you Sam?" Jake asked. "It's not very warm in here." Sam smiled and continued about his work.

Later that day Jake came and opened the big doors in the rear of the shop. It was a warm day. Who came strolling by but Sarah. She stopped out side the door. Looking in she asked in a loud voice. "Is this where the guns are made?" She hiked up her dress and stepped into the shop.

Jake saw her first, he took off his glasses and hurried to meet her. "Miss Sarah," he said, "How good of you to bring such beauty into this old shop."

"I've never been in a gun shop before," she said. "It smells of fresh-cut wood, oil and gun powder, kinda smells good to me. Smell's like men should."

Jake said, "Come I'll show you around." He took her by an arm and to each working station to show her how the guns were made.

Hal the lock maker leaned over to Sam and said, "Ain't that the God damn best looking woman you ever seen?"

Sam said, "Mighty pretty."

She could hear them, turned and smiled. Jake walked her to the door, every eye in that shop was on her until she left. Jake turned to his workers and said, "Hope she don't come back, her presence could destroy this shop."

That evening most of Hawkins workers were eating at Miss Sarah's Café. She was at the shop with a tray of food for Sam. They sat at his bench and talked as he ate the meal. She asked him to come to her apartment. He refused. Said he had work to finish.

"I'll come up soon, soon as I get rested." They both had a good laugh. She took the tray and left. He followed her out the door and watched until she entered the back door of her café, he returned to his work.

The next day a man came to the shop. He was well dressed, with a well-groomed beard, looked to be in his fifties. He had a younger slightly built man with him.

Jake asked the workers to come look at the guns this man had brought with him. On the counter lay several revolver pistols. The man introduced him self as Colonel Sam Colt owner of the new Colt firearm's company. "This pistol is our latest make, an 1847 model .44 caliber Colts Army Revolver. I'm on a trip looking for dealers for these fine pistols. Mr Hawkin would you be interested to be a dealer for me? We sell them for 28 dollars a piece, in a case with accessories delivered to your shop, we have orders for one thousand from the Government. Soon we'll have another model we call the Dragoon. How about it Mr. Hawkin?"

Jake rubbed his face with a left hand said, "We make guns here, never thought about being a dealer of some other gun maker."

"These pistols are selling for thirty-five to forty dollars in Texas. You can make a handsome profit." Sam Colt was some salesmen. "How many can we send you?"

Jake asked his brother, "What do you think?"

Sam Hawkins said, "We don't even know if they'll shoot."

"You got a place to shoot? My man here will show you how well they shoot," returned the Colonel.

Jake told him he had a range out back where he could shoot the pistols. Colonel Colt turned to the young man with him and said, "Let's show-em how well these pistols shoot."

They all went out to the range behind the shop. Jake had Sam set up six metal, six inch round trip targets. They stood thirty yards away. The young man had loaded one pistol.

"Go ahead Henry-hit em." Henry fired six times hit one target.

Jake said, "Not very good, let my boy Sam here try."

Colonel Colt agreed. Henry loaded the pistol again and handed it to Sam. He cocked the gun and in rapid fire, cocked, fired and hit all six. Handed the pistol back to Henry.

"My God," said Colonel Colt, "this boy can shoot."

He asked Sam, "How ya like a job with me?"

Sam shook his head no, turned and went back in the shop.

Jake told the Colonel, "We'll take twenty to start, so we can see how well they sell."

Later in the day George came to see Sam. "Miss Sarah wants you to come to supper tonight, will you come?" Sam told him to tell her he would.

It was after dark when he knocked on the kitchen door. Sarah opened the door. She was a beautiful woman even in the dim light. "I've been waiting supper on you, come on in."

Sam followed her up the stairs to her rooms. The table was set with lighted candles. She turned to him said, "After supper I have a surprise for you. Please set and let's eat."

Sam did as she asked. The meal was baked turkey and mashed potatoes, gravy and all the trimming. After supper they sat on the settee and had coffee. They talked for over an hour.

Sarah then said, "Want to see my surprise for you?"

Sam told her not to spend her money on him. She went into the other room and returned with a wrapped box, handed it to Sam. "Open it," She insisted.

In it was a new blue wool suit with a vest and two pairs of pants, also a pair of high button shoes.

"Now," She said, "you gotta have a bath. I've new underwear for you too." Sam shook his head no.

She said, "Look I have a tub waiting for us." She took his hand and led him to a tub in the bed room. Three foot deep, four feet across it was steaming with hot water.

Sarah said, "It's big enough for two." She undressed so did he, they both took a nice warm soapy bath.

Next morning Sam had over slept. He jumped out of bed and dressed and ran to the shop. He did his chores as fast as he could before anyone would come. He sat and waited. No one came. He had forgotten it was Sunday.

Sarah knocked on the back door. "Are you in there Sam?" she called.

He opened the door. "Let's have breakfast and go for a buggy ride. I want to take you on a picnic." Sam had one of the most pleasant mornings he could remember.

She had a new single seat black buggy and a fine stepping bay gelding to pull it, she let Sam drive. They stopped in a small grove of willows and had a picnic of fried chicken.

While they were eating, Sarah asked if there was any thing in the world he would want? It didn't take long. He told her he always wanted a horse of his own.

She said, "I own a farm not far from here. It has lots of horses. You want a' go look?"

He told her, "Lady, you are full of surprises. You own a farm?"

"Yes, let's go look at horses."

As they drove, she told Sam that her Pa had the café and the farm. When he died, he left them to her. She told him she never went out there.

"A man runs it for me and brings the money after the harvest."

"What do you grow on your farm?"

She said, "I don't know, some corn, and all kinds of things, but I know we have lots of horses."

Soon they turned into a lane with large cottonwood trees on both sides. The trees hung over the lane and covered the sun from sight. In about a mile they drove into a farm yard. A large old house with two stories stood before them. An older man came out on the porch. He had long white hair and a long white beard. As he approached the buggy, he walked kinda stooped over. He looked to Sam to be in his early sixties. When he saw who was in the buggy, he said with a big smile, "Miss Sarah what brings you to the farm today?"

"Mr. Cartwright, meet my friend Sam Duncan."

As they both got out of the buggy, she said, "We've come

to look at my horses."

The older man moved to shake Sam's hand, "Call me Al, I ain't seen Miss Sarah in a coon's age. Glad she finally come to see us, I'll have the boys go bring up the horses."

He called to two young black boys in a demanding voice, "Go get them horses. Bring em up here."

Soon there was twenty head in a pen by the barn. Sarah told Sam to look them over. "See if you'd like one."

Sam went in the pen and studied the horse herd for some time. Then he told her, "I like the big sorrel gelding with the blaze face."

"You can have him," Sarah said with a flip of her hand.

Al said to Sarah, "This man knows horses. This horse is the best on the farm. He's worth four or five hundred dollars."

Sam turned to Sarah and said, "You can't give him to me. I'll buy him."

"No, you won't." Sarah looked mad. "If you really want to pay, I'll split the difference with you, two hundred dollars, Okay Sam?"

"It's a deal Sarah."

She told Al to tie the horse to the back of the buggy. Sam was delighted with the horse.

All the way back to town Sarah jabbered and jabbered. The horse meant nothing to her. Sam had to keep looking back to make sure he wasn't dreaming. He owned a horse.

Monday morning Jake had a surprise for Sam. Colonel Colt had given a pistol to him. The Colonel told Jake to tell him, "A man who can shoot like that needs a good pistol."

Then Jake said, "I need to talk to you sometime today. You gettin the Itch Sam?"

Sam smiled and shook his head yes.

After work hours Jake asked Sam to come in the office. "Set Sam," he said, "You getting pretty thick with this woman

Sarah. I'm gonna tell what I know of her. You can take it for what it's worth."

"Fine. I would like to know all you can tell me about her." He was ready to listen to what Jake had to say.

Jake starts talking. "I didn't know her Pa at all. He was a big fella, always in a hurry. I don't think he made friends very easy. Most of the folks around here never got to know the man. When he come to town, his little girl was just a little tyke. He had that café for ten or so years. When he died, she got all he owned being his only kin. She went kinda wild at first. She was about your age, maybe a little older, to be handed a lot of money, it was bad. Lots of people took advantage of her, she be-n so young. She met a river boat man and took up with him, he was probably forty years old. He moved in with her, in that up stairs' apartment. She spent a lot of money redoing it, so we heard. One Saturday night they had a big fight. I heard the yelling and screaming could be heard all over town. In two days he was found a float-en in a back water slue south of town. Been told she had given him an expensive gold watch, it was never found. Some say them blacks that work for her will do any bidding she wants. They're all free and married men they all live in the same location she had built for them south of town. Sam she's had several men since then and they all disappear never to be seen again. I tell ya it's kinda strange. You walk softly around that woman."

Sam thanked him. They never talked of Sarah again.

Sam began gathering horse equipment. A saddle, pack saddle and camp gear. He made a leather saddle scabbard for a rifle and a pair of saddle bags. He had talked to Sam Hawkin about making a two-foot barrel for his colt pistol. Sam made it in a few days and he and young Sam screwed it into the gun. He had made a wooden shoulder stock for it and mounted the same on the pistol. The two fired the rifle-pistol out back on the range.

He asked Sam Hawkin, "How far you figure she'll shoot?"

"Pack all the power in the cylinder you can get, set the ball deep and she should be good for two hundred yards." Sam did and Hawkin was right.

The winter turned to spring, it was 1849. Word came gold had been discovered in California, the gold rush was on.

Many men started west and needed a rifle and pistols. The shop was booming. Sam was lucky, he found and purchased a ten-year old mare who had been used as a saddle and pack horse.

A shipment of a hundred colt pistols came in. Sam purchased one and an English 10 gauge double-barreled shot gun. Now he was ready to go west.

By June prices went sky high. Flour, sugar, corn went for a hundred dollars a barrel. Teams of oxen, mules and horses went for a thousand dollars if you could find any. It was a true seller's market.

Sam talked to an Army officer who told him mounted troops were going to a new post named Fort Laramie. Six hundred miles up on the Oregon trail. "There's gonna be need for all kinda help up there. A man could make good money."

Sam told Jake he was about ready to go. Jake knew how he felt. "If you want ta start a repair gun shop up there, we'll send anything you need. Mail has started coming in from that fort and going that way. Write and let me know, we'll ship supplies to you. Them emigrants need all kinds of help by the time they get that far."

Sam said he would take him up on the deal. "Just as soon as I get set up."

He told Jake he planned to leave Monday morning. "Good luck and God go along with ya," Jake hugged him, turned away and left the shop. It would be a long time before they saw each other again.

Sam was busy packing. Sarah knocked on the back door. "You in there Sam?" she called.

He went and let her in, it was raining hard. "Why you out in this rain?"

"You won't come down, so I came here." She acted angry. "I'll be up there in a little while. You go back, I'll come up and eat." She reluctantly returned to the café.

The two had a nice supper. After supper he let her know his plans of going west. She went into a fit of rage, started throwing things at him calling him names, fell on the floor screaming and kicking, saying she hoped the Indians would kill him. He told her he didn't like to see her act this way.

"I just gotta go Sarah," he told her. "I'll miss you." He went down to the kitchen. George heard it all and said, "Come by on your way, I'll have a food sack for you's." Sam did.

At sunup, with his saddle horse and pack horse he rode to the docks and onto a steam boat he had booked passage on to go up the Missouri River to the town of Independence. The jumping off place for most of the wagon trains headed west and to Fort Laramie on the Oregon Trail. Sam was on his way west.

Chapter 6

Fort Laramie

Sam rode into Independence, after leaving the paddle wheel steamer. There were three wagon trains being made up to go west, one a Mormon with a hundred and fifty Saints. Many a pretty girl was with this train.

Sam missed Sarah already.

Sam asked a wagon boss when they expected to leave. "Not for another week." The other trains were waiting for one thing or the other. No one seemed to be in a hurry.

He decided to push on by himself. He followed a well worn trail west. As he moved past settlements and farms the plains became empty of civilization. He could see that the wagons moved four wide abreast. He guessed it was for protection from Indians. The grass was stirrup high, small streams ran to the north toward the Missouri river. Game became plentiful, rabbits bounded away every few yards, deer stopped to watch them go by. Antelope herds grazed in the distance. Coyotes and wolves hid in the tall grass, not moving unless Sam and his horses disturbed them. Late in the evening of the first day out, two wolves followed along for some time, staying out of gun range. He surmised them had been shot at before. A crippled antelope appeared. The wolves went after it and Sam watched as the two got a meal.

Moving on he found where unshod horses had cut across

the trail. Quite a bunch, maybe ten or more. He made camp in a slight draw. No fires tonight and no hot coffee. That night he had a fitful sleep. Morning light came. He felt tired all over.

He saddled, packed and rode on, without eating. The dried meat he ate as he rode took much water to get down. It was a pleasant, cool morning. By noon a thunder storm hit the prairie. Lightening and thunder rolled across the plains. Soaked to the skin he looked for a spot to camp, none could be found to his liking. He rode on late into the darkness.

Then the rain stopped, it gave the prairie a fresh smell. A fire appeared in the distance. As he drew near, he could see a covered wagon, there were people standing by a fire. He yelled, "Ho the wagon."

A women's voice came back, "Who are you?"

He rode on in. He could see two women with bonnets and heavy coats on. When he stepped down, they both ran to hug him and almost knocked him down, one was saying, "God has answered our prayers." She said, "Thank you God."

He asked what they were doing out here on the plains by themselves? Both women tried to tell him at once. He stopped them, "One at a time."

He pushed them both back and held them by an arm. The older one, he pushed her bonnet back so to see her face, he could see she was very young, she started talking so fast he couldn't understand her. "Whoa, whoa, slow down."

She told him her story. "We're from Illinois, on the way to meet my husband's folks at Fort Kearny on the Platte River. This girl is my little sister, my husband stepped in a gopher hole. He was out in front of the oxen they ran over him and broke his leg yesterday afternoon, we been here ever since, he's in the wagon asleep, my baby and two children we picked up in Iowa are in there too. We been scared to death Indians would come and get us, will you help us?"

Sam asked why they were out here. "Why didn't you follow the river?"

"We were told this is a short cut, my husband was in a hurry to catch his folks."

Sam climbed on the tail gate to look at the man. Struck a match. The air was filled with the smell of fresh blood. He asked if they had a lantern. The young girl went and got one and handed it to him, he lit it and removed the quilt covering the man. His leg lay in a pool of blood, Sam felt his face, he was burning hot.

Sam held the lantern high, he could see three little children asleep father back in the wagon. Sam told the woman, "This man is not asleep, he's unconscious, his leg is shattered, it looks to me like it's got to come off."

The young wife started crying, "No, no, he'll die if you cut his leg off."

"Lady he'll die if we don't, let's get together and get it done."

Sam unsaddled his horses and put the saddles under the wagon. He asked if the oxen were in the yoke all day.

The woman said, "They've been yoked since we started, we were afraid they might run off."

Sam unyoked the team and turned them loose, they started in eating grass.

He told her, "They ain't going nowhere, they'll eat all night."

Sam asked if she had a sewing kit. She did and went to get it. He told the sister to keep the fire going. They had a big pile of buffalo chips.

"We gathered chips all day to have something for the children to do," She said.

"Get it hot as you can but not too high, we don't want the Indians to see it."

Sam looked for something he could make a hot iron out of. A sharp pick hung on the side of the wagon. He knocked the wood handle out, gave the steel pick to the younger girl. Told her, "Get the tip red hot, and bring it to me when I ask."

He went to the wagon told the wife to get something for bandages, heat plenty of water. He set his Bowie knife in the fire to get the blade hot.

"You got whisky?" he asked.

"We're Mormons, we don't use spirits," she said.

"It's for his leg not his belly, I have some in my pack. I'll get it."

Sam got his bottle, climbed in the wagon, the wife was there. "Let's get this quilt out, hand me that pillow." He worked the quilt out and pushed the pillow under the fractured leg. He lifted the leg, pushed the pillow so the bad part of the leg hung loose. He called for his knife and with the knife cut the pants all the way to the hip.

What a sight, pieces of bone were protruding in every direction. He sent the knife back to be heated some more.

He asked, "How long's he been out?"

"Since early this afternoon."

Sam studied the leg. He told the wife, "I ain't no doctor but this leg must come off. You want me to do it? Or do you wanta do it?" Tears streamed down her face.

"I can't do it." Now she was crying hard. "I can't do it."

"You gotta tell me to do it. If you want me to."

"If it's gonna be done, you will have to do it."

"Fine, let's get to it. Get the biggest needle you have and a heavy thread."

Sam called for the hot water. They cleaned the break as best they could. Sam grabbed the wife by her shoulders with both hands, shook her hard saying, "You gotta help me, if you do what I say we'll be okay." She wiped her eyes and shook her head, yes.

Sam slit the skin four ways and peeled it back. Next he cut the leg where the break was, the leg came right off. He laid the leg on the tail gate, cut the meat back to where the break was clean, almost to the knee. He called for the pick and pushed the red-hot end against the meat. A sickening smell of burning flesh filled the wagon. Next he tied an artery and blood vessels with thread. Pulled the skin down, trimmed it to cover the flesh and sewed with needle and thread. Poured the whisky over it and made a pad, he pushed it against the cut. He asked the wife to bandage the leg.

He got down, went to the fire and asked the young girl if they had some coffee.

"We don't drink coffee," she said.

Sam went back got the whiskey and took a big swig. Told the girl, "I don't drink whiskey. It don't like me. I don't like it."

He got his pot and coffee, took water from a barrel on the wagon, made a full pot. While it cooked, he got his bed roll, unrolled it by the fire. Drank his coffee and lay down and went to sleep.

The sun woke him from a deep sleep. He heard children playing. Opening his eyes, the two women were standing above him. They both said, "Good morning, we made your coffee and breakfast."

Sam asked, "How's your man?"

"He woke early this morning, cried out and went back to sleep."

Sam ate a breakfast of bacon, eggs and cold corn bread. "Where the eggs come from?" Sam asked.

"We have chickens in a cage on the other side of the wagon."

This was the first time Sam got a good look at these

women. He asked, "How old are you women?"

The wife replied, "I'll be seventeen in December. My sister is fourteen. My baby is one year, the other two are orphan children we picked up in Iowa. Don't know how old they are, maybe six and eight."

Sam told them, "We gotta get moving." He told the women to get loaded. He went and got the oxen. They were grazing fifty yards away. He yoked them, saddled his horses and tied them to the back of the wagon. He carried his rifle, pistol and became a bull whacker. The children and the women walked beside the wagon. Only the baby and husband rode. Sam turned the wagon north toward the Platte River and Fort Kearney.

At noon they stopped to eat something. Sam unyoked the oxen and unsaddled his horses and put the saddle and packsaddle in the front wagon box. He kept his rifle and shot guns handily. He asked the women their names.

The wife told him, "Our name is the Wards. My husband is Jess Ward. Mine is April. My sister is June, my baby Easter, the children, Andy and Mary Jo. What is yours?"

"Sam, Sam Duncan," he replied. He then asked why they were going west. April said the people in Illinois don't like Mormons. "They forced us to leave. We're going to Salt Lake City."

Sam asked more questions. "What did your man do? You know what kind of work?"

April told him. "Jess worked in his Pa's hardware store. His Pa sold out. His folks wanted to get going west. Jess and I stayed to help the new people get started. Jess has three younger brothers. They went with the folks. Jess being the oldest was asked to stay. His Pa gave us some money to buy this outfit. We got this wagon and oxen in St Joe and outfitted it there."

Sam asked if there was a rifle in the wagon. April said there was. He asked her to get it. She went and brought an old double barrel cap lock shot gun. He checked it out. It wasn't loaded. She went back and got a bag that went with the gun. Sam showed her how to load it.

She said, "I'm a town girl, I don't know a thing about guns and neither does Jess."

"Look," Sam said, "It's not hard to shoot a shot gun, just point and pull the trigger. The gun is safe until the hammers are pulled back." He showed her how. "See the caps I put on the nipples."

She started laughing. "Nipples?" she said.

"Not the kind your baby uses, these caps are what makes the gun shoot, you under stand?"

"I'm afraid of guns." She cringed all over as she spoke.

"You gotta get over that, you'll have to use a gun sooner or later, what if Indians come? You'll have to help me fight-em off." He told her to be sure to set the hammers and not to pull both triggers at once.

A groan came from the wagon. April hurried to see Jess.

She came back said, "He must be awake, his eyes are open, but he's not saying anything."

Sam told her to try to spoon feed him some water. "I saw some wild chickens, I'll try to shoot some." He walked out a hundred yards and circled the wagon. Sure enough two hens flew up, he got them both with the shot gun and returned to the wagon.

"April you can dress these hens on the move. The children can ride my horses."

Sam put both Andy and Mary Jo on his horses, told them to hang onto the horse's mane. "Try not to fall," Sam told them. Both seemed pleased to be riding a horse. June got in the wagon to help April. Sam yoked the oxen, with the horses tied

F. M. Worden

to the wagon they moved on.

They had gone several miles when Sam spotted three mounted Indians to their front. He stopped the team. Told everyone to hide in the wagon. "I'll see what they want. Stay hid, I don't want them to see you, none of you, do you understand me?" Sam had anger in his voice. April said they would.

Sam walked out to meet the riders with his rifle in the crook of his left arm.

As the braves approached within ten yards, Sam raised his hand in friendly manner and spoke to them in Choctaw. They didn't understand. Then he tried sign language. They talked back. Soon the riders gave the wagon a wide berth and rode onto the south. He watched until they were out of sight.

Back at the wagon, April asked what happened. Sam told her the Indians said the river was a sun away.

"Why did they leave?"

"I told them we had white mans sickness in the wagon. The other wagons made us leave, I don't think they will bother us." They moved on.

It was well before sunset when they came upon a large clump of trees. "We camp here tonight," Sam told them.

The children gathered wood and chips for a fire. A good meal of prairie chicken was prepared. Sam told April to make chicken soup for Jess and spoon feed him.

"He's awake but not saying a word," April said.

"At least he's alive. Looks like we'll have a storm tonight, there's lightning in the south, we better get prepared." He made a leanto of canvas between two trees. Before turning in he tied the animals to big stout trees. The people slept in the wagon.

Around midnight the storm hit, lightning danced across the prairie, thunder rolled over head, heavy black clouds and

71

strong winds accompanied the storm.

The animals pulled at their leads trying to get away, the rains came, the animals turned their rears to the rain. It was a heavy down pour for more than an hour, it stopped as soon as it came.

Sam had a fitful sleep. When he did sleep, he dreamed of Sarah's café and the fine meals she used to have for him. He was awake most of the night off and on.

At day light he opened his eyes. He saw the women had a fire going and the smell of bacon frying was in the air. Sam felt as hungry as he had ever been. Coffee, bacon, eggs and corn bread stopped the hunger. He was in a hurry to move as he saw many birds in the trees. "We must be close to the river," he told the women. They loaded and pushed on.

On a rise, just before noon they could see the Platte River some distance before them. Everyone was jumping for joy, to see this beautiful sight. Sam said "Let's push on and camp by the river."

In a few hours the animals were drinking in the Platte River. Camp was made and a meal was prepared.

"How's your man?" Sam asked.

"He's awake and moving a little, still not talking."

Sam told her to keep pushing the chicken soup down him. "Let's stay here and rest for a few days." They all agreed.

Next day Sam saddled his horse, rode west looking for a ford to cross the river. In just a mile he found one, crossed and saw there had been many wagons moving along the trail to the west. He hurried back to tell the women what he had found.

They rested another day. Then loaded and forded the river and turned west. Two days travel put them in sight of Fort Kearney. Jess was awake and talking. April was so happy. She could hardly contain herself.

Sam talked to Jess and Jess asked for everyone to pray and

thank God for their survival. April told him, "Thank Sam, too, he brought us thru."

Next day they were in Fort Kearney and found the Ward family. Much joy and happiness were displayed in the family. Jess was unhappy about having only one leg. Sam told him he was a lucky man to have such a wife and he would be just fine if he tried, many men live a good life with a missing leg.

Next day Sam bid the Wards goodbye, saddled and rode west toward Fort Laramie.

Sam rode the wagon trail, watching for Indian signs. He could see the wagons traveled spread four breasts across the trail. Late that day he found tracks where many unshod horses crossed the trail and moved to the north. He followed them for over a mile, fresh, maybe this morning or late last night, he thought. He turned west again, stayed off the high ground. Camped in a ravine, slept a fitful sleep. He dreamed of many Indians killing many people. He sat up startled. A coyote was howling on the ridge above him. No more sleep, by sunrise, he was on the move again.

As he rode, he watched the ridges to the north, no stopping, he kept moving. At noon hunger gnawed at his stomach. He had to keep moving. Then he saw Indians on a ridge to the northwest. He ducked into a ravine and turned south toward the wagon trail. Reaching it, he rode west. Dust filled the sky to his front. He surmised it must be a wagon train, circling for the night.

For some reason he turned and looked to the back trail. There three Indian horsemen, not more than three hundred yards away, saw him at the same time. They yelled their war hoops and came running their horses toward him, lances at the ready.

He knew he couldn't outrun them, not with the pack mare. He turned her loose. Turned his mount sideways on the trail and dismounted, laid his pistol-rifle across the saddle to help steady his aim. As the warriors came closer, he fired at the lead rider. The bullet hit him square in the chest. He tumbled from his mount. Another bullet found its mark too. A second warrior slumped to the ground and fell in a heap. The last painted brave was charging with his lance. At twenty paces, he too took a bullet in the chest. A surprised look filled his face, big eyed and gushing blood from his wound, he too fell to the ground. Sam could see this brave was just a teenager. His painted face made him look older.

As he looked on this young boy, he got deathly sick. He had never killed a human before. The Indian ponies had stopped by his pack mare. It was easy to gather them up and tie them head to tail with the rawhide reins in their mouths. He rode on toward the wagon train.

This was the train that had circled for the night. Men were busy driving their animals into the middle of the circled wagons. As Sam rode in, the wagon boss came to see him. Asked him what the shooting was about. Sam told him, "You got Indian trouble, there's a bunch coming this way, you better get ready. I have three Indian ponies you can have." He gave the reins of the horses to the wagon boss.

The people became much excited and began preparing to fight. The wagon boss asked if Sam had seen three wagons coming this way. Sam said he hadn't, but he had seen Indians on the ridges to the north and the ones he shot were painted for war.

Just as they talked, three wagons came in to sight. Everyone started yelling and cheering. These were their relatives and friends. No sooner had the wagons appeared so did the Indians. With war hoops they swooped down on the wagons. The men never had a chance. They were either lanced or tomahawked when they tried to keep moving their teams of oxen toward the wagon train. The women and children came running and screaming toward the train, they were lanced, tomahawked and savagely killed by the riders.

Some men of the circled train fired at the riders, but they were out of range, their bullets only kicking up dirt in front of the warriors. Sam saw two young girls run south toward the river, an Indian horseman scooped one up, she fought like a wild cat, he had to drop her to the ground. The rider stopped, with a mighty stroke he drove a lance into her body as she lay screaming on the ground. The other girl was fighting her captivity as hard as the first one.

Sam mounted his horse and with a pistol in hand rode as fast as he could after the Indian warrior with the girl. The brave saw him coming, he threw the girl to the ground and drove a lance into her stomach. By then Sam was on top of the brave, he fired three shots at point blank range into his head, the Warrior tumbled from his horse. Sam reined his mount back to the girl, dismounted and pulled the lance from her body, he picked her up and held her in his arms. Her young beautiful face was pouring blood from mouth and nose. She mumbled the word, "Momma." She died in his arms, Sam wept unashamed. Men from the train came and pried the girl from his arms.

All the dead were loaded in the wagons and taken to the train. That afternoon, four men, three mothers, two young girls and five children were buried in a mass grave down by the river. Much crying, sobbing and praying went on for hours. Then the people sang religious songs for another hour. An elder told the people that God works in strange and mysterious ways, they should go on as God and Brigham Young had planned for them.

The women prepared meals, an older man brought Sam a plate and sat and talked to him. He could see Sam was in bad shape, he asked if Sam was a religious man. "No, I'm not," Sam told him with no hesitation.

The man asked if he knew these people were Mormons. "Yes," Sam answered.

"Do you know about us?"

Sam told him he didn't know too much.

"Let me tell you about us Mormons. Our leader was Joseph Smith. He founded our church in 1830 in the state of Illinois. We are the Church of Jesus Christ of Latter-day Saints. We've been shoved and pushed in every way possible known to man. Brigham Young is now our leader and has founded Salt Lake City in Utah territory for us. The Government said they would let us alone if we sent our young men to fight the Mexicans in California, most of our young men have been lost in the fighting. We're asking all men of Christian faith to join us in Utah and come join our Church."

Sam was impressed with this man and his people. The man asked if Sam would like to join them in Utah. "We would be pleased to have you."

Sam thanked him, said he was leaving in the morning for Fort Laramie. The man said no more.

Sam made his camp for the night down by the river. He wanted to be alone. He made a small fire and made coffee and his supper. He thought back to April and Jess and hoped they were having a safe passage.

He had just unrolled his bed, when two young girls from the train came into the fire light. "Can we talk to you?" they asked.

"Sure, set and talk, I need company about now."

The girls talked for some time, telling him of their lives in the east and the church they belonged to. The older one who was near Sam's age asked him to come to Salt Lake City with them. "We need young men to marry, would you like to marry us?" she asked.

"Oh - no, I'm not ready to marry anyone yet, I sure don't want to be a farmer."

"You don't have to be a farmer, there's lots of things you can do in Utah."

"Not me, I'm leaving in the morning, I thank you both for your offer, now you girls scoot back to the train, I need to get some sleep." He tried to be as easy as he could with these fine girls.

The older girl asked if she could hug him. He said, "Yes." The other wanted to also. She did and they both returned to the train.

Sam had a fitful sleep. He dreamed of the young girl that died in his arms. Dreamed of another massacre, he tried to stop it but couldn't. He sat up stunned, it all seemed so real to him. It was almost morning as the light in the east was breaking thru a cloud filled sky. He got up, made a fire and fixed breakfast, saddled and packed his horses ready to leave.

The elder came and stopped him. Told him some soldiers on horse back had come into camp and wanted to talk with him. He tied the horses and walked with the elder to see the soldiers.

A Lieutenant, who looked to be in his thirties was the commander of the troopers. He asked Sam if he was the one who had killed the warriors back on the trail. "Those Indians were from the Cheyenne tribe, they where Cheyenne Dog Soldiers, they have sworn to stop all immigrants on the trail. We're from Fort Kearny, we've been sent to put them back into their territory."

Sam shook his head as he told him, "You're just a little too damn late."

The Lieutenant took objections to Sam's words. "We do the best we can, we been after this bunch for days, this country is so big we can't be every where, you people have to protect yourselves. We're here just to slow the Indians down. Which way did the warriors go?"

"After the massacre they headed north. Their trail should be easy to follow."

"We'll find them and take revenge for these killings. Will you come with us?" the Lieutenant asked.

"No Lieutenant, I'm on the way to Fort Laramie."

The Lieutenant mounted his horse and bid them all good luck, good by and with a command turned his mount and the troop north.

"They make enough noise, they'll be heard miles away," Sam remarked. "They couldn't catch a cold in those hills, the Indians can hear them coming and never be seen."

Sam told the Elder goodbye and mounted his horse and headed on the trail west.

That night he camped by the Platte River. The grass was plentiful and his horses never raised their heads as they grazed the night away.

The next day he encountered unshod horses' hoofs by the hundreds. The sign was every where. It puzzled him. He surmised there must be some big doings going on or the Indians are attacking the fort in force.

As he approached the Fort, hundreds of tepees were pitched on the east, south and west sides of the Fort. The trail went right thru the tepees, horses were eating grass everywhere, Indian children played games on both sides of the trail. There were dogs by the hundreds, some came nipping at his horses heels, several got kicked by the pack mare. Sam laughed and thought it was funny, as the hounds went yelping away.

"Those dogs have lessons to learn about a white man's horses, serves em right to get kicked," he said to himself.

He rode past many squaws that were doing their chores. Young boys and girls came out and followed along with him for some distance, most had their hands up wanting Sam to give them something. He would shake his head and motion for them to get away, he spurred his mount into a long trot and headed to the fort.

Approaching the fort, he met two mounted officers. A Captain and Lieutenant. He stopped them and asked, "Why are all the Indians camped here?"

The Captain, a stout looking man in his early thirties with a large handle bar mustache answered, "This is a treaty meeting for the first time on the plains. Most of the tribes in this area are here. We think there's more than ten thousand Indians and more coming. The Crows and Shoshones haven't come yet, the Cheyenne have refused to come. Who knows what's gonna happen when Crows and Shoshones get here, they're old enemies of the Sioux, and Arapahos. Are you on the way to the gold fields?" he asked.

"No, soldiers I had met in St Louis told me there's plenty of work here, I'm looking for work."

"We've imported a lot of Mexican people to work around the Fort. They're working on the buildings and grounds. You might get work with the wood cutter, north of here, see the Dutchman, he's the contractor for supplying wood to the Fort, tell him Captain Mack sent you."

"How far north is he?" Sam asked.

"Eight or so miles in the timber, you can't miss them, take your horses up to the stables and tell Sergeant Kelly I said to grain and feed em, you can stay here for the night, we have supper call at five, you're welcome to eat with us."

The Captain was very cordial. Sam thanked him and rode up to the stables.

Sam asked a private if he would call the stable Sergeant. A

Sergeant heard and came out and asking what he wanted. Sam told him, "Captain Mack said to stable and feed my two horses."

"Okay by me," He said. "I'll show you where to stow your saddles and gear."

After he unsaddled his horses the Sergeant led the two and stalled them in the stable. A bugle sounded the mess call. Several troopers came from the stable and headed for a huge tent set up a short distance from the stables. The Sergeant gave orders to two privates to stand guard until he got back.

He said to Sam, "Come on, let's go get some chow." Sam went with him to the tent, long lines of troopers were going past tables where soldiers were putting food on their plates, Sam followed the Sargent. This was the first hot meal he had in days he hadn't fixed himself, he also managed to get a large cup of black coffee. The two sat at a long table with benches on each side, troopers filling the benches, most of the conversation of the troopers was of the Redskins camped on the grounds around the fort. Sam listened to their talk, one soldier said he had heard the wagon train with the presents for the Injun's was late and the Chiefs were getting mad. Sam heard some of the troopers complain about the Government giving the Redskins gifts.

Sergeant Kelly started telling Sam of the building going on. "We're gonna have one of the best posts on the Oregon Trail. A new mess, three barracks, a power magazine, nine houses for officers and a Sutler's store will be finished before summer is over. It's gonna be a great place for us enlisted men to serve. Been in this mans army fourteen yar's and I kain't sees a better place to be stationed."

After supper, Sam thanked the Sergeant and asked if he could sleep in the harness room tonight.

"Okay by me," the Sergeant said.

Sam took a short walk around to stretch his legs. Then rolled out his bed and went to sleep.

Next morning he rode the ten miles to the wood cutter's camp. Finding the Dutchman and getting a job, he was shown by the Dutchman a tent that would be his home for as long as he worked there. The Dutchman also let Sam keep his horses in a pen where the mules were kept.

"The men call me Dutch, we're glad to have another cutter as many men have run off to the gold fields in California. The big tent is where we eat. We keep a guard on the mule pen just in case the Redskins decide to steal some, most Indians don't care for mules so we ain't had no trouble."

Sam was given an axe and a stone to sharpen it with. His job was to trim all the limbs off the fallen trees, to make firewood, he worked at that job for over a month. During that time some troopers stopped and told of the treaty with the tribes and said the Indians had to be moved to Hat Creek thirty miles west, the wagon bearing their gifts was late and the forage for the Indian ponies became such a problem the council site had to be moved. Many more tribes and sub-tribes came to take part in the talks, making this the first great peace council with the plain's Indians.

The meetings took on the color of a powwow like the Indians had never seen before, the tribes showed off their regalia and ponies, the chiefs smoked peace pipes and promised to not fight among themselves and not to attack the emigrants on the trail. Each tribe got a territory of their own to live and hunt in, plus an annuity of fifty thousand dollars worth of trade goods. The commissioners declared peace on the plains forever.

Sam was still working for Dutch and became a teamster. He would drive a timber wagon to the horse drawn saw mill at the fort, two or three times a week. On one of these trips he asked a Mr. Tuller at the Sutlers store if he knew of any cabins near the fort for sale. He was told several old trappers were getting ready to go east, he should go and ask them. He had no luck in finding them.

The next Sunday Sam rode down to the fort. The wood contract had been fulfilled and the men would soon be on their own. Sam stopped again at the Sutlers store to ask about the cabins. Mr. Tuller owner of the store told him a trapper by the name of Jim Bridger had a cabin he hadn't used in a long time. The trapper had been living with the Snake Indians for sometime.

Sam asked, "Jim Bridger? My Pa told of a man of that name he trapped with, when he was a mountain man. This must be the same man?"

"I'm shore he is. Why don't you take the cabin, he won't care?"

Sam asked Mr. Tuller if he knew of a place he could start a gun repair shop. "We have a room here in the store you can use, we been looking for something to help bring emigrants to our store. Be glad to have you, you'll need to have a stove in that room, it'll be cold this winter, the emigrants have thrown all kinds of household goods down on the trail, to lighten their wagons. I'm sure you can find a stove, take my spring wagon and go look."

Sam said he would as soon as he came back from the wood cutters camp. Sam figured things were going good for him and was a pleased young man in the fall of 1851.

Chapter 7

The Maiden Fawn

Sam found Jim Bridgers cabin and moved in. While Sam was setting up his shop in the Sutlers store, he asked Mr. Tuller if he knew of someone to help him write a letter to send to Jake Hawkins in St Louis?

"My wife can help you, she teaches at the fort school. When do you want to write this letter? You'll have to send it soon. The mail only goes once a month. The last will go soon. There'll be no more mail till spring."

Sam wanted to get more tools sent from Jake, he needed to send a letter right away. "I have a few tools but will need more to do a good job."

Mrs. Tuller came in that afternoon and asked Sam if he could write. "Not very well," he admitted. This woman in her mid fifties, shiny black hair and a ready smile said she would write the letter for him.

This winter she would help teach him to write, if he wanted. Sam told her his Ma had started to teach him before she passed. "I can write my name," he said proudly.

"That's great. Let's get going on your letter this evening."

"I've moved my belongings into a cabin west of the store. I'll come back this evening. We can do the letter then."

Sam was very impressed with Mrs. Tuller. She was a woman with a fast and witty mind. Reminded him of his Ma.

He often thought of his Ma and Pa, and Jack.

Mrs. Tuller had brought a book of a-b-c's and a primer for Sam to take and study. "Read these books as best you can and I'll help you all I can." She asked Sam to call her Amanda.

Sam asked if she and Mr. Tuller had any children. "No." She told him she had lost a boy baby some years earlier. "He would be about your age now, we've never had another, I can't have children. It almost killed Mr. Tuller when the baby died. Please never ask Mr. Tuller about him." Sam promised he wouldn't say anything.

The letter got finished and was mailed the next day. Sam asked for wood stock tools, a vice, and any other tools Jake would think he would need to complete his shop. He wrote that freight wagons would be coming in the spring. "Be sure to let me know how much I will owe you. Money will be sent right back."

The next day a light snow was falling. Sam was on the roof of the cabin doing some repair and didn't hear the horseback riders come up.

"What the hell you's doing on my cabin?" a loud voice almost sent him off the roof. Sam turned to see a white man with a long beard and several Indians on horseback looking at him.

"What the hell does it look like? I'm trying to patch a hole in this damn old roof."

"You know who's cabin this is?" the old white man asked.

"An old trapper named Jim Bridger, I was told. Folks said he wasn't use-n it no more, if he comes I'll see him about it."

"Wa'll you're a looking at him, get your ass down here and we'll talk." The man sounded angry.

Sam dropped to the ground and stood before the man on horse back. "You old Gabe?"

"Who the hell are you?"

"Sam, Sam Duncan, you knew my Pa."

The old man was off his horse in a shot and giving Sam a big bear hug. "How the hell is your Pa?"

Sam told him that his Pa had passed some time ago. Gabe wiped his nose on his coat sleeve, with his eyes full of tears, he told Sam his Pa was one of the finest men he had ever known. "What in God's name you doing here at Fort Laramie a fix-n this old cabin?"

"I planned to stay the winter and live here in this cabin if you don't care."

"Hell no. I'm living with the snakes and have a warm lodge and a warm woman, no man can ask for more." He reared back and laughed until his whole body shook. The Indian horsemen all laughed with him. It was so funny Sam began to laugh too.

Gabe finally controlled himself and suggested going in the cabin and have some coffee and a snort, Sam had a pot made, Gabe and the Indians had the snort. The Indians and Gabe enjoyed the coffee so much Sam had to make another pot.

Gabe offered a snort to Sam. "I never been a drinking man, it don't like me and I don't like it."

"Ever man to his own poison, I always says." Gabe reared back and laughed and laughed. The Indians laughed with him, Sam laughed too, it was all very humorous.

Gabe told Sam that he was going to be the chief of scouts for Fort Laramie the coming spring. "How you's like to scout for me?" he asked.

"I know nothing about scouting, but I'm sure willing to learn."

"I have one of the best durn scouts a comm-n to work for me this spring, Old Lonesome Charley Reynolds. I'll pair you's up with him, He's the best. If-n you's like your Pa, it won't take you's long to larn this scout-n business." Gabe said as he shook Sam's shoulder.

Sam told him he could count on him. "I'm a looking forward to it."

Gabe said Sam could have the cabin. "Fix her tight as it's gonna be a cold windy winter. What you's need is a damn good woman, they makes them winter nights a hole lot better." He sat back and laughed again, so did the Indians. Gabe told Sam they had to get a going. "Gotta make thirty miles before resting. I'll be a seeing you's when the snow melts."

Gabe and his Indian companions mounted and rode off toward the west. Sam watched them go and felt a sense of loneliness for the first time since he had come west.

Sam spent all his time fixing the shop and his cabin until the snows got too deep to work on either.

The post commander heard Sam was repairing guns and sent many rifles for him to repair. Sam cut a trap door in the back wall and set a target fifty yards out so he could check his work, this went on all winter.

Mrs. Tuller and Sam became good friends as she taught him to read and write, she found he was a quick study and enjoyed her time helping him.

The spring came with heavy rain that made the trails deep in mud, the scouting didn't start until late May.

Sam along with Charley and four Shoshone Indian scouts kept a close watch on the Cheyenne Dog Soldiers. The Dog Soldiers raided the Sioux and Blackfeet villages to take horses and captives. The war chief Rain in the Face led the warriors. As long as the Cheyenne stayed away from the Oregon Trail the white soldiers paid little attention to what they did. Old Gabe warned the new commander of Fort Laramie, Colonel Phil Sheridan that an all out war between the tribes would be forthcoming if something wasn't done to stop the raiders. The Colonel only said, "The best Indian is a dead one." The raids continued.

A party of commissioners was sent from Washington to try for a treaty between the tribes, to try and stop the killings between the tribes and the raids on the trail.

Old Gabe was a friend of one of the commissioners, Tom Fitzpatrick who knew Sam's Pa, he asked Gabe and his scouts to get the Chiefs of the Sioux, Cheyenne, Arapaho and Paiute together for a friendly council meeting.

Sam was assigned four Crow scouts to help find the various Sioux clans. Iron Fist was the oldest, Black Elk was Sam's age, the other two were young teens, Curly and White Man Runs Him.

Sam and the scouts found the clan of the old Chief Flying Eagle some eighty miles north east of Fort Laramie. Sam and Iron Fist rode right into the center of the village. They carried no weapons and raised their hands in a show of peace. It was a chance they had to take, the old chief came out and spoke to Iron Fist. "Why you come with this white man to our lodges? No white eyes should be in our country, you Crows have turned against all your Indian brothers, now you come with the Shooter to our village. Why you come?"

Sam was known as the Shooter to the Sioux, the killing of the three Cheyenne Dog soldiers on the Oregon Trail had filtered down thru the tribes, the Dog Soldiers named Sam, the white man who kills Indians.

Iron Fist told the chief the whites wanted to have another treaty with the Sioux and all the clans. A meeting was going to be held on the Little Powder Creek near the Stone Tower the First day of the new moon. "Will you come?" Iron Fist asked.

Before the chief could answer, a young warrior rode his horse hard against Sam's, in a loud voice he told all the Indians gathered there, "I know this Shooter, soon, he will be mine."

Iron Fist told Sam what the warrior said. Sam dropped from his horse. Pulled his belt knife and spoke, "Talk is easy."

Sam stood six feet four inches, weighed two hundred pounds. The warrior was near his equal in stature. They squared off both had knives at the ready. War hoops were heard thru out the village from the warrior braves.

Chief Flying Eagle came between the two. "No fight! These white eyes has come in peace, no fight now," he demanded. The warrior sneered and turned away.

The chief said he would come to the meeting. Sam and Iron Fist rode safely out of the village. Iron Fist told Sam, "Is good you show no fear. That warrior is the war chief Red Cloud. He says he will drive all white eyes from this land. He is much respected by all the tribes. I say he is wrong. Our Crow Chief, Plenty Coups say too many white men to fight. They like birds of the sky. Too many to count. If we be friends, the whites will treat us well."

Sam replied to him, "I hope your chief is right." They talked no more of the Crow chief and his logic.

Three more villages the scouts found and made the invitation to come to the meeting. No trouble until the last clan, another brave challenged Sam. The village chief stopped the challenge, No harm was done. Iron Fist said that the War chief was Sitting Bull, another hard head who was making war talk.

Sam and the Crows returned to Fort Laramie and were told to accompany Old Gabe and the commissioners to the meeting.

The party left Fort Laramie with four officers, fifty troopers, four white scouts, twenty Indian scouts, the two commissioners with a pack train of fifty pack mules, loaded with presents for the Indians.

In three days the party made camp several miles from the meeting place. Only the officers, white scouts and the commissioners were to enter the camp of the Indians. The camp numbered more than a thousand men, women and children.

Old Gabe told Sam to stay close with his Crows. "We may need you." That's all he said.

Sam and the Crows moved to a wooded hillside above a creek and a half mile from the village of tepees. Sam had the Crows hobble the horses and keep guard and let the horses graze the new green grass. Sam took his bed roll and moved down the hill away's to where he could see the creek and listen to the rushing stream. He lay down and fell asleep.

Some time later he was awakened by female laughter. Looking down to the creek he could see two females bathing in the stream, standing in the water up to their knees, their naked wet bodies gleaming in the sun light. Sam could see their buckskin dresses hanging from tree branches in the woods across the stream. The girls were gently splashing each other and enjoying them- selves in the clear cool stream. The older girl was tall with soft black loose hair that hung to her hips, her creamy tan complexion, her round firm breasts and girlish laughter, set Sam's heart beating so fast he felt it would leave his chest. Never had he seen a more beautiful woman, she looked more white than Indian. If lighting strikes a man once in his life time, it hit Sam hard that sunny bright summer day on that hill side, Sam fell deeply in love with this Indian girl.

He said to himself, "I must have her."

One of the Crows coughed or made some noise. Sam looked to see who or what it was, when he looked back, the girls were gone. Their buckskin dresses and moccasins with the maidens, had vanished into the woods across the way.

The picture of the young Indian girl was imbedded in his mind forever. He told the Crows to stay put, he was going to the village. He crossed the stream and looked for the girl's trail. Finding it, he followed it to the village. The sun was setting in the western sky, a huge fire was being built in the center of the village.

Sam went straight to Old Gabe and told him of the Indian maiden. "I must find this girl, I'm in love, will you help me?" he pleaded.

"Why shore Sam." Gabe could see on Sam's face the love bug had hit him and hit hard.

"Set yourself down with me by the fire, the Indians are gonna have a meal and a circle dance for us to see. She'll be one of them dancers, I'll bet my life on it."

Sam sat crossed leg as did all the other white men. The Squaws had tin plates filled with cooked meat and a flat kinda bread served to each man. Gabe asked what was the meat. A squaw only said "bow-wow." He asked no other questions. To Sam's surprise a cup of coffee was given each of the men.

The Indian Men in their finest feathered war bonnets, the squaws with a feather in a head band, stood one man one squaw in a large circle around the fire, the shadows of the people made them seem larger than life.

The drums started, the dancers began their chanting "hy-ya-ya-hy-ya-ya." They moved in a sideways dancing rhythm, the drums grew louder and louder, the chanting and dancing faster. No white man had never seen this dance before.

Sam watched intently as the dancers moved by, the smoke from the fire made his eyes water. It was hard to distinguish the dancing squaws apart. He got up and moved closer, staring closely into each squaws face as they passed, there she was, her dark eyes flashed as she passed. Sam waited, when she passed again, he entered the dance next to her. He took her hand and looking down at her, smiled the biggest smile he could make, she smiled back and he squeezed her hand hard. Old Gabe came and pulled him from the dance saying, "You's want-a start a war here and now, them braves ain't gonna take lightly to your love make-n, your time will come."

Gabe made Sam set back down, and each time she passed,

she turned her head and gave him a big smile. He couldn't take his eyes off her, she was so beautiful.

Gabe put his arm around him saying, "Sam get back to your Crows, you's gonna have a war here right now. I'll find all about this gal you so interested in."

Sam went back with the Crows and went to bed, he couldn't sleep, all night he rolled and tumbled in his bed roll, he saw the maiden in his mind all thru the night. "God she is beautiful. I must try my best to have this girl." He said this over and over to himself. "Somehow she must be mine, I'll get Gabe to help me."

At sunrise a scout came to tell him that the treaty was not signed, the gifts had been left in a pile in the middle of the village. Flour, tobacco, coffee and rolls of cloth were scattered all over after the Indians picked thru the piles.

The entire treaty party saddled up and started for Fort Laramie, a failed mission. Sam rode with a heavy heart.

Gabe rode up beside him. "You's want-a hear about this gal you're a looking for?"

"What did you learn for me Gabe?" He rode close to hear what Gabe had to tell him.

Gabe told him, "The girl's ma was a Mexican. Captured as a small yung-n in Mexico and swapped and traded thru the tribes, as a young girl, she ended up in this Sioux tribe. Man Afraid of His Horses took her for his wife, she had a boy baby first, he's named, Afraid of his Horses too, he's a war chief. This gal was her second baby, her Ma died having her, she's been raised by her Pa's wife's, he has four Squaws, maybe more."

"Sam," Gabe said, "this here gal is all Indian, I got a good look at her, she's as purty as a picture. I'll tell you right now she's all Sioux and you'll never take the Indian out-a her."

"I don't care, I want her, tell me Gabe, what have I gotta,

91

do to get her?" Sam listened hard to get every word Gabe said.

Gabe looked away, a frown on his face, looked up at the sky, then he looked Sam square in the eyes. Leaned over and said, "I'm a bet-n a lot them bucks want her too, the family was camping at Fort Laramie last spring, I see-d her old Pa there, I'm a bet-n thar'll be thar next spring. If-n she ain't take-n by then, if-n them young bucks ain't got her, you's may have a chance. All you's can do is wait and see."

Gabe could see Sam was excited. Tell me Gabe if she ain't married what will I have to do to get her?"

"Wa'll I'm a gonna tell ya, Mind ya now if she ain't been took, we'll find out what her Pa likes. I know he wants and likes lots of ponies, we'll find out what else he likes and I'll tell ya, them squaws will have some-m to say. If-n they want's to get rid of her, it'll be easy, we'll just have to wait and see."

Sam shook both clinched fists and said, "By God Gabe, I'll do my best too make it work, whatever it takes."

The rest of the summer and into the fall the scouting was slow. Sam and his Crows had made a swing north and turned east looking for the Cheyenne dog soldiers, they were not to be found, they turned south to the Oregon Trail. Stopping on a high ridge there was a sight down on the trail he couldn't believe, men, women and children pulling and pushing two wheel carts. There must have been near a hundred such conveyances, ever now and then a wagon and oxen was in the mix.

Sam and the Crows rode down to the trail slow. Sam kept a hand up to show they were friends. A rider came up and asked who they were. Sam told him they were scouts from Fort Laramie. Sam asked about these people. "They're Mormons, on the way to Salt Lake City, most are from Europe. I'm hired to get-m thru, toughest bunch I ever saw, you gonna see a lot more comm-n .Their make-n them carts by the hundreds in St

Joseph, next spring thar'll be thousands a comm-n." He asked, "How far to the Fort?"

"Yu'll make it by noon tomorrow if-n you get an early start, I'm sure a troop will come to take you in. Have you seen any Indians?"

"No, it's been real quite, we ain't seen hide nor hair of red skins."

"When we get to the fort, I'll let the commander know you're a comm-n."

Sam and his Crows rode hard for Fort Laramie.

Chapter 8

Fawn and Sam

As soon as Sam reached the fort he reported to the commanding officer and told him of the cart train coming on their way to Salt Lake City. The officer sent a troop to escort the train in to Fort Laramie, the train left the fort in a few days, winter was fast approaching. They were told to hurry or be caught by the snow in the mountain passes. A report came later that the train made a safe passage.

Winter made an early entrance. A blizzard hit in October and stayed for two weeks. Sam spent most of his time in the shop refurbishing military rifles. The weather let up for a month then hit with a vengeance and stayed for weeks.

Late one afternoon, Sam was working in the shop. Amanda came in and asked if he had seen the Indians huddled on a bench out against the store wall. Sam said he hadn't. "Go see what they want?" Amanda asked him.

Sam put on a coat and opened the door to a biting cold wind and saw four figures trying to cover themselves against the cold with blankets. Sam motioned to the man to come with him inside, the four followed him in to the store, inside the Indian man pushed a rifle at him. "You fix-em?"

Sam took the gun, he could see it was an old trade rifle converted to a cap lock, the hammer would not stay cocked. "Me fix-em," Sam told the Indian.

Again he motioned for them to follow, he led the four Indians into his shop. The Indians went to the stove, put out their hands trying to get warm. He could see by their hands three of the Indians were women, they were shaking and shivering all over.

Sam took the rifle to his bench and went to work. Taking the side plates off he could see the sear chocking notch had sheared off. Removing the sear, he began with a piece of flat steel to make a new one. This took several hours. Finished he installed it into the gun with a new hammer spring, he turned to show the man it now would work.

To his amazement, there looking at him was the girl of his dreams standing by the stove, he looked her in the eyes and said, "You are the most beautiful woman I have ever seen." She only smiled at him.

Amanda standing in the door, heard his words and said, "Is this the girl you've been mooning about? Lord-E-Lord I say she is a beauty, you sure can pick-em. Sam show-em some hospitality, take them to your cabin and fix some of your elk meat. Make points with her family. You'll never have a better opportunity than this."

Sam put on his hat and coat and motioned for them to come with him, the four Indians followed him to his cabin. In the cabin Sam lit a lamp and started fires in the stove and fire place. He cut meat from a hanging elk on his enclosed back porch and set to cooking. The two women helped him prepare the meal of meat, beans and fresh baked bread from the fort bakery.

After eating, the man, his squaw and little girl wrapped in their blankets, laid down on the floor next to the bed and went to sleep.

Sam sat in his rocker facing the Indian girl, she sat on the fireplace hearth and put out her hands. Sam took them in his and asked in sign language her name? She said proudly, "I can speak American."

"You know all the things I've said?" He was surprised. "Tell me your name, what are you called?" He leaned close to hear, she spoke so softly he had to listen closely.

"My name is Little Fawn." She was smiling all the time as she spoke.

"The name fits, you're as beautiful as a new born deer, I love you Fawn." Sam stood, pulled her up to him and kissed her on the lips, she pulled away, then came back and rubbed her nose against his face.

"I love you too, Sam."

"Fawn, do you know what love is?"

"Yes, a Momma loves her baby and a Papoose loves their Momma, I must sleep now." She wrapped herself in a blanket, lay down with her family and went to sleep.

Sam sat for awhile watching the sleeping figure on the floor. "I can't believe she said she loves me." He said it over and over to himself, finally he removed his boots and lay down on the bed, pulled a robe over himself and went to sleep.

Day light had come into the cabin when he woke up. The family was gone, the cabin cold, he jumped from his bed, pulled on his boots and ran outside calling, "Fawn, Fawn where are you?"

The fresh fallen snow had covered their tracks. He returned to the cabin, made coffee and then went up to the store. "Have you seen the Indian family this morning?" he asked the Tullers.

No one had seen the family. Amanda said, "They couldn't get far in the deep snow, why don't you take a horse and go have a look? They must have a lodge somewhere close."

He did as she suggested and rode a big circle, but found no trace of the Indian family, he did find two soldiers that were missing, their frozen bodies were in a group of trees a mile from the fort, they must have lost direction as they had moved away from the fort.

Sam was disappointed and spent his time in the shop, just to keep busy, the winter drug on, Spring came early the year of fifty seven.

Sam was working in the shop when Gabe came in and asked if he had seen the Indian girl and her family camped down on the flats east of the fort.

"What did you say Gabe, did you see them?" Sam couldn't believe what Gabe had said "Are you sure?"

"Rode as close to her as I am to you, just ten minutes ago, why not go see?" Gabe had a big smile on his face.

"Come on Gabe, I gotta go see her myself." Sam went running to his cabin, saddled a horse. He and Gabe rode to the camp of the Indians, there tending a fire sat Little Fawn, she stood as they rode up.

"Where have you been Sam?" she asked. "I been waiting for you to come for me."

Sam was off his horse in a flash and took her in his arms and was kissing her face.

Gabe was yelling, "Sam this ain't no way to be a court-n. You're gonna get us killed, back off, back off boy!"

Sam pushed her away and said to Gabe, "I plum got carried away, I love this girl."

Gabe was off his horse and with his hat in his hand leaning down and looking in the teepee, asked if the man of the family was at home in the Sioux language. Man Afraid of His Horses came forth, followed by two squaws and a little girl. "What you want of me old white man?" he asked in sign language.

"My friend here," pointing to Sam, "wants your daughter Little Fawn for his wife, he's willing to pay the great chief for his daughter's hand."

The Indian father went to Fawn and in whispers talked to

her, she shook her head, yes, yes. Gabe gave Sam a high sign, he and the Indian walked off talking. It took an hour for them to return.

"Sam," Gabe said, "he wants five ponies, a new rifle and plenty powder and shot. And a little whisky won't hurt. What them Squaws will want, I don't know but we must bring lots of gifts for them, I'll get them ponies you get the rest."

Sam told Fawn, "I'll be back tomorrow at high noon, you're gonna be my wife."

She stood looking at him and shaking her head, yes.

Gabe told Sam, "I can have them ponies here in the morning, you's round up the rest." Gabe mounted and loped off to the west. Sam went to the Tullers and asked Amanda to help him. They loaded the buckboard with all kinds of things they hoped the squaws would like. Sam was so happy he hardly slept that night, he had never been this happy in his whole life.

Next morning he rose before sunup and went to the store to load the gifts for her Pa. He walked back and forth like a caged lion, the Tullers tried to get him to eat. He just drank coffee and walked around the buckboard and every few minutes he would ask if he had got enough to satisfy her family. Amanda told him he was paying more for this girl than any man ever had. Still Sam wondered if he needed more gifts for the family.

Old Gabe came in before noon, with him were five Shoshone braves and five paint ponies. Gabe said to Sam, "Let's get on with this before the old Chief changes his mind, they been known to be damn changeable."

Sam with the Tullers and some off duty soldiers, a few civilian workers, Gabe and his Shoshones, all converged on the Indian village and stopped in front of the family's tepee. The old Chief came forth and stood, arms folded, dressed in his finest war bonnet and buckskins, not saying a word he looked the crowd over.

Gabe was the first to speak, "Great Chief we have brung you many ponies and gifts, our hearts are open to your kind ways, let your new son bring gifts to you." He motioned for Sam to bring the ponies. Sam came forward and in sign language gave them to the Chief. The Chief walked slowly around them, and grunted, "Good, good." A young boy led the ponies away.

Sam came forward with the rifle, shot, powder and caps. The Chief took the rifle and looked it all over again he grunted, "Good, good." He was pleased.

The Tullers being helpful, started unloading the buckboard. The squaws came from the teepee and stood stone cold behind the Chief not cracking a smile until the gifts were laid at their feet. Then the smiles came. The chief called for Little Fawn to come out. Took her right hand and Sam's right hand and tied them together with a leather thong saying some words in Sioux. He shook his head yes and untied the thong. Gabe gave a big yell and told Sam, "You're now a married man."

The Sioux wedding ceremony was over. The celebration began. Fawn and Sam sat on blankets on the ground as young boys and girls began dancing to flute music and drum beats. They danced in circles making whooping sounds and shaking their hands on raised arms over their heads, all the time turning and dancing in small circles. Fawn rose up and joined with them. This dance was the Sioux wedding dance. The white people started clapping and singing a religious song, "We'll All Gather by the River." The singing was led by Amanda. A jug appeared and was passed around. It was soon empty. Another came forth and it too was soon emptied. Everyone was having a gay old time. Gabe was as happy as Sam and laughed and made hooping sounds of his own. Fawn and Sam were two happy people. Sam hugged and hugged his new bride. She laughed and smiled and danced around him. No two people could be more happy that sunny spring afternoon on the plains of Wyoming.

The celebrating went on the rest of that afternoon. The squaws came with plates of food for the new married couple. Cooked meat, Indian bread and a drink made from an herb. The drink was to make the sexual juices flow, all new Sioux couples tasted this rare treat. As they drank, the squaws and young girls giggled and acted in giddy ways pointing at the couple. The young Indian men smiled, laughed and clapped their hands. All the Indians knew what was in store for this newlywed couple. Except the very young. They too danced and laughed with the elders.

As the sun set in the western sky, Fawn took Sam by the hand and led him to a tepee set up in the trees near the Platte River. Inside in the center of the tepee a fire was made ready to be started. With a fire stick she lit the fire. By the light of the fire Sam could see buffalo robes covered the ground. A strange smell came from the fire. It was also for newlywed couples. It was to encourage the making of papooses. The newlyweds spent an enjoyable night together consummating their marriage.

The next morning Sam took Fawn and her belongings to his cabin. At the cabin, Amanda had prepared a breakfast for the newlyweds. All morning well wishers came to the cabin with food and gifts for the new married couple.

Amanda asked Fawn if she would like to be married in the white man's church. "Oh, yes," she said, it would make her very happy. Sam agreed. That evening being Sunday the couple were married in the post Chapel. The Tullers, Old Gabe, Sam's Crow scouts, several officers and their ladies attended. The wedding was preformed by the post Chaplin. Another celebration was held at the post commander's quarters.

Sam Duncan was the happiest man in the entire country to have this beautiful girl for his wife.

The only sad time was when old Gabe came and told Sam he had had enough of frontier life. "I'm going to Missouri and get to farm-n."

It was a sad day for Sam when he left. "I'll never forget you Gabe. I love you like I did my Pa."

Old Gabe would die on his farm in Missouri.

Chapter 9

Life with Fawn

The summer slipped by so fast, one could hardly believe winter was here again. One winter evening Sam sat by the fireplace and watched his bride preparing the evening meal. He marveled at this young woman. The way she had fit into his life. The ladies of Fort Laramie had fallen in love with her and she with them. She made buckskin shirts, vests, coats and moccasins. The beaded work she put on the garments was beautiful. The white people of the fort all wanted her work and at the same time she taught Sam to speak the Sioux language. His knowledge of Choctaw helped to make it easy.

That winter she made Sam an elk hide coat, a soft buckskin fringed shirt and a pair of boot moccasins. He liked them so much he wore them all the time. Not one person had ever called him a Squaw man. At least not to his face.

Fawn loved to watch the ceremonies at the fort and what the soldiers did. The changing of the guard, the raising and lowering of the flag, the marching, the horse troopers maneuvers. She loved the band music. Most of the soldiers admired her and none ever spoke a bad word of her.

The officers of the fort gave dances at every opportunity. Fawn loved to go and watch the officers and their ladies dance. It was the evening of a Fourth of July dance that Fawn and Sam watched the dancers from the porch out side of the Old

Bedlam building. Fawn insisted that Sam try to dance with her. Sam tried but had two left feet. Captain Ryan's wife, Sue, saw them thru a window and came out and asked if Fawn would like to learn the white people's dances. Fawn was overjoyed. "Yes, yes," she answered. Sue told her to come to her quarters, bring Sam and she would teach them. Fawn and Sam spent many evenings with the Captain and Sue dancing to Sue's music box that played the Blue Danube Waltz. Fawn became very good at the dance. Sam and Fawn found they liked to dance together, they were good.

That winter the officers and noncommissioned officers held a Christmas Eve dance and Sue saw to it that Fawn and Sam had an invitation. All the ladies dressed in their finest, the soldiers in their dress uniforms made an impressive sight. Fawn wore the most beautiful white fringed and beaded buckskin dress anyone had ever seen. She was stunning. Her shiny long black hair hung in two braids. Her flashing black eyes and rose-colored cheeks had all the men wanting to dance with her and most did. She was by far the most beautiful woman at the dance. Sam was so proud of her. He also was outstanding in his best suit. He danced with every woman there. Sue was so proud of her teaching the couple to dance, she told everyone what good students Fawn and Sam were.

Sue was a good horse woman, and rode almost every afternoon. The Captain asked Fawn to ride with her. Fawn also a good horse woman taught Sue her ways of Indian riding. The two women loved to ride together.

The years flew by. A new President was elected in the States and word came that the South had seceded from the Union. Then came the news of Fort Sumpter and War between the States. The Army pulled most of the troops from the western forts to fight in the war. The Oregon Trail was wide open to Indian attack. The Indians thought the soldiers were leaving because of them. Raiding became wide spread. The Oregon Trail was shut down most of the war years.

The spring thaw of 1862 was slow to come. Sam and his Crow scouts had come in from their first scouting trip and reported the tribes to be mostly peaceful and hard at hunting game and stealing horses from each other.

Returning to his cabin he found his wife in tears and in a terrible state. She told him thru crying words that Major Ryan's wife, Sue, had been raped and murdered. "If I had gone with her, it would not have happened." Thru her tearful words she told her husband that Major Ryan now the commandant of the fort, wanted Sam to come to his office.

At the office Sam found the Major in an awful state. The Adjutant Lieutenant Adams was trying to soothe him to no avail. When the Major saw Sam he said, "Sam I want you to go get that son-of-a-bitch who killed my Sue so I can hang the dirty bastard. I'll give you a letter of permission to go anywhere. Take the best horse in the stable. He has taken my grey gelding and headed east. It was Corporal Schmidt. I sent him as her escort. He raped and killed her. Go Sam as soon as you can."

Sam promised he would bring him back. "I'll start as soon as I get my gear together." Sam left within an hour. Fawn begged to go with him. He refused her. He took the Oregon Trail east. A light rain had washed all tracks away. He would lope and walk his steed so as not to use him up. Second day out he found the telegraph wires had been ripped down by Indians for several miles. He knew no word of the Corporal could have been sent ahead.

Late that evening he met a wagon train coming west. He asked the wagon master if he had seen a soldier riding a grey horse going east on the trail. "Yes, came in our camp late last night, said he had a message to take to Fort Leavenworth. We

104

gave him a meal, fed his horse and he went on his way."

Sam told him the story, thanked him and rode on. Everyone he met he would ask about the Corporal. Many said they had seen him. Sam rode into Fort Leavenworth two days later and talked to a Captain Bates. He told him the Corporal he was after had taken a steam boat with troops on the way to a battle somewhere down on the Tennessee River. Sam got permission to go on a troop boat bound for the fighting.

Three days of travel put Sam at a place called Pittsburgh Landing. A major battle had just finished. Boats were being loaded with wounded men from both sides. Sam asked of the Corporal with the grey horse and was pointed to the battle field. He had been seen on his way there.

What a terrible place. Sam led his mount thru many dead men laying in every direction in both uniforms. He found a party picking up the dead. A Sergeant told him a man answering to the description of the Corporal had been seen robbing the dead. He had killed wounded men if they resisted. He was last seen on the road going east on the south side of the river. Sam thanked the Sergeant and took the road east.

Within a few miles two horsemen blocked his way. Two more came in on his rear. All had their guns leveled on him. "Where ya going Yank?" a rebel Sergeant asked.

Sam could see these men meant business. "I ain't no Yank" Sam answered. "I'm after a blue belly who's been a robbing and kill-en wounded men back on that battle field." Sam was wearing a fringed buckskin shirt and grey pants and looked more like a reb than yank.

"We done see'd him," one of the men spoke up. "He was a tearing along the other side o the river, we never got a shot at him. He was a riding a grey horse."

Sam asked where he could cross the river.

"Thar's a ford a mile or so on down," he was told. "Go get

the son-of-a-bitch and kill him for us," the Sergeant said.

Sam pushed on and found the ford and crossed. He rode fast on the road east.

It was after dark when he saw a fire thru the trees a short distance off the road. Tying his horse he slipped up on a sleeping figure by the fire. There sleeping was the man he was after. A blow with a pistol on the head knocked the man cold. Blood streamed down the side of his head. Sam felt like killing him right then and there. No, he had to take him back to Major Ryan. He rolled him over and tied his hands behind his back. Went back for his horse and from the saddle bag took a rope and tied his feet up to a limb of a tree. Then completely drained of energy lay down and went to sleep.

The man's groaning woke him up. Day light had come. He could see a strange looking rifle laying a few feet away. He picked it up and examined it. On the barrel it read New Haven Arms Company 44 rimfire cartridge. It had a lever, out side hammer and no fore arm. There also was a pistol on this man with Remington Model 1861 on the barrel.

The man finally came around. With one eye swollen closed, blood matting his full black beard, he said in his German accent, "That you Duncan? You hit my head too hard. Why didn't you kill me?"

"I'm taken you back to Fort Laramie so's Major Ryan can hang your sorry ass. Where did you get this rifle?"

Schmidt spit at him. Sam shoved the barrel hard into his gut. "I ain't gonna ask again, you no good bastard."

The Corporal told him he had picked it up on the battle field with a pouch of cartridges. "I was a high ranking German officer, I get no respect from you people. I'm better than any of you." He was as belligerent as a man could be.

"Why did you kill her? Wasn't raping her enough?"

The Corporal could see Sam was mad as hell. "She could

fight like the devil. I told her I was gonna have her even if she was dead. She asked for it. I don't care if I live or die, I'm no good in this country," he said with a snarl on his lips.

"You're gonna die mister. If they don't kill you, I will." As he spoke, Sam's whole body shook with anger. Sam loaded the man on the grey, with his hands still tied behind him. He tied his feet to the stirrups and headed for Pittsburgh Landing.

It was noon when they reached the landing. Got a ride across to the west side on a ferry boat and asked an officer where he could keep his prisoner. "This the man who was robbing the dead?" the officer asked.

"This is him."

"General Grant wants this man, come with me." Sam followed the officer, pushing the Corporal ahead.

In a tent sitting behind a field desk was a stocky man with a full beard, smoking a large black cigar. He looked to be a man in his fifties. "Sir," said the officer, "this man has brought in the man accused of robbing the dead and killing the wounded on the battle field."

"How do we know this is him for sure?" asked the General.

"We have several men who saw him, I'll go get them."

Sam spoke up, "Here's a bag of watches, rings and money I found on him." Sam handed the bag to the officer. He took it and dumped the contents on the desk in front of the General.

The General stood in disbelief. Looking at the loot he said, "This has to be the worst crime I have ever seen. What have you got to say for yourself, Corporal?"

The Corporal spat out, "Go to hell General."

The General called for the guards. A Sergeant and four privates came up. The General said, "Take this son-of-a-bitch out and hang him right now."

Sam turned to leave. The General called him back. "I want you to see him hung. Then come sit and talk with me."

Sam went with the officer and watched Schmidt kicking air. It was short and quick. He didn't say a word before he was hung.

Back in the tent the General introduced himself. "I am Ulysses S. Grant. How are you called?"

"My name is Sam Duncan, I came from Fort Laramie to bring this man back. He raped and killed Major Charles Ryan's wife, Sue."

"Charlie Ryan's wife?"

"That's right sir"

"I went to the Point with old Charlie, what a beautiful woman she was. I'll wire Charlie we got the bastard and hung him. Now I want to ask you to join my staff. A man like you can be useful to me. How about it?"

"No sir, I promised the Major I would bring his grey horse back and I am needed there. I must return." Sam was flattered the General would ask. "I would like to ask if I could keep the guns I took from the Corporal?"

"Keep them, I'll see that you get passage as soon as it comes available" the General told him. He boarded a steam boat that afternoon on the way to St Louis.

The boat docked at St Louis three days later. Sam went straight to the pens behind the Hawkins gun shop. Unsaddled and put his horses in the pens. He knocked on the back door of the shop. To his surprise Jake opened it. What a happy reunion. Jake was so surprised to see Sam standing there he was almost speechless. When he found words he was overjoyed. All work in the shop stopped. Everyone came to welcome Sam. Questions came thick and fast. He told them he had married and had come east to catch a soldier killer. The job done, he had to return to Fort Laramie as soon as he could. He asked Jake about Sarah. Jake told him she had married a river boat gambler and had sold her holdings here to the black people working for her. She was last reported to be in New Orleans. George now runs the café.

"You should go see him. He always asks about you."

Sam showed Jake the guns he had taken from Schmidt. Jake had heard of the rifle, had not seen one. He said, "It's called a Henry. The pistol by Remington has been made for a few years. We can convert it to use the same cartridge as the Henry if you would like."

"What a great deal that would be, I want to do it," Sam told him and the process was started as they talked.

Sam, Sam Hawkins and Jake had supper at the café with George. He was so glad to see Sam he told him all the things that had happened to the blacks since they owned the café and Miss Sarah had left. "We shore didn't want her to leave. She was so good to us. We didn't want her to marry that gambler man. Now we hears she and him ain't together no more, we hears she has a café down in New Orleans town. She is one fine lady, we shore do's miss her."

"I missed her for a while myself."

Sam told them all he had to get back to Fort Laramie and would be leaving in the next few days. "I am so glad to see you all, I'll be back one day with my lady."

Two days later Sam took a river boat to St Joseph and headed up the Oregon Trail. The first stop he made was at an old pony express station that, he was told, was being made into a stagecoach relay station. One of the workers said that the line was being started by Ben Holladay. It would go from St Louis to Salt Lake City. Relay stations would be placed twenty miles apart. A new line was coming from California to Salt Lake City. Sam stayed at stations being built all along the way to the Fort. Thought to himself the Indians will have plenty of places to get horses.

He rode into Fort Laramie in mid afternoon. He went to the

cabin, Fawn was overjoyed to see him. The sad note was she told him Major Ryan had taken his life, just after he got the wire Schmidt had been hung. She was the last person to talk to him. He had told her, "Life was no good without Sue." She had been out of his office a few steps when the gun shot was heard. Fawn was so sad to have lost them both.

A new Commanding officer had come from the states. An older man who had never had a command before. A Captain John White. This man Sam could see was uneasy in the job.

The summer of 1862 flew by as Sam and the Crow Scouts were kept busy keeping track of the Cheyenne Dog Soldiers. They made a raid in mid July and had to be put back on their reservation. A company of Colorado volunteers came up to help with the Indian problem.

In late summer with the war in the states raging, word came that the Sioux on the Minnesota reservation went on the warpath under Chief Little Crow. Seven hundred settlers on the frontier of Minnesota, Iowa and the Dakotas were killed and over two hundred captured.

Washington telegraphed and asked if Ft Laramie had scouts available. The commanding officer telegraphed back, "We have Sam Duncan, a man who can track a pissant across a flat rock."

Sam and his Crow Scouts were ordered to go north and locate the guilty perpetrators and send word to General John Pope who was coming from Fort Leavenworth with a unit of cavalry. After a long hard ride the scouts found the Indian camp. The village of tepees was set up in a long flat valley with hills rising on both sides. The east and west ends were open. There must have been at least two hundred lodges and a thousand head of horses.

Sam and his scouts found a covered spot on the south hills. From there they could observe the village without being discovered. The Crows told Sam they thought this Sioux clan had intentions of staying the rest of the summer.

Iron Fist told Sam, "War Chief not afraid. He think he safe here. Soldiers no find. This sacred land. Indian no be killed here."

The young scouts, Curly and White Man Runs Him were sent to find and bring the troopers. Sam told the young scouts to keep their blue coats on. "You might be taken for the Sioux hostiles."

For two days the three scouts lay in the high grass watching the Indians and their captured white people. With a spy class they saw the horror the whites had to endure. Men were staked out over anthills. Women were beaten by squaws unmercifully. They used stick and stones whipped and beat the women and children at will. It was hard for Sam to watch and not try to stop the punishment. There was no way he could intercede.

Curly and his companion found General Pope and his cavalry units. They were two days march from the valley. It was almost dark when the General and two of his staff officers came to see Sam. They parlayed in a ravine a quarter mile from the observation post. Sam laid the village and valley situation out to the General.

The General asked, "Tell me scout, you got any ideas on how we should take this village?"

Before Sam could answer a Captain piped up and said, "I'll bring my cannons up, put em on this hill and blow that village into kingdom-come."

Sam was beside himself. "What the hell you gonna do? You damn fool. That village is plumb full of white captives, women and children and Indian women and children." He was hot under the collar and showed it.

General Pope said, "We're not foolish enough to kill that many people. Give me your plan scout. By the way what's your name?"

"Sam, Sam Duncan."

"I know of you. You're damn good at what you do."

"Thank you General. These are my Crow scouts." He pointed to the four Crows. "They're damn good at what they do."

The General asked again, "You got a plan?"

Sam laid his plan out. "General these bucks have been drinking a lot of firewater. We think they're sick and hung over. You know they're feeling pretty bad. They won't give you too much trouble. The horse herd is down the west end of the valley, maybe a thousand head. They ain't got many guards on the herd. Me and my Crows will take the guards out. Then we'll get in position to drive the horses west at first light. Them bucks will all come out to see what's go-n on. You have your troopers on this ridge. They can move down in the valley and get the bucks. They will have good targets. They won't have to kill the captives or the Indian women and children. Have your horsemen up at the east end. They can charge thru the village and clean up the rest. For God's sake tell em not to be kill-en the women and children."

"By God you got one hell of a plan." The General was all excited. "We got all night to get ready." He turned to his staff, "Let's get crack-en." He was giving orders fast and furious.

Sam said again, "Tell your troopers not to be kill-en the women and children."

Sam and the Crows took their horses way around to the far end to the valley. Sam, Iron Fist, Black Elk and Curly slipped up on the guards and used their knives. At first light they started the horses stampeding. The plan worked.

Sam rode back into the village. The troopers were killing everybody. He was screaming and waving his arms for them to stop. A trooper was about to kill a young girl. Sam drove his horse into the trooper's knocking both of them down. He picked the girl up and put her on his horse. Warriors were surrendering everywhere. The defeat of the Sioux was complete. This engagement captured over one thousand Indian men, women and children.

Sam dismounted in the village on the last charge by the troopers. He had done his best to stop the killing of the Indian women and children. As he stood near a tepee, a young blonde woman crawled out and put both arms around his legs. She was crying uncontrollably. He couldn't understand her words, she was a Swedish immigrant new to this country. They found over a hundred captives in the village.

A prairie military trial was convened at Mandate, Minnesota. All the warriors were found guilty and sentenced to hang. President Lincoln intervened and ordered thirty-eight to go to the gallows. Sam was asked to help make the selections. It was the hardest thing he would ever have to do. He would spend many sleepless nights thinking of the men he had selected. It was the largest mass execution in U.S. history. The thirty-eight were hung the day after Christmas 1862.

Sam had to hear their eerie death songs the night before the hangings. Then he and his scouts returned to Fort Laramie with heavy hearts.

More trouble was found at home. Seems a cow had wandered away from a wagon train and a young Sioux boy had found and taken it to a village across the Platte River. There a feast was had by the villagers. The wagon master demanded the Indians pay for the cow. They refused. A Lieutenant Louis fresh from West Point was sent to bring the boy in. A fight ensued and the Lieutenant and four Troopers were killed.

Next day the Fort Commander surrounded the village and with cannon and rifle fire killed all the villagers, men, women and children. Captain White was recalled to be an instructor in the states. Sam blamed himself. "If I had been here it wouldn't have happened."

Fawn was so upset over the tragedy, she wanted to go back to her people. Sam and Amanda spent several days convincing her to stay. Only her love of Sam kept her from leaving.

A new commander came to Fort Laramie. An older Major. He was another officer with no command experience. This man was a bit better as he had been stationed with the Cherokee nation and understood the Indian problem a little better than Captain White. Fawn and Sam liked this man. They felt things would be better for all the Indian tribes.

The war dragged on in the states. The Indians began to raid more often, causing Sam to stay in the field with his scouts all summer long.

In '65 the war was over at last and troops began to return to the western forts.

In 1866 Sam was used as an interpreter for a group of Sioux and Cheyenne Chiefs on a trip to the east. They made a visit to see the great white father in Washington D.C. There they met President Johnson. He made many promises to the chiefs. On the way back the group made visits to New York City and Chicago. The old chiefs were impressed and one told Sam the white people were like stars in the sky. "Too many white eyes for Indian to fight."

The visit didn't seem to do any good for the raids and fights between the Indians and soldiers continued. The years 1866 and 67 kept Sam and the Crow scouts in the field most of the time.

It was fall of '67 and Sam had been gone for over a month. He returned to the fort just at sun down. He went to his cabin. It was dark and cold. Fawn was nowhere to be found. He went to the store looking for her. Amanda with tears told him Fawn was at the fort hospital. She went there with Sam. The surgeon met them and broke the news that Fawn had died in child birth earlier that very day, both she and the baby boy were dead. "We did all we could to save her." The surgeon wiped tears away as he spoke.

Sam was devastated with this loss, he turned white. A blank look filled his eyes. Amanda took a hold of him and told him that Fawn had two miscarriages in the last years. "She was such a petite little thing, I don't think she was meant to have children," Amanda told him thru her tears. "She didn't want you to know she had the miscarriages."

Sam told them Fawn had hid the problem very well. "I never knew." He cursed God with all his might. Took his knife and started slashing his arms. Amanda and the surgeon stopped him. He fell to the floor in a pool of blood, he had passed out. The doctor acted fast to stop the bleeding or he would have died. Too weak to go to the service for Fawn he lay between life and death for days. The loss of blood kept him in the hospital bed for weeks. He couldn't go to the fort's cemetery for Fawn's burial. When he was well enough he told everyone he couldn't stay at Fort Laramie. He gave away most of his belongings. He wanted to burn the cabin. Amanda stopped him. He told his Crows and the Tellers's good by and how much he thought of them. "You people will always be in my thoughts."

Early on a late fall morning, he saddled his horse and with a pack horse headed on the trail east. The first heavy snow of the season was falling as he rode the Oregon Trail. A very dishearten, lonely and sad sick man.

Chapter 10

Hunter, Lawman

Sam took two months to reach St Louis. He had camped by the Missouri River and just did nothing. Total despair and depression had come over him. He cared for no one. He had no ambition to do anything. He only took care of his horses. Did little for himself. Only ate enough to stay alive. He stayed away from people. A total recluse. Wouldn't even talk to any one who happened to come by his camp. If someone stopped at the camp, he would motion for them to leave. Even pointed a pistol at one party who tried to talk with him. He yelled at them to move on in no uncertain terms. In all, Sam Duncan was a very sick, lonely and unhappy man. He dreamed of Fawn night after night. She was on his mind constantly. He kept asking himself, "Will I ever get over her?"

It happened on a cold sultry evening. A thunder storm hit the plains. Lighting danced across the prairie and struck a tree Sam had camped by. Both horses and Sam were knocked down and out. When he came to, a young couple was bending over him.

"You're a mighty lucky man to be alive. We saw the lighting hit. Was sure it was gonna hit our team and wagon. We saw your horses go down. We came over to find out if we could help."

Sam could not speak he only shook his head.

"I'm Daniel Harper this is my wife Clair. We just been married a week. We're going to California. We're gonna try to help until you get on your feet." He smiled and told his young wife to get blankets from their wagon.

The couple stayed with Sam for two weeks. They attended to his every need. It made him realize he wasn't alone and people, even strangers were willing to help him and they cared. The young couple prayed to God out loud every morning, evening and at each meal. Sam was always in their prayers. He was getting better.

A wagon train came along. Sam told Daniel he should take his wife and join the train. The couple wanted to stay to make sure he would be okay. Sam assured them he was now in his right mind and could take care of himself. Daniel and Clair packed and joined the train.

Sam stayed in camp for several more days. He missed the couple badly so he packed and moved on to St Louis. He arrived at the Hawkins gun shop late one afternoon. His old friends at the shop made him feel at home and Jake offered him a job working in the shop. He accepted and went to work as a stock maker once again.

Sam was uneasy working indoors, the days dragged for him. A month passed. He wanted something but did not know what. He discussed it with Jake several times.

Late one day a stranger came to the shop looking for buffalo rifles. Jake showed him two he had in stock. A Sharps fifty caliber, with a thirty-six inch barrel. A real buffalo gun. He showed the man another. A Remington rolling block. It was also a fifty caliber.

"I'll take em both," the man said. "Would you know where a man can find a good shooter. I'm goin' a hunt-un buffalo."

Jake called to Sam, "Man here look-n for a shooter. Says he's go-n hunt-un buffalo. Maybe you's outa talk with him."

Jake knew in his heart Sam needed to do something else.

Sam came to the counter and asked, "Where you goin' to hunt these buffalo?"

"Down Texas way. There's big money in hides and buffalo robes. They're paying two to four dollars a hide, five to six for robes and fifty cents for tongues. Man make a right tidy sum if he can shoot. There's buyers that will come and pay cash for all you can get. You know a good shooter?"

Sam asked the man, "What's your deal? How you gonna pay a shooter?"

"Well," he says, "I have a wagon and team and some camp equipment. I got a few dollars. What I need is a pardner who can supply the same and shoot. You know someone like that?"

"I have a few dollars and I'm a damn good shot. What kinda deal you gonna make me?"

"Fifty- fifty right down the middle if-n you got a mind to. My name's Otto Clinger. I been down in that country and seen, I tell ya thousands of them buffalo. They're there just for the taken."

"Now just one minute friend. That's Comanche land. Them savages will be a lift-en your hair as soon as they see you's." Jake didn't care for this deal. He turned to Sam, "I wouldn't be ago-n with this fella, no sir- ree."

"Ah hell, the Army and Texas Ranger got them red skins on the run. They got a reservation for em up in Indian Territory. They ain't no problem at all. Fact is the Army will buy the meat if you can get it to em. They want's all them critters dead so's them red devils will stay on their reservation. How about it young fella you's wants to pitch in with me?"

Sam turned to Jake and said, "Gotta good mind to join this man. I feel like a chicken in a coop around here."

"Hell yes Sam. You're free, white and twenty-one. You's can do anything you's a mind to."

Sam turned to the man and said, "You just got yourself a pardner." The two shook hands.

Right away the two started to make plans. "I'll buy another wagon and team. We can buy our shoot-n stuff right here from Jake. We gotta have lots of ammunition. Need two hundred and fifty pounds of lead and a fifty caliber mold, four thousand primers and seventy pounds of powder. We need at least two thousand cartridge cases."

Sam was ready and willing for this adventure. In the next few days the needed equipment was procured.

Sam traded his Remington pistol for a new six shot forty-four caliber Colt. The two started for Fort Dodge, Kansas. On the trip the two men talked of their troubles. Otto, a German had lost his woman. This big man, six feet four, two hundred fifty pounds, broke down and cried as he told of losing his wife. He told Sam, "I will never get over her, she was my whole life. I'm gonna try real hard to get over her."

Sam knew just how he felt. He told Otto, "It'll take time."

The two became fast friends. They had their lost women in common.

Arriving in Fort Dodge the two looked for hide buyers and men who could be used as skinners. They wanted at least two men. They found buyers who said they would come down and pickup and pay for the hides at least every two months. They found two men for skinners, one a Mexican, the other Irish. As they pulled out on the road south, a woman in a buckskin dress carrying a blanket, covering her face with her hand, stood in the middle of the road and stopped them. She called and said she was a good skinner and needed a job.

"I hear you's a need-n skinners." Sam and Otto dropped down to talk with her. She told them in her broken English, she could out skin any man alive. Sam told her to get in his wagon. In a flash she was over the tail gate.

Sam turned to Otto and told him, "She's a Cherokee been thrown out of the tribe, she covers her face because her nose has been cut off. She was unfaithful to her man."

"By God we gonna have to look at that all the time?" Otto asked. Otto didn't seem too happy to have her along.

"We'll fix her a mask, you'll get used to her," Sam told him. "Hell, who knows you may be sleeping with her before it's over. She's got a real nice body on her."

They both laughed and Otto slapped Sam on the back. "Why not, it's one way to get over my wife." They went to the wagons and continued on their way.

At night camp the woman disappeared. Sam set a plate and a cup of coffee out and called to her to come and eat. No one saw her but next morning the plate and cup were by the fire. She was asleep in Sam's wagon. He pushed her breakfast and coffee over the tail gate. They broke camp and journeyed on. The next several days were the same.

Just before noon on a bright sunny day, Sam's wagon topped a small rise. There below in a shallow valley was what looked like a thousand buffalo contentedly grazing away.

Sam in the lead, pulled his team around and waved to the others to follow him. He told them what he had seen. "I'll do some shoot-n. You pull back and make camp." He found a spot, set up and dropped fifty beasts that afternoon. Mostly bulls.

Next morning the herd had moved on. The skinning began. Sure enough the woman was an expert skinner. That afternoon Sam saddled his horse and followed the herd and dropped another fifty. Back at camp the work began. The woman showed the men how it should be done.

Otto was impressed, "By gar she has a good looking body on her, even in them man's clothes."

Sam laughed, "See, what did I tell ya, ya may be sleeping

with her before long, nose or no nose."

They moved camp and followed this herd. Sam took forty to fifty a day most days. The hides were piling up. They ate buffalo meat three times a day. The herd disappeared and they had to move to another location.

Otto began talking of the woman a lot. "I could take to her except for that nose."

Sam told him he had seen that before. A doctor had made a fake one and no one could see the difference.

"Sam, this is one good looking woman, I may be falling for her, what do you think Sam?"

"She's a real worker and I bet she was a pretty gal before they cut her up. You ain't get-n no virgin, I can tell you that."

Otto was laughing, "I sure got a hanker-n for her." No more was talked about her for some time.

The buyers came and the two partners made several thousand dollars each. The hunting continued.

One evening two lawmen came into camp and asked if a lone rider had come by. None had. The two were Texas Rangers. They were after a man named Bass Outlaw, a killer and robber. The Rangers stayed the night and their talk interested Sam. They told him if he ever wanted a job to look the Rangers up. "We always need good men."

A few days later a lone rider rode into camp. Sam was reloading cartridges, when he saw a man on horseback coming, he slipped his colt on to his lap. The man demanded something to eat.

"There's coffee on the fire and some jerked meat hang-n," Sam said in a curt tone as the man dismounted.

"Who the hell you think you're a talking to you son-of-a-bitch." The rider acted mean. He placed his right hand on the revolver in his holster.

Sam displayed the cocked colt. "I be talk-n to you, you

asshole, now climb back on that pony and make tracks before I put holes in your worthless hide."

The man mounted and rode out a few yards, turned in his saddle and yelled, "We'll meet again, you lousy bastard."

Sam called after him, "I'll be looking forward to the day." The horsemen spurred his horse and loped away to the east.

The next months were uneventful, Sam was knocking down twenty to fifty buffalo a day, the hides piled up. Otto called the woman Sunny as she was always pleasant and cheerful and kind to all, and a very good cook. All the men were amazed at her hard work and know how.

Sam was on a stand when the Mexican skinner came riding on a well lathered horse and told him to get back to camp. "We got Injun trouble."

When Sam reached the camp he could see half a dozen mounted Comanches sitting on a hill watching the camp. They were about a quarter mile away. Otto was watching them thru a spy glass. "They all got war paint on Sam. Here take a look."

Sam looked thru the glass. "I think we're in for a fight, let's throw up some breast works under the wagons, go get your guns and get ready."

Otto still watching thru the spy glass. "There's three braves riding out, one has his hand up."

Sam told them, "He wants to parlay, I'll go talk"

"I'll go too," Otto said.

"Me too," Sunny was already walking out.

Sam put the Henry in the crook of his left arm and the three walked boldly out to meet the three Warriors.

Drawing close Sam could see one of the Warriors was a black man. Sam raised his right hand in friendly fashion and in sign language asked what they wanted. The black man rode forward.

"You men kill our Buffalo. You stop or we kill you all."

Sam looked long and hard at this man. Something looked familiar about him. The black man said. "You're in our land, if you want to live, go, go now."

Sam asked, "Who are you, what's a black man doing with these Warriors?"

The black became visibly angered. "Who are you to question me? White eyes. I'm a free man and can do as I damn please, you go to hell white man."

Sam tried to be calm and asked, "What is your name? I must know you from some where."

"My name is Joe, Joe Duncan. My Comanche name is He Walks Fast, what is your name white man?"

With a big smile he said, "Duncan, Sam Du—." Before Sam could finish his name the black was down off his horse, rushed to and with both arms was hugging Sam with all his might. Sam was hugging back and the tears flowed freely from these two adult men. Sam's people looked in amazement at this outward show of affection to each other. The two warriors looked to each other in disbelief.

Sam finally composed himself and told Sunny and Otto, "This is my friend from my boyhood days." Joe told the two Comanche warriors the same in their language.

Sam invited all three warriors to his camp where meat, bread and coffee were served to the Comanches. This Pow-Wow went on the rest of the day and late into the night. Sam and Joe talked of their lives and families until they were talked out. Joe told Sam he was a happy man, he had three wives and many children. "The Comanche're good to me." He told of his life in the free states as a young boy.

Next morning Sam told Otto he was tired of killing and wanted to go back to Fort Dodge. "I have enough money to last awhile."

Otto agreed, "Tell em we're leaving."

Joe and Sam told each other they love one another and would be brothers forever, then they parted.

Within the next week the party reached Fort Dodge, the fort was now Dodge City, it was a railroad town for shipping cattle to the east. Otto said he wanted to go north and hunt more buffalo, the two sold their hides, paid the help and divided the rest. Sam sold Otto his wagon and team. Said he was going to do something else didn't know what. Otto had Sunny's nose fixed and she was now his common-law wife. Otto and the skinners headed north.

Sam stayed in the Long Branch hotel and saloon, he sat on the porch smoking a corn cob pipe and watched the town's goings on, it was very entertaining.

He was down in the livery stable checking on his horse when a well dressed man approached him. He carried two pearl handled six guns on his side, butts forward. He stood six foot tall, two hundred pounds, a handle bar mustache and long blond hair hung over his shoulders. "Can I talk with you mister?"

"Sure. What can I do for you?" Sam had seen this man around town and knew he was the law.

"I'm the Marshal in this town and in bad need of a deputy, been watching you, I see you can handle yourself, how's about you hire-n on? I'm in need of a good man. Pays good and you don't do a whole lot, just kinda keep the cowboys in line. My name is Hickok, Bill Hickok, what's your handle?"

"Sam, Sam Duncan, never thought of bein' a lawman, sounds good, you just hired yourself a deputy." Sam was sworn in that afternoon. He purchased a new blue suit, with a vest where he pinned his badge. He had to have a new hat, the work was easy. In the two years he was with Bill Hickok, he didn't kill anyone, he had busted a few heads but no real trouble, mostly young cowboys from Texas who had come with trail herds of long horns, they were just look-n for a good time, no real trouble.

Sam tired of this job. He heard that lawmen were being hired in Fort Smith, Arkansas. He told Bill that he had been in that country as a boy and would like to go take a look.

"I can't stop ya, I'll write a letter of recommendation."

In two weeks Sam walked into the court house of Judge Isaac Parker in Fort Smith Arkansas. He was ushered into the Judge's office by a Marshal Crump. The judge was a man in his late fifties, he sat behind a large desk. His piercing eyes could look right thru a man, a big smile was on his face that his white beard could not hide, his hair was snowy white. He stood and extended his hand. "I understand you want to come work for me, I've looked over your record and I believe you will make a fine deputy. Marshal Crump will give you a booklet to study and in a few days you'll be sent with another marshal to get to know the ropes, that ok with you?"

"Okay, with me."

"Any questions Sam?" The judge leaned close to listen.

"How and when do I get paid?"

"When you bring in a criminal you will get money, try to bring them in alive. Did I answer your question?"

"Until the time comes, you did."

Sam rented a hotel room, he went to look for something to eat. He went to a café in the same block as the hotel. Entered and sat at a table with his back against the wall. Dodge City had taught him that. A very fine looking woman came to take his order, Sam smiled and said, "Are all the ladies in this town as pretty as you?"

"You must be a new marshal, all you guys are full of shit." She had a big smile and then started laughing.

Sam gave her a wink. "Are you a single lady?"

"Free, white and twenty-one."

125

"I'm gonna get to know you lady," Sam said as he looked her over.

"You can bet on it." She took his order, turned around, shook her hind-end and walked away.

When she returned with his food, she sat down next to him and they talked as he had his dinner. She asked about him, he said very little of himself. He said he had a wife that died, he was having a bad time getting over her, he asked questions about her.

She had been married, her husband got sick and died. That's all she would tell him except her name was Nell Snyder. She did tell him she baked the pie he was eating. He bid her goodbye and told her he would be back soon.

"I'll be right here a-waiting," she said with a big smile.

Sam looked up a gun shop to buy some ammo. The owner placed a new hand gun on the counter and told Sam this was the newest thing out, a Smith and Wesson Schofield revolver. "I think you'll like it, see how it breaks open to load." He then handed the pistol to Sam, he looked it over.

"I really like the feel of it, a man can load this son-of-gun on a dead run on horse- back, you got a place I can shoot her?"

"Right out back, come on let's try her out." The shop had a range with iron targets set up. Sam loaded and hit all six targets just by pointing and shooting.

"Man that's great shooting, how you like her?" The owner was impressed.

"Can I trade in my colt and gun belt?"

"You bet, let's go in and make a deal."

Sam got a new Cavalry model with an eight inch barrel and another with a four inch barrel and two new gun belts and holsters.

Sam went to the nations the first time with a Deputy Tolbert, known as Pad. The man had blue eyes that would look deep into your brain and almost tell what you were thinking. He had a southern drawl and he was awfully polite. He seemed too easy going to be a lawman, Sam soon learned when Pad got on a trail he always got his man.

On their first outing, they rode thru the Choctaw, Sam met people he remembered and they said they remembered him as a boy. Pad was impressed, Pad told Sam about the nations. "Each tribe has its own lawmen, they call them light horse men, they take care of the Indian problems. We're after the whiskey peddlers, bootleggers, robbers, killers, horse thieves and all who commit crimes against the U.S. government."

Sam rode with Pad several months, Pad suggested that Sam should get a new Winchester rifle, the Henry was outdated. Sam followed Pad's advice, the next time in Ft Smith, he purchased a 73 saddle ring carbine in 44 caliber, same as his Scohfield. Pad and Sam worked together for two months and in that time brought in three men that Judge Parker hung for crimes of robbery and murder.

Sam would stay at a hotel when in town and eat at the café where Nell worked. He had many conversations with her and came to want to see more of her, as he needed female companionship. After one evening meal she invited him to move in with her. "I have a house and barn on the out skirts of town, you will like it there, you've got nothing to lose."

Sam was puzzled. "Why me Nell, there's plenty men in town that wants to move in with you."

She told him she liked his company. "You don't cuss, you don't drink, you're always clean and you're clean shaven, I likes that in a man. I ain't never been married, never found a man I would want, I ain't the marry-n kind. When I told you I was married once I lied, besides if we can't get along or you don't like my bed we can split, Okay Sam?"

"I'll give it a try," He said with a big smile. He moved in

127

the same day.

The next deputy Sam rode with was Sam Brass, a much younger man than himself, a black man who over the next few years became the most feared deputy out of Judge Parker's court. If he was sent to get a law breaker, it was a sure bet he'd bring em in.

The Sam's called each other by their last names, so did most other people when they saw them together.

The two were sent to bring in one Bob Cook, he was twenty-two years old, a horse thief, robber and raper of any woman he happened to come across. He was last reported to be in the Kickapoo Nation. Sam and Brass were traveling the road north by Turkey Creek, in the nation when a shot rang out and hit Sam's horse knocking him and the horse down. The shot came from the trees to their right, Sam scrambled up and threw a pistol shot at a figure moving thru the trees. Brass did the same and a scream could be heard, a bullet had found its mark.

The two deputies were on him in seconds, Cook lay in pain, a bullet had hit him in his left side and leg. He was cuss-n something terrible, he called the two deputies every dirty name he knew.

"You shot my horse you worthless bastard. I should finish you off right now." Sam was mad as hell.

"Don't shoot, don't shoot, I'm hurt bad, get me a doctor," the young man cried in his pain. The deputies managed to get the bleeding stopped.

Sam returned to look at his horse, the big Red Roan was hit just below the neck line, he was trying to get up, his big sorrowful eyes pleaded for Sam to help him. One shot stopped his pain, Sam loved the old roan, he had him for five years, a true and faithful friend.

Sam would have shot the kid but Brass stopped him. He looked for and found the kid's horse, a big powerful Dunn, maybe twelve hundred pounds. Sam asked repeatedly where he got the horse. The kid told Sam the horse was the only thing he had paid money for. "Got-em when he was two years old."

"He's mine now." Sam went and retrieved his saddle and took off and threw the kid's saddle into the road.

Brass looked for and found an Indian with a wagon. They took the kid to a federal jail in the town of Guthrie and had a doctor treat him. "He's got blood poison in his leg, he's lost a lot of blood, gonna die soon," the doctor told them.

The two stayed in a hotel, the kid died three days later. The Sams paid two dollars to have him put in the ground. They returned to Ft Smith and reported to the Judge.

The next time out Sam and Brass were after the Cherokee Kid, a half Indian boy, who was twenty-five years old and as mean as a snake. The two deputies shot and killed three of his companions, but missed getting him.

They had been out for three months. They were on the way back to Ft Smith on a road running along the north side of the Red River. Four horsemen blocked their path. Both deputies drew their pistols and held them by the right leg ready for action. It turned out the men were Texas Rangers look-n for the kid too, he had been in Texas and killed a rancher, his wife and two little girls.

The men camped together that night. The Ranger leader was Captain John Hayes, a man of some notable reputation. He asked how the deputies liked working for the US Government in the Nations? Both said it's okay. Sam said that the pay was slow and the deputies were being killed regularly. The Captain invited the two to come down to Texas and join the Rangers. "We need good men all the time, the pay is good and on time, we're treated well in Texas."

Sam told him he just might do that.

"Come on down to Austin and tell Captain McDonald I

sent you," Hayes said.

Two days later the two rode into Ft Smith, Judge Parker was mad that they didn't get the Cherokee kid and they had killed the others, he wanted them alive. Sam asked if their pay had come? It hadn't and the Judge didn't like Sam asking.

Sam told the Judge of the Ranger's offer.

"Go on if you don't like it here." The judge had anger in his voice.

Sam took off his badge and laid it on the judge's desk. "I just quit. You can send my pay to Austin in care of the Texas Rangers."

"Good," the Judge said. "When you get home you'll see that woman you been sleep-n with has run off with a Mississippi River gambler."

Sam thanked the Judge, shook hands with Brass. "Nice know'n ya. I'll see you again some time." They parted friends, Sam rode home.

When he entered the house he found Nell coming from the bedroom, putting on her clothing. A sinister looking man with dark features followed her from the bedroom. He was half dressed.

"Sam, she said. "You been gone a long time, I...."

Sam cut her short. "I don't want to hear about it, I'll get my belongings and get out."

He took his things in a war bag, put his horses in the livery stable in town and stayed in the hotel that night.

Next day he got some grub, packed his pack horse and riding the Dunn, he rode west into the Choctaw. He remembered the day as a boy when he went the other way toward the Mississippi. Memories came flooding back into his mind some happy most sad. Some things change, some don't, he said to himself, he was happy to be on the move again.

Chapter 11

Sylvia, Texas Rangers

As he rode west on the road to the Choctaw agency, his mind wandered back to his boyhood days, when he came to the Choctaw with his family. It was a good time and a sad time, he had to leave his friend Little Joe. He though of Joe and his Comanche family, he thought of Jack his brother, will I ever see them again? It was almost dark when he rode into the Agency.

He reined up at agency headquarters. An older rather heavyset woman came out on to the porch. In a very unfriendly voice with a German accent, "You got business here?"

"I need a place to camp tonight. Can I camp in the trees by the horse pens?"

"Sure you can, don't make no big fires and no trouble."

"Thank Ya Ma'am. I'm no trouble maker."

Sam put the horses in a small pen, fed and watered them, made a cooking fire, fixed his supper and turned in for the night.

At first light he was up and fed the horses and fixed breakfast and walked to the agency cemetery, it wasn't far from the horse pens. There he saw chiseled in a marble head stone his Ma and Pa's name. It read, "SAM AND LIZ DUNCAN." No date of death, nothing else, next to them was his Aunt and Uncle with their names on a stone, nothing else, just Walter and Jane.

He talked to them as if they were there and told them all he missed and loved them.

Said out loud, "May you all rest in peace." Tears ran freely as he returned to his camp, he saddled and packed the horses and rode the road west from the agency.

He rode in the Choctaw all day, turned south and reached the road that ran on the north side of the Red River, he rode into the setting sun. Just at sunset he made camp, figured he was at the southwest edge of the reservation, he camped off the road thirty or so yards in a clump of trees.

After seeing to the horse's needs he made and ate his supper, he lay back in his saddle and watched the stars fill the darkened sky. A quarter moon came up, it shed a dim light thru the trees. He started to roll up in his blankets when a voice came from the dark, it spoke in Choctaw, asking to come in. Sam held his pistol so the one who called could see it. He called, "Come in slow and easy," in Choctaw.

Soon an old Indian, followed by a woman and three young girls came into the fire light. The Indian said, "We've lost our way in the dark, saw your fire, we mean you no harm."

Sam returned the pistol to its holster. "Come in and warm yourselves by my fire," Sam spoke in their language again.

One of the young girls complained of being cold and hungry.

"Come set by the fire, I'll fix you all something to eat." He went to his grub bag and fixed beans and bacon and put on a fresh pot of coffee. When the food was ready, he gave the old one a plate full, he ate heartily using his fingers and as each person ate a plate full, Sam would fill it again and it was passed to the next. Same with a coffee cup. After they ate and drank, the three girls lay down and rolled up in blankets and went to sleep. The older woman came close and looked Sam in the eyes and said something like, "I know you."

He replied, "Maybe, maybe you do."

She took a blanket, lay down by the girls and went to sleep.

The old Indian man wanted to talk, he started by asking questions. "Who are you? Where you from? Where you go? How you speak Choctaw?"

Sam stopped him saying, "I lived at the agency as a boy, my Ma and Pa passed on and are buried in the cemetery here."

The old one looked hard at Sam. "You a boy Indian Medicine Man saved with water and sprits?"

"I am that boy."

The old one said, "I am that Medicine man." He put both hands out to Sam, palms up, Sam placed his hands on the old ones.

"I wished many times you had come sooner." Sam's voice quivered as he spoke.

"The Great Spirit moves in you my son, the Spirit One told me in a dream you would be a great man." He looked to the sky. "Oh Great Spirit guide and be with this man."

The old one prayed out loud to his God, he told Sam, "I must sleep now, old people need much rest, if we are to be here tomorrow." He joined the others, rolled up in a blanket, lay down and went to sleep.

When Sam woke up, it was barely daylight, the Indian people were walking away toward the road. Sam called, "Wait, let me fix you some food."

The old one turned and called back with a raised hand, "May the Great Spirit walk with you always." He turned and led his little group east on the river road.

Sam fed the horses, cooked his meal, saddled and headed west on the river road.

By noon he had reached Colbert's Ferry, he crossed the river on the ferry into Texas, stopped and paid for a meal from a vendor on the Texas side. He then rode on the Colbert road south. At sundown he started looking for a spot to make camp. Finding none he liked, he rode on.

After dark he spotted a fire off the left side of the road in a group of trees. "Must be a good spot to camp," he said to himself. He turned off the road and approached the fire.

He called, "Ho, the camp, comm-n in."

In the dim light he could see two men setting facing his way at the fire, a man yelled back, "Come on in friend."

Drawing closer he saw things he didn't like, he slipped the Schofield out of its holster and down by his right leg. Two dirty, scroungey looking men, one had a pistol laying on his stomach, his feet stretched out to the fire. The other one was leaning against a large rock, a winchester rifle leaning against a tree to his left side. Sam saw a pile of blankets just in the light of the fire. There was motion and much movement in the blankets. Whimpering and groaning sounds were coming from there.

The man with the pistol spoke, "Get down friend, we have fresh coffee, meat and beans on the fire, come and have some."

Sam tightened the reins, squeezed with both legs and started the Dunn backing up. "No thanks, just passing thru, I'll be move-n on."

"Don't like our company, Friend? That's a nice pony your-a ridden, I'd like to make you a deal for him," he said as he pulled up his knees.

"He ain't for sale," Sam almost yelled.

"I ain't a buy-n, I'm a taken," the man called back in a loud harsh voice. He started moving the pistol up and pointed it at Sam. The Scohfield spoke, fifteen inches of fire and a half ounce of lead. The bullet hit the center of the man's chest, sending him reeling back into the ground. The other man reached for the winchester, the bullet hit him just below the right ear angling down, tearing away most of the left side of his neck and face, a red blood mist filled the air above his limp body. Out of the corner of his eye, Sam saw movement coming from the blankets. A man threw off the blankets and fired a shot over Sam's right shoulder, it made a swishing sound as it passed his ear. The Schofield spoke again, the bullet hit the man in the right arm pit, killing him instantly.

At the same time Sam could see in the dim moon light a white bare naked woman had jumped from the blankets and started running thru the trees screaming. "Don't kill me! Don't kill me!"

Sam was off his horse and after her in a flash, in a short chase he caught her, knocked her to the ground, picked her up, threw her onto his left shoulder and carried her back to the fire, kicking and screaming. He tossed her on to the blankets and said in a commanding voice, "Shut up, I ain't gonna kill you. Please, shut your mouth, cover yourself with a blanket."

She was still whimpering as she wrapped a blanket around her bare body. She kept on crying. Sam kneeled down and tried to console her.

Looking at this woman he saw she was in bad shape. Her face was bruised, her lips split and bleeding, her eyes blacked and red, her sandy blond hair was dirty and matted.

"I'll go get you some clothes," he told her. He went to his war bag and came back with wool pants, a shirt and a pair of wool socks. As she dressed he could see her arms, legs and body were a mass of black and blue bruises, her feet cut and bleeding.

He asked, "What in the hell is going on here?"

Thru her crying, she told him she had been stolen by these men after she started to calm a bit, Sam asked if she was hungry. "I ain't had nothing to eat in days, they gave me some water this morning, they been taken turns beat-n and rape-n me, I hoped I would die."

Sam was so mad he said, "I ought to go shoot them low down dirty bastards again."

For one minute she thought he might, he walked over to where they lay. He then pulled the dead men out of the fire light and laid them side by side. Then set about his horses needs.

He returned and fixed a meal of beans, bacon and coffee for the woman and himself, as she ate she told him her story. "I worked in a dance hall and saloon in a town on the Arkansas and Texas border, the older one you shot last, came in the saloon and tried to make me go to his room. I had the bar keep throw him out. Early the next morning they came, gagged my mouth, tied my hands and stole me from my room, they took away my shoes and clothes and said I would be shot if I tried to run away."

Sam asked her name.

"Sylvia Loveless, I can never thank you enough for coming to get me."

Sam sat there shaking his head in disbelief. He told her, "I have never heard a story like yours. These men must be the worst lowdown dirty white trash in the whole damn world, how does God let people like these live?"

Sam used his blankets, made a bed, lay back in his saddle, and asked her to come and lay down, she did. He put an arm around her, she laid with her head on his chest, they both fell into a fitful sleep.

Sam got up at sunup, fed his horses and looked to the three dead men's horses. They had been tied to trees all the time and were still saddled, he fed each with the last of the grain he had.

Sylvia told him, "Those men hardly ever fed the horses, only saw them watered once."

Under his breath Sam cursed the men. "Dirty, low down, no good for noth-n snakes, lousy sons-a-bitches, a man who treats horses that way needed kill-n."

Sam made coffee and breakfast. After eating, saddled his horses, and loaded the three dead men over the saddles of their horses, with Sylvia riding double with him, rode south a few miles to the little town of Denison, Texas.

Entering the town, this procession attracted a crowd. Sam asked for the sheriff, a citizen told him. "We only got a deputy, he'll be down at the saloon, I'll go fetch him."

A young man in his late twenties came out to meet Sam, Sylvia and seeing the dead men over the saddles asked, "Where'd you get them dead men?"

Sam paid him no mind. "Where's the sheriff's office?"

The deputy said nothing, he ambled back to look at the dead men.

Sam asked a citizen standing there about the sheriff's office.

"It's down in Sherman, the county seat, it's 8 or so miles on south."

Sam asked if anyone with a team and wagon would take them there. The man he was talking to said he had a team and wagon. "I'll go hitch up, be right back." He returned in a few minutes.

They loaded the dead, tied the horses to the wagon and with Sam and Sylvia on the seat with the driver, they headed for Sherman. Sam had to hold her, to keep her from falling, she was so weak, she had a hard time keeping her head up.

They drew a crowd as they entered the town. The driver pulled the wagon up in front of the sheriff's office. Sam hopped down and carried Sylvia into the office and sat her in a chair. The sheriff with his feet on a desk asked, "What can I do for you stranger?"

"I have three dead men in a wagon outside, you want-a go take a look?"

The sheriff got up and walked slowly out to the wagon, looked over the side board. "Wa'll, I'll be dammed, them boys been around here before, I"ll bet money there's a price on their heads."

"Can we find out?" Sam asked.

The sheriff yelled to a man standing in the office door. "Bring them wanted posters out here LeRoy." Looking over the posters the sheriff said, "I knowed I was right, that one." He pointed to the older one, "He's got a price of five hundred dollars, dead or alive, the other two worth fifty, dead or alive. Looks like you made a right nice bit of change, mister."

Sam asked, "You got a doctor in town?"

"Right across the street up them stairs above the barber shop," said the sheriff as he pointed.

Sam went in and picked up Sylvia and carried her to the top of the stairs. On the door a sign read, "Doctor B.S. Sanders MD - knock before entering." Sam kicked the door lightly with a booted foot.

An old man with a grey beard and long grey hair opened the door, spectacles sat on the end of his nose, looking over them he said, "Come on in."

Seeing Sylvia he asked, "Is she hurt?"

"No. She's been beat up pretty bad, I want you to look her over." Sam laid her gently on a table.

"I'll call my wife," the doctor said.

As Sam held her hand the doctor said, "This gal is shore pretty, ain't she?"

His wife came in, a friendly looking heavyset woman. "My goodness, what do we have here?" Sylvia looked like a waif in men's clothes.

"She's been beat up, this man wants me to look her over,"

the doctor told his wife.

Sam turned to leave, Sylvia grabbed his arm. "Don't leave me Sam, please don't leave me alone."

Sam told her, "These people won't hurt you, they're gonna help you, I'm just going across the street, be back in a minute."

Sam asked the Doctor's wife if she would go buy Sylvia some ladies clothing. He gave her a twenty dollar green back.

"I'll be glad to," she told him.

Sam walked back to the sheriff's office.

"There's an undertaker come-n to get them boys, I telegraphed Austin and told them to send the rewards money."

"What about the horses, saddles and guns of the dead men?" Sam wanted to know.

"I reckon they're yours, ain't nobody gonna claim em, you gonna sell em?"

The sheriff and Sam walked outside. Sam answered him, "Yeah, I plan to sell them all."

The undertaker drove up in a spring wagon with a young black boy. He asked, looking at the three dead men, "Who's paying to bury these men?"

The sheriff told him, "Greyson County ain't got no burying money."

Sam asked how much it would cost. The man put his left hand on his chin, rubbed his face, looked at the sky, looked back at the black boy and finally said, "Five dollars a head."

Sam told him to load up and put em in the ground. "Come to the hotel this evening, I'll pay ya."

Just then a man came running and gave the sheriff a telegraph.

"Wa'll you'll be a get-n six hundred dollars reward in the morning, Austin is a sending it right up."

The undertaker heard, he wanted more money. "I'm too cheap, them feller's worth that kinda money needs to be put in a box."

Sam turned on him with fire in his eyes and in his voice he said so everyone there could hear, "You better get your ass down the road and put them boys in a box and in the ground before I give you one hell of a butt kick-en you money grub-en jackass."

The undertaker loaded the dead men and drove off grumbling. "Man's only trying to make a dollar." When he looked back, Sam shook his fist at him. He drove on a little faster, still grumbling.

The man with the wagon that drove them down started to leave, Sam stopped him. "How much do I owe you pardner?"

"You don't owe me a thin dime, I was proud to bring you and the little lady down here."

"I thank you kindly," Sam told him.

The man flipped the reins, clucked to his team and drove away, he turned in the seat and waved goodbye.

Sam asked the sheriff, "Will you put the guns and horses up till I find a buyer."

"I'll take care of em and find a buyer." The sheriff was getting friendly.

Sam went back to the Doctor's, Sylvia sat in a chair with a big smile on her face, she had been cleaned up and had new clothes on, her hair was all clean and combed. Sam told her she sure looked pretty.

The Doctor took him in the other room. "We treated her cuts and bruises, she should heal up real good, her problem is gonna be in her head, take a long time for her to get over what they did to her."

"I know, she's a strong girl, I think she'll handle it okay."

Sam asked the Doc's wife, "Did you have enough money for the clothes?"

"Sure did, got her a night gown too and slippers, have some

money left."

"You keep it."

He picked Sylvia up and carried her down the stairs, she wanted to walk. When he set her down her feet were so tender she couldn't walk. He picked her up and crossed the street and set her in a chair back in the sheriff's office.

The sheriff told him the livery stable man had come and got all the horses, for the three the dead men's horses, he'd give twenty dollars apiece and ten dollars each for the saddles.

"He took mine to the livery stable?" Sam asked.

The sheriff shook his head yes.

"I'll see him later, I'm gonna take this girl to the hotel and get her something to eat." He picked her up and walked to the hotel and rented a room with two beds. He took Sylvia to a café and had supper. When they returned to the hotel the undertaker had sent a boy for his money, Sam paid for putting the three dead men in the ground.

He told Sylvia to go to bed, he had to go get his war bag at the stable. When he returned, she was in bed fast asleep.

Next morning he sold the guns and collected the horse and saddle money, with Sylvia and his two horses they took the Missouri, Kansas and Texas railroad train to Austin.

In Austin they got a hotel room. Sam went to Ranger headquarters, she stayed at the hotel.

At Texas Ranger Headquarters Sam was ushered into the office of John B. Jones, Major in charge of the Frontier Battalion, a man in his late thirties. He was well dressed, in a frock coat, white shirt, black tie sporting a well groomed mustache, dark set brown eyes. He came form around his desk with a friendly smile, and a hand shake.

"Sam Duncan, I believe. We had word you were coming, I hope you're here to join the Rangers? We need men of your caliber."

Sam was a little taken back to hear his coming preceded him, he thanked him and said, "Hope my age won't be held against me?"

"Why hell no, my Grandpa forked a horse at eighty-five, my Pa is as good a shot as any twenty year old, he just turned ninety. Sam you're not that old, I heard how you handled yourself on the trail. I want to tell you about the Rangers, we have six Companies of about forty men each, we're to uphold the law and peace in Texas, we don't give badges. I'll give you a Warrant of Authority you should have it with you at all times. Captain Leander McNelly has a special force and needs more men, he's operating down in the big bend country along the Rio Grande River on the Mexican border, I plan to have you join him. Cattle and horse thieves come in from Mexico and steal and rob at will. I think you'll like the man he's a real straight shooter."

"Sounds good to me." Sam felt good hearing from the Major.

"This woman you rescued, is she with you now?"

"Yes she is, I have no idea of what to do with her."

"Sam, why not bring her and come have supper with my wife and me. My wife has had some experience with women captured by Indians. She's done real good helping them get over their ordeals. She might do some good for this woman."

"I'd shore be thankful if she could." Sam was happy to get some help with Sylvia.

"Sam I'll have the lady in the outer office give you my home address, come around six this evening."

Sam returned to the hotel and told Sylvia of their invitation, she was pleased as she could be.

Six o'clock found Sylvia and Sam in the setting room of Major Jones and his wife. Mrs. Jones and Sylvia took to each other right off, Mrs. Jones was a very handsome lady in her late twenties.

The supper consisted of fried chicken, mashed potatoes, mixed fresh vegetables topped off with sliced peaches and cream. Sam told Mrs. Jones he had never had a meal as good, Mrs. Jones told the couple most of the food Mr. Jones had grown or raised.

After the meal Mrs Jones and Sylvia retired to the sewing room to have a chat, the Major and Sam went to the setting room to have coffee, a smoke and some conversation.

"After you left my office I had some news you might be interested in, did you ever know a man named Bill Hickok?" the Major asked.

"I shore did, worked for him as a deputy near on two years in Dodge City, Kansas, why do you ask?"

"I have bad news, the man was shot and killed last week up in the Dakota Territory, in the town of Deadwood, shot in the back while he was playing poker."

"Good lord he must have forgotten all he taught me, he always told me, 'keep your back to the wall.' Damn he was a good friend, some called him Wild Bill, he was never wild when I knew him. The law lost a good man." Sam buried his head in his hands. "I shore hate hearing that."

The Major told him, "We're all sorry to lose a good law man, I have more news, looks like the Comanche problem in Texas is over."

"What's that about?" Sam asked.

"The U.S. Cavalry with Colonel Mackenzie in command and a company of our Rangers put a war party of Comanches back on their reservation. The Indians were playing havoc with whites in the panhandle, my report states as many as fifty Comanches were killed."

"Was there a mention of a black man with the Indians?" Sam asked.

"No, do you know of such a man?" the Major inquired.

"Yes, I have a friend who was with the tribe, he was with them in the panhandle."

"How do you know this man Sam?"

"I was raised with him on my Pa's farm over in Louisiana, I sure hope he wasn't killed, he saved my hide a while back."

"I'll try to get news of him and let you know, Sam things have changed since we talked this morning, I have a different job for you, the sheriff and his deputy have vanished in the west Texas town of San Angelo. They've been gone five or six days, the town council have asked for rangers to come and provide law enforcement until they find out what happened to theirs or they can hire new ones. You're just the man to fit the bill, since you've been a lawman, will you take the job?"

"Sure I'll go and see what I can do."

"Great, I'd like you to go soon as possible."

Mrs. Jones and Sylvia came in and announced the two of them have decided that Sylvia would stay with the Jones' for a while. Sam told them. "That's real good, I know Mrs. Jones can help you Sylvia, I'll go bring your things."

The Major told them he would take Sam to the hotel in his buggy and bring her things back.

As the two men started to leave Sylvia stopped Sam, "I'll always love you Sam for what you done for me." Sam smiled and told her she would be a friend forever.

The two men went about getting her things, Sam gave the Major seven hundred dollars. "It belongs to Sylvia, give it to her when she leaves." The Major assured him he would.

The next morning found Sam and his Dunn horse on the Texas and Pacific railroad bound for west Texas. He dropped off at a station that was in a short days riding distance of San Angelo. When he rode into town he found the Mayor and had a meeting with the town council.

"I'm only here til we find yer Sheriff or ya hire a new one."

He asked if anyone had gone to look for the lawmen. He was told the two lawmen had gone west along the Middle Concho River to see about some stolen horses. "When he didn't return his deputy went to look for him, he ain't come back either."

Sam told them he would go take a look the next morning and asked if anyone would like to go with him, no one volunteered, he was put up at the local hotel.

The next morning he and the Dunn rode on the Middle Concho road west, at each farm house he came to he asked if they had seen the lawmen, no one had.

About ten miles out he rode into a farm house yard to ask questions, no one answered his call. He ground tied the Dunn and walked to the back of the house, he heard voices coming from the barn. He walked over and peered through a crack in the door, he saw a woman and two men, having an argument, he strained to hear their conversation. The woman was telling the men they must kill and bury the men in the root cellar, Sam had found the lawmen.

With the Schofield in hand and cocked, he burst through the door. In loud voice called out, "Raise your hands high, I'm the law, move and you're dead."

With their hands raised the three screamed, "Don't shoot, don't shoot."

He made the woman tie the men to a post and asked her, "Show me the root cellar, keep your hands where I can see em." She let out a string of cuss words that burned his ears.

In the cellar he found the two lawmen, both in pretty bad shape, neither one was able to talk or walk. He went back, untied the two men and made them carry the two lawmen and put them in a wagon. He retied them and made the woman hitch up two mules, then loaded all the men in the wagon, made the woman drive and proceeded to town, there he locked all the perpetrators in jail.

The two lawmen came around soon to tell their story, the law breakers got the drop on both the unsuspecting officers, each one was put in the cellar and forgot about, both men thought they had seen their last days, both men thanked Sam for finding them.

Sam telegraphed Major Jones with his report, the Major sent orders for him to proceed to Fort Stockton and report to Captain McNelly.

It was gonna be a long hot ride, on the second day a light rain was a welcome change. Moving southwest he hit the Pecos River and made camp for the night. Some time near morning a sound of cattle being driven woke him up. He moved on foot along the river bank and saw a herd of cattle being driven across the river by a half dozen Mexican Vaqueros.

The next morning he followed the tracks all the way to the Rio Grande River. He returned back northwest to Fort Stockton, and reported to Captain McNelly and told him of the cattle taken into Mexico.

The captain asked Sam to go back to the place he saw the crossing and watch for any others crossing. "My company is strung out and will take a few days to round the men up, I've been after a man named Juan Cortina, he's been rustling cattle and horses for some time, it's time we put a stop to him. Before you leave have you heard of the massacre of Colonel Custer and the whole Seventh Cavalry in the Dakota Territory?"

"No, not a word, I've known some of the troopers in that unit, I have a good friend who is a scout with Seventh, did you hear any names?"

"No, what's his name?"

"Charlie Reynolds."

"I'll try and find out about him."

"I hope he wasn't killed," Sam said with a lot of concern in his voice.

"What I can surmise, a lot of the tribes, got together to make the attack," Captain McNelly said.

"I left that country in 67, all the tribes were unhappy with their treatment by Washington, I'm sure the war chiefs were spoiling for a fight, Sitting Bull and Red Cloud wanted to have an all- out war years ago, now they can have it. I'm sorry it happened, I knew it was gonna get bad up there, I better get on my way."

After gathering up some chuck and grain Sam rode back to the crossing he had found and camped in a grove of trees near the river bank. It was near the Big Canyon creek where it emptied into the Rio Grande. That night he observed another herd crossing into Mexico.

The next morning he took a walk to the Big Canyon creek, he saw a horse stuck in a bog, the horse was sunk in up to his belly. Sam went back and saddled the Dunn returned to help the horse out of the bog, with a rope around the neck of the struggling animal he managed to free him. After he got the horse out of the bog, he took him back in the trees, the horse was so tired from his ordeal he could hardly stand. Sam could see, even though caked with mud, this was a well bred animal. To his surprise this beautiful horse was a black stallion, Sam fed a little grain and the horse began to revive. He hobbled his front feet and let him graze on fresh green grass.

Captain McNelly came with his company of twenty-five rangers. All the Rangers the next morning crossed into Mexico, this was an illegal maneuver as no Ranger company had made such a move before.

After a day's ride the Rangers found the stolen cattle in a small ranch, the Rangers surrounded the small casa and captured ten Mexican cowboys. Unknown to the Rangers the rustlers were in cahoots with a Mexican General, the General came to get his share of cattle and had with him a large contingent of troops, seeing the situation he surrounded the Rangers.

McNelly wouldn't give in, even after the U.S. Government commanded him to give up, he refused a direct order from the President of the United States. Many telegraphs were exchanged, the siege went on for several weeks, McNelly was steadfast in his demands of the return of the cattle and the surrender of the rustlers. Finally a compromise was made, the cattle would be returned, the rustlers were to go free.

The Rangers and the cattle returned to Texas. At Fort Stockton Captain McNelly was ordered to Austin and was relieved of his command for provoking an international incident, he left the Rangers. Sam was ordered to San Antonio and given a six month unpaid suspension for his part in the fiasco.

On the way back to Fort Stockton Sam had picked up the black stallion and was told the horse had been stolen from the King Ranch. "Where's the King ranch located?" he asked the commander of Fort Stockton.

"Way down south, damn near in the Gulf of Mexico. You should turn that horse loose, he'll find his way home."

"I think I'll take your advice and let him go."

Sam and the Dunn with a pack horse started for San Antonio, out a few miles the stallion was turned reluctantly loose, he ran, jumped and kicked, ran circles around the horses and rider, made quite a show. As Sam rode off the stallion fell in beside the Dunn and stayed there the rest of the trip.

"Guess we will have to take you home old feller." He was talking to the horse, they were on the long hard trip to south Texas and the King ranch.

The three rode into the ranch land of King. A sign told Sam

they had entered the ranch land of Richard King. It took several more days to reach the headquarters, on the way they met many cowboys and vaqueros who laughingly told him the ranch house was just over the hill, fifteen or so hills later the horses and rider entered the fenced grounds of the hacienda of the King ranch.

A crusty old cowhand came out to meet them, after spitting a long stream of tobacco juice, this long bearded face asked, "Where in hell ya get our old hoss? He's been gone a long time."

Sam was impatient. "I want ta talk to the boss of this outfit. Can ya go fech him?"

The bearded one spun on his heels went into the house and returned with a man, who said he was Richard King.

Sam spoke to the two men. "I brung this old horse a long ways, I'd shore like to buy him, if you'll sell him to me."

King looked at Sam hard. We thank you for your time, but he ain't for sale at any price, you can put him in that pen over there." He pointed to a horse pen west of the house. Sam dismounted and the stallion followed him into the pen. Sam shut the gate, returned, mounted the Dunn and started to leave, the black stallion went crazy, rearing, kicking the pen and pawing up a storm.

King yelled, "Turn that damn horse loose before he tears the whole pen down."

The bearded one rushed over and opened the gate. The horse trotted to Sam and stood pushing against him with his head.

"That's the God damn'est thing I ever saw," King told the people standing there. "Mister, whatever your name is, you just got yourself a horse. Put your horses in the pen and come on in the house, I gotta have a talk with you."

Sam unsaddled the Dunn and pack horse, all three horses

were put in the pen, then he went to the house.

In the house King invited Sam to have supper with his wife and himself. Sam asked if he could wash up first, he was shown a wash basin and after washing he sat down at the King's table.

At supper Mr King told him he had never seen a horse take to a man as the stallion did.

"I saved him, got em out of a bog, guess he remembers me for that."

"I want to hire you to oversee my horse herd, a man like you don't come along every day, you have a way with horses, I like that. Give you top hand wages."

"No sir, I can't I'm with the Rangers, been ordered to Sam Antonio, I just came to see if I could get the stallion."

"I knew you were no ornery cowhand the way you carry yourself and wear that pistol. The trail north of this house will take you right up to San Antonio, we'll see you have enough grub to get there. You can stay the night in our bunk house, I want to tell you about this horse you now own, he's one of the best Kentucky has ever produced, I purchased him as a yearling several years ago, we used him as the ranch stud for two years. We don't know when he was stolen, possibly last fall. He was out on the range with his mares, we have six of his sons, they're out of our best mares. You are a good judge of horse flesh, take him and keep him, he'll be as good for you as he was for us, he's the fastest horse on four legs I've ever seen."

Sam said he would and thanked them kindly for their hospitality and the black stallion.

After a hardy breakfast of steak, eggs and plenty of good strong black coffee, cooked by a Chinese cook, he took the trail to San Antonio. Four days later he reined up at the headquarters of the Rangers in San Antonio, Major Jones welcomed him as he entered the office.

"We been expecting you for some time, where you been?"

"I took a little detour to the King ranch," a smiling Sam told him.

"My God man you took that horse all the way down there? Guess you know you're on suspension? I'd call it a small vacation. You can bunk over in the Ranger barracks and eat at Lupe's Café. No pay, but the State of Texas will take care of your bills while you're on leave."

"Sounds good to me, don't ever recall have-n a vacation before, I like this State of Texas."

"Was it pretty rough down in Mexico?" the Major asked.

"We damn near starved, McNelly was right, the government was wrong to have him fired." Sam was bitter and showed it as he spoke. "I know you're right. McNelly is a good man and friend, it's a shame to lose a man like him."

Hayes seemed as mad as Sam. He told Sam that he had no news of his black friend, who was with the Comanche Indians.

Sam put his horses in the Ranger barn. Fed them and went to the Ranger barracks. A young Mexican boy showed him his room, Sam met two other Rangers living there.

"It's time to eat," Jay Jones said. He was the brother of Major Jones, Jay and Hop Anderson invited him to Lupe's Café for supper. "You're about to meet a good looking woman."

As the three entered the café Jay told Sam, "This is the best looking woman in all of Texas, I tell you she's a pretty thing, they say she's a real hellcat when she gets mad."

The aroma of Mexican cooking filled the air. Sam told the two he was hungry enough to eat a whole cow. Then he saw her, his heart jumped a beat just look-n at this Mexican beauty, black haired, black eyed with cream colored skin, this voluptuous woman came to greet them.

"How's the Rangers doin this fine evening?" she said in a seductive voice. A big smile on her face. With a hand she leaned on Sam's shoulder.

He couldn't help himself when he said, "If you ain't the best looking woman in Texas, I'd shore like to meet her."

Lupe took the flattery in stride and motioned for a white coated Mexican boy to come and take their order. She introduced herself to Sam, as she presented her hand for him to shake. "I'm Lupe Moreno, I own this café."

Sam took her hand in his right hand he squeezed hers and with his left he rubbed the top of her hand and up her bare arm a-ways. Anyone could tell she liked it. She gave him a big beautiful smile, she pulled a chair next to him and sat with a hand on his shoulder and asked his name.

"Sam Duncan."

"Where you from? You make my blood rise, how come you so handsome?"

He laughed hard and told her, "My Ma and Pa had a little to do with that."

"They did a good job, you are one good looking man."

All during supper she sat and watched every move Sam made, he had a bad time eating as he did the same to her. She asked him to walk out with her, she wanted to show him some of San Antonio since he had just come to town. Sam was ready for a relationship with a woman, this woman could fill the bill very well.

They walked down by the Alamo, she told him the history of the place. Then they sat on a bench and watched the river flow by as it turned dark. He walked her back to the café, her apartment was next to the café. He took her in his arms and planted a gentle kiss on her lips, breathlessly she asked if he wanted to stay the night? He backed up, hands raised and told her, "Not tonight, maybe tomorrow night."

Back in his room he washed up and went to bed and tried to sleep, was he ready for this woman? he asked himself. Sleep came and he dreamed of Fawn and his love of her. All the rest of the night she was in his sleeping subconsciousness.

He was awakened by the crowing of a rooster off in the distance, he was wringing wet with sweat. After dressing he went to the horse barn, fed and groomed the horses, his mind kept thinking of Fawn, her presence seemed to be everywhere, she was like a beautiful memory hanging over him. He saddled the Dunn and took a long ride, Fawn's presence rode with him, she told him many times, "Be your own man Sam, be your own man."

Her Indian father always said he was his own man, she liked that in a man, he knew Fawn would understand. A light rain was falling when he returned to the barn, the night was fast approaching. He felt hunger for the first time that day, time to see Lupe.

At the café he had ordered and was eating when Lupe came in and asked, "Where you been? I sent a boy to look for you, you afraid of me?"

"Ho no, I took a ride, let's take a walk after I eat." Again they walked to the river and sat on a bench and talked.

He told her he had a wife that died and he didn't think he could ever love another. She said she didn't care, she just wanted a man to make sweet love to her. "I'm not the marrying kind, ya take me that way or not at all." Sam agreed to that kind of relationship.

The days and nights that followed the two became good friends and lovers. Sam had a lot of time on his hands, spent a lot of the time with his black stallion, the horse was the best he had ever been on, he had a stride so long he fairly flew over the ground on flying hooves. He loved to ride the horse. He was also the smoothest one he had ever been on.

The blacksmith's son told him match races will start soon. He should race the black one. "You'll make lots of dinero with him."

Sam told him, "I have no rider or race saddle."

"I, Charlo Lopez, will be your rider, I have a saddle, I rode last year and won many races, we win many together now with your Negro Caballo."

This small Mexican boy meant what he said. A more wiry boy Sam had never seen, he agreed to go in partners with him. "We'll split his winnings 50-50."

The first of the year the races started and the black and Charlo did win every race they matched. Sam made so much money he hoped it wouldn't end.

Lupe became jealous of his horses and told him so. "You spend more time with your horses than me."

He could see they were drifting apart fast, she became more bad tempered and hard to get along with. Jay told him she had put a knife in one of her lovers as he slept, that was enough for Sam, he broke it off, in three days she had another lover in her bed.

Spring time in south Texas is a beautiful time of year, Sam was enjoying his horses and the forced time off, some how he was ready for some action. Time hung heavy on his hands. Tom Gilman, another Ranger who had been put on unpaid leave, became a close friend. Tom backed Sam at the match races when needed, they rode together and practiced their shooting together, in the few months they were buddies and became good friends.

In the last of April, Major Jones came to San Antonio and wanted to have a talk with Sam. Sam asked about Sylvia. Major Jones said, "She worked in a dry goods shop for a while, all she talked about was going to San Francisco, California. She felt her ordeal was finally behind her and she was ready to go on her own, she had a thing about California. We hope she has done well there. I gave her the seven hundred dollars and she had saved some more. With misgivings we put her on a train bound for the west coast. Sam, I came down to see you, the United States Government asked me to find a man and recommend him for the U.S. Deputy Marshal's job in the Arizona Territory, in the town of Tucson. I told them you're the man for the job. How about it, will you take the job, Sam?"

"Sounds good to me, I'm ready for new places, When do I have to be there?"

"Come back to Austin with me, you can catch a train to Arizona, you'll be on your way in a few days."

Sam made arrangements with Tom to ship his horses by rail, filled a trunk with his belongings. Then he went with the Major to Austin, four days later he was on a Southern Pacific Train en route to a new job in Tucson, Arizona Territory.

Come December Sam would be 50 years old.

The Arizona Saga Begins

Chapter 12

Tucson, Arizona Territory

A long hot dirty ride from Austin, the train engine blew cinders thru the open windows. As the train slowed a dust devil made its way toward the adobe houses off in the distance, Sam was glad the trip was over. The train screeched to a stop. He stood, stretched, rubbed his butt. He was sore all over, the wood seats in the train became hard as a rock. "I'd rather be horse back," he said to himself.

Hungry, thirsty and tired, He picked up his carpet bag and stepped off the train at the depot in Tucson, Arizona Territory. It was May First 1880, the railroad had just come to Tucson three months earlier. A man dressed as a railroader was standing in the depot door.

Sam called, "Can you keep my trunk in the baggage room til I can come for it?"

"That it, they're taken off now?"

Sam turned to look. "Yes that's it."

"Sure we'll take good care of it, it'll be in the baggage room."

Sam then asked, "Where's a hotel? I need a room."

The man pointed, "Just around the corner across the road."

The sun was setting behind the pointed mountains in the west. Sam walked a few feet and looked at a two story building around the corner and across a dusty road from the depot.

"That's the San Xavier Hotel."

"Thanks."

As he walked toward the hotel, he could see the two story building had a covered porch all the way around on both levels. The dust kicked up by his feet blew up the road to the east toward town. Sam climbed up a few steps and entered a lobby room. The man behind the desk asked, "What can we do for you, mister?"

"I need a room and some eats."

"We have both." He turned a ledger book around. "Can you write your name?"

"Sure can." Sam took the pen and wrote, Sam Duncan.

"You can get eats thru that door," pointing to his right.

Sam picked up his bag, walked to and opened the door. He saw a small room with four tables. A man and well-dressed woman were eating at one, the rest of the tables were empty. He sat down to the one at his right. He sat with his back against the wall.

A white aproned young Mexican boy came and asked in broken English, "What you want to eat?"

"How about a well done steak, potatoes, coffee and some water."

Without a word the boy turned, went thru swinging doors into the kitchen. Sam heard him speaking to someone in Spanish. He returned with a glass of water and a pitcher. Sam drank several glass fulls. "Been on that damn train two days and nights."

The boy said nothing, looked away and returned to the kitchen. Sam could smell and hear his steak cooking. Soon the boy brought the food.

After eating, Sam returned to the lobby. He asked the desk man how to find his room.

"Room 14, out the door, turn left, third door on the left," he said as he handed Sam a key. Sam followed the directions, found the room, unlocked and entered.

Being dark he struck a match, found a lamp and lit it. Looking around he saw a bed, a dresser, with a wash pan and a pitcher of water, and a table the lamp was on. He hung his hat, coat, and vest on pegs on the door, hung his gun belt on the bed post, pulled his boots off, took off his shirt and pants .Washed as best he could and fell in the bed and went fast asleep.

He woke up hot and sweating .He reached for, found and looked at his watch, it read twelve midnight. He got up raised the only window, not much air. Then he opened the door, and lay down again. Couldn't sleep, too hot, got up pulled on his pants and walked out on the porch that looked out over the town. Mexican music and a lot of noise in the distance was coming from town. He stretched and said out loud, "At least it's cooler out here."

He backed up and sat in a chair against the wall, he yawned and looked around and discovered he was not alone.

A woman's voice said, "Too hot to sleep isn't it?"

Sam agreed. "It sure is."

She moved her chair closer to him said, "My name is Mamie Dunning. I'm from Pittsburgh, Pennsylvania."

"Where is Pittsburgh?" asked Sam. "Is it near Gettysburg?"

"Oh no," she said. "It's far from there, were you at Gettysburg?"

"No, ma'am, everyone has heard of the town. A lot of good men died there on both sides."

She changed the subject. "I'm here for my health, are you?"

"No, Ma'am, I have a job here, I understand a lot of people come here for their health."

"Yes, I have T.B. My husband sent me here to be cured.

There's a village out of town where people go to get treated, I hope someone will come and give me a ride in the morning out to the village."

Sam told her, "I'll find a way to take you out there if your ride don't come."

"I'm sure they will come. I must try to get some sleep now. What is your name?"

"Sam Duncan. I'm gonna try to sleep too."

They bid each other "good morning" and went back to their rooms.

Morning found Sam sleeping late. When he woke he was wet with sweat. He checked his watch, ten o'clock. "Good Lord, I overslept."

He washed the best he could, dressed and went out on the porch in time to see the lady he was talking to early this morning getting in a carriage. She looked up, saw him, waved as they drove off. It was Thursday, May the second, 1880. Sam's first day in the Old Pueblo had begun.

He hurried down to the lobby, where he asked the man behind the desk if the kitchen was open. "I need a cup of coffee."

"I'm sure you can get one, it's late for breakfast, see the cook, she's a real nice lady."

Sam hurried in to the eating room and on in to the kitchen. The cook was glad to give him a cup. He drank it down, asked, "Can you tell me where I can find the United States court house?"

"Go out on the road here, that's Congress St, go up to Stone St, then turn right, the next street is Broadway the court house and post office are just to the left, you can't miss, it's the biggest building on Broadway."

Sam thanked her and followed her instructions.

On the way he passed a manure pile, a dead dog and lots of

trash laying in the streets. He said to himself, "Guess the folks here don't give a damn what this town looks like or smells like."

Sam found the court house, a sign over the door read, U.S. POST OFFICE - U.S. 10th DISTRICT COURT - JUDGE J. J. HENRICKS PRESIDING. Sam went in, a sign told him the court was up the stairs to his left. He climbed them to a door at the top, a sign in the glass in the door read, 10th District Court.

In the room he found a desk with some file cabinets and a comely woman with auburn hair. She looked up as he came in and asked if she could help him. He handed her his papers, he told her, "I'm the new Deputy U.S. Marshal assigned to this district."

She acted upset. In a demanding voice she asked, "Where have you been? We've been looking for you for weeks."

"What? I just got my commission last week."

"I'm sorry, we asked for and thought you were coming weeks ago." The lady gave him a warm smile.

Sam asked, "Where's the judge, when can I see him?"

She said, "Now, if you want to go to San Diego."

"What are you saying, why there?"

"Since the rail road came, some people who can afford it, go where it's cooler, he won't be back until this fall."

Sam asked, "What am I supposed to do in the meantime? Set on my rear til he decides to come back?"

"No, I have the authority to take care of your business."

"That's just great, a women boss." Sam acted perturbed.

"I'm not so bad," she said. She stood up, turned around and showed him her shapely figure. "You have lots of work to keep you going until he gets back, you get two dollars for a summons and fifty dollars for serving a warrant."

"When do I start?" he asked. "I may get rich at these prices." He began laughing.

"Do you have a place to stay?" she asked.

"No, I stayed at a hotel down by the train depot last night. I must find a better place, it was hotter than hades there."

The woman said, "I live in a boarding house, I think there's a vacancy there, would you like to go take a look?"

"Sure, when?"

"We can go now."

Sam asked, "You can close this office anytime you want?"

"I told you I'm the boss when the judge is gone." She reached in a drawer, took out and handed him a U.S. Marshals Badge, then she took it back and said, "Let me pin it on your vest." She moved close, her perfume smelled so good it made him shiver.

He said, "You're the best smell-n boss I ever had and I might add the prettiest."

She pinned the badge on his vest and said, "You're the best looking Marshal we've ever had and the most cocky."

She gave him a wistful smile. They closed and locked the office and went down the stairs. At the bottom she stopped and leaned against the rail out of breath. She said, "I've got to stop a minute."

"Are you okay?"

She looked wobbly on her feet. "I- I'm just fine, I must catch my breath." She breathed deep and said, "Let's go."

They walked out into the bright May Arizona sun, then turned west on Broadway and crossed Stone St, crossed over to the south side of Broadway. As they passed the Shu-Fly café she said," This is the best eating place in town, if you're good to me, I'll let you take me there some time, they have wonderful food, fresh vegetables and fruit since the railroad came and I believe we're going to have ice from El Paso anytime now."

They walked on down to Meyer St and turned south. Sam

saw a long high adobe wall with windows and a door every so often.

She told him, "These houses have been here for years and years, they're all made of adobe, cool in the summer and warm in winter, I just love living here, I love this town of Tucson."

Sam told her, "The smell could be better, don't they ever clean the streets?" as they passed a pile of horse manure. She let his words pass.

He asked, "How long have you been here?"

"Almost a year. I came from New York."

"New York City?"

"No, I'm from upstate, Albany, the state capital, you ever been to New York?"

"Yes, a long time ago on government business, I was with a group of Sioux Indian Chiefs, we came from the Wyoming Territory to show them the white man's cities. We took them to see some of the eastern cities, even Washington, D.C. Saw the President, it was just after the Civil War."

"Doesn't sound like much fun to me." She stopped short, "Here we are. This is the Martinez house."

She opened the door, he followed her in. He could see a long hall with doors on both sides, there was a double glass door way in the back. At the first open door on the right she stopped and called. "Dolores, I have a new boarder for you."

An older pretty Mexican lady answered, "Wonderful I need another one."

The lady with Sam said, "You're gonna like this one, he's our new U.S. Marshal and he isn't too bad to look at, only trouble he has a big mouth."

Sam corrected her, "Deputy Marshal."

She said, "Whatever." She introduced Mrs. Martinez. "Our very good house mother, the best cook in all of the Arizona, Territory."

Mrs. Martinez blushed. "Go on Louise," she said. "You're so good and kind, makes me sad you have no man." She smiled at Sam.

"Louise," he said, "the name fits, I'm Sam."

"I know your name, it's Sam Duncan."

A young, very attractive Mexican girl looked up from the tortillas she was making and said, "I'm Rosa, the best looking, the most beautiful and the best Mexican girl in all of Tucson." They all laughed.

"Can I see the room now?" Sam asked.

All three women led the way down the hall to the last door on the right. Entering the room Sam could see a four poster bed, a table with a lamp, a dresser, a rocking chair, a wall closet and a picture of a Mexican bull fighter hung above the bed, various paintings of beautiful Mexican women hung around the room. Two double glass french doors opened into a patio. Sam opened the doors, walked out to take a look. He saw a porch covered the full length of the house, a high wall enclosed the patio. Flowers bloomed in pots on the porch and by the wall. The floor was of some kind of red brick. Strings of red peppers and several hollas hung from the porch beams.

Mrs. Martinez spoke, "Thru that door in the back wall leads to our outhouse."

Louise told him, "Dolores has cots we can sleep on out here when it gets too hot in the rooms, how do you like this?"

"Looks good to me." He turned to Dolores and asked, "How much do you want?"

"Seven American dollars a month, two meals a day, breakfast and supper."

"You got yourself a new boarder Mrs. Martinez."

"We're glad to have you, Senor Duncan."

"No, no Mrs. Martinez call me Sam, please."

"You call me Dolores, okay?" Sam said he would.

The three women left the room. Sam slumped down in the rocker and said to himself, "This is the best place I've had in sometime."

For most of an hour he sat and contentedly rocked back and forth almost asleep. He took his pocket watch from his vest, it read one fifteen. He got up, hung his coat, hat and gun belt on pegs on the door and started to set back down.

A knock on the door. "Come on in," Sam called.

The girl Rosa pushed the door open, she carried a pan, a pitcher of water and a towel. "Momma said you should come and eat with us now, here's water to wash up with, there's soap in the dresser drawer." She smiled, turned and went out.

Sam washed and went to the kitchen. At a small table the three women sat talking, Dolores motioned for him to sit down. Green peppers, frijoles, sliced cheese and a hot flour buttered tortilla, reminded him of Lupe in San Antonio. Rosa gave him a cup of coffee. She wanted to know, "Where you from tall man?"

"I just came from Texas, and a lotta other places."

Louise asked, "Were you with the law there too?"

"On and off, I been with the law a long time"

After eating he stood and took seven dollars from his billfold and handed it to Dolores and asked to be excused.

The women all shook their heads yes, as they looked at each other. "What a polite man," he heard one say as he left.

He returned to his room, lay down and fell asleep.

When he woke up, the evening light was streaming into the room, it helped him to wake up. As he rubbed his face, I need a shave he thought. A knock on the door, the young Mexican girl called in a loud voice, "We're waiting supper on you Texas."

He heard her walk away. He washed again and hurried down the hall to an open door across from the kitchen. He went into a room with a long table and lots of good smelling food sat on it. Colorful pictures hanging on the walls of Mexican people and places. A wagon wheel hung from the ceiling with lighted candles. There were candles on the table. The smell of the food hung in the air, Mexican cooking has an aroma all of its own. It smelled wonderful. In all, a very pleasant place to be.

Dolores said, "Come sit by me."

He slid into a chair next to her, Louise sat across from him. She stood, "I want you to meet the other boarders Sam. This is Mrs. Ruiz."

He saw a rather heavyset older Mexican lady. "She's a seamstress, she has a sewing shop up town. The man with the beard is Jake Holbrook an old timer here. Next to him is Ramon Leon, he's always smoking a cigar, he works at the wagon factory. The lady with the beautiful smile is Hilda Swanson." She smiled and nodded her head.

"And this handsome man is Mr. Stein, he works in the only bank in town."

Stein rose and came to shake his hand saying, "I'm glad! We need a good lawman in this town."

No more was said and everyone started eating. All the people seemed to enjoy the meal of baked quail, brown gravy, fresh tomatoes, corn, frijoles and fresh made tortillas .It was finished off with sopas, honey and goats milk.

After everyone finished eating, Dolores brought a jug of red vino from the kitchen and insisted all have a glass in celebration of the new boarder. After the drink, Sam returned to his room. He opened the double doors and went out in the patio and sat in a leather tub chair. From a pouch, he filled his pipe, tamped the tobacco with a forefinger and lit it with a match, sat back and watched the smoke he blew go up in the air and fade away.

Rosa the young girl came from the hall. Seeing Sam, she sat in a chair next to him. She told him, "It's nice out here, it'll be dark soon, it stays light longer this time of year. When the darkness comes it'll cool off. When it gets too hot to sleep in the rooms, momma has cots for everyone to sleep out here. Only bad thing, the sun makes us get up too early."

Sam said to her, "I'm going to bed." He stood and went into his room, she followed.

"Time for me too, Texas."

"I'm not a Texan, it was just a stop in a long line of places. Don't call me Texas." He had some anger in his voice.

"What will I call you? Ha!" She said, "I'll call you the handsome gringo."

Sam pushed and shoved her out the door, saying, "Good night."

He opened the patio doors, undressed, washed and went to bed the first night in his new room.

Chapter 13

Shooting of the Greek, Dance

When he woke up, he dressed and opened the door to his room. He could hear people talking in the eating room. He hurried down the hall and into the eating room. Most of the boarders were already eating. He slipped into a chair next to Louise. She greeted him with, "Good morning Sam, sleep well in your new room?"

"Too well, I overslept, I do that when I'm tired. A train ride makes me tired."

Louise asked, "What's on your docket for today?"

"I have to go to the depot and get my trunk. Do you know where I can rent a rig?"

Rosa spoke up, "Manuel's corrals are just down the street by the river, he rents rigs."

Louise got up and said, "I have to get to the office, people will be waiting, they always are in the mornings." She hurried to her room.

Rosa said, "I'll go to Manuel's with you, Sam."

"I'll go get my things," he told her. He hurried to his room, returned with his hat, gun belt and coat.

Rosa took the coat from his arm saying, "It's too hot for a coat." She hurriedly returned it to his room.

The two went out the front door. Louise came out behind them carrying a parasol. Sam turned to her saying, "How beautiful you look in that blue dress and matching hat. The blue parasol sets it all off."

"Yes it's new." She turned away and strutted up the street toward Broadway.

Sam and Rosa watched her go, they turned and walked south down a slight hill toward Manuel's corrals.

As Sam and Rosa approached the corrals he could see a large adobe barn with a tin roof. It had large openings in the front and back with many mesquite pole corrals on each side of the barn. He could see several large corrals in the back. They almost reached the bank of the Rio Santa Cruz River.

As the two entered the barn, a stout Mexican man who looked to be six feet tall with a heavy mustache, came from the harness and saddle room. He greeted them saying, "Buenos dias."

Rosa told Sam, "This is Manuel, the owner here." To Manuel she said, "This is Momma's new boarder." She spoke to him in Spanish. "He's the new U.S. Marshal."

Manuel in perfect English, "Welcome amigo to my stable. We need a good law man in this town."

Sam asked, "Do you board horses? I have two coming from Texas soon."

"For you Senor Marshal, no problem."

Sam asked if he could rent a rig to go to the depot to get a trunk.

"Si," Manuel replied. "I have a rig already harnessed to go." He yelled, "Hector bring the mule and the wagon."

A young Mexican boy came leading a grey mule and a buckboard. Rosa sounded her displeasure, "Not that old grey mule."

"Hush Rosa, we're just going to the depot she'll do fine," Manuel said. "That old girl is a good worker, I go and get mesquite poles to make corrals with her all the time, she's a good one."

"She'll do fine." Sam wanted no arguments.

Rosa climbed on to the seat and took the reins. Sam moved up beside her. When he reached for the reins, she jerked them away saying, "I will drive, I can drive!"

Sam saw it was no use arguing with this girl. They drove upon the road to Meyer street and north to Congress, turned west down to the depot, she turned the buck board to the left between the tracks and the depot platform, pulling up by the baggage room. Sam jumped on to the platform. He asked a railroad man standing there if he could get his trunk from the baggage room.

"Yes, you shore can." He yelled to two young Mexican boys to bring out the big trunk. When the boys tried, Sam could see they were having a bad time dragging the trunk, he went to help.

Just then a man came running from the waiting room yelling, "There's a man in there with a shot gun, saying he's gonna kill everybody, he wants to kill them all, he's yelling he's been cheated."

Sam rushed to the waiting room door. Looking in, what he saw made his blood run cold. A short man with a long black beard was swinging a sawed off shot gun around pointing it here and there. All the people had their hands in the air, backs to the walls, big eyed and some were shaking uncontrollably.

Sam with his right hand pulled his Schofield from its holster and dropped it by his right leg out of sight. He entered the station waiting room, he said in a loud clear voice, "WHAT'S THE TROUBLE HERE?"

The little man with the shot gun spun around, pointed the shotgun at Sam, saying in a loud broken English voice, "I'll kill you, you son- a-bitch." He said it again, only not as loud, "I'll kill em all, you sons-a-bitches."

Sam said slow and loud as he could, "You don't want to hurt anyone, put the gun down! Do it now! You can't shoot that gun no how, it's not cocked! Cock it and I'll kill ya!" He said it slower and louder so all could hear. "Touch those hammers, I'll kill ya."

The little man said, almost yelling, "You can't cheat me, nobody gonna cheat me." His thumb touched the hammers. In a flash Sam's Schofield spoke, fire and lead, the bullet hit the man in the right shoulder spinning him around, he fell face down to the floor. Quick as a cat Sam scooped up the shotgun, broke it open spilling the shells on to the floor.

As he kneeled down to see if the man was dead or alive. A man came thru the front door yelling loudly, "What the hell is the shooting about?"

Sam could see this big man was with the law. The star on his vest told him this must be the town marshal. A colt pistol hung at his side. "I did the shoot-n," Sam said as he rolled the little man over. "This man needs a doctor."

"Is he dead?" asked the law man.

"No," Sam replied. "The bullet went clean thru his shoulder"

When Sam straightened up, the town marshal said, "You must be the new U.S. marshal?" He saw the badge on Sam's vest. Sam shook his head yes. "I'm the town Marshal, Tom Henry. Who's the wounded man?"

Sam shook his head. "I don't know, he was threatnin to kill the people here."

The marshal took a long look. "Hell, it's that damn Greek, he's been shoot-en his mouth off all over town. Didn't think the little bastard was dangerous." Sam handed him the shot gun.

The marshal said, "He must have stolen it from one of the casinos, he's been gambling and hanging out in most of them for the last few weeks."

Sam told the Marshal, "He needs a doctor bad."

"I've got my buggy at the hotel," the Marshal said. He asked one of the men there to go get it and bring it over. As soon as the buggy arrived, Sam and some of the men carried the wounded man out and put him in the buggy.

As the Marshal drove off he asked Sam to come to his office and make a shooting report. Sam said he would and he returned to loading his trunk.

Rosa and Sam drove to the Martinez house, he drove this time. The girl babbled all the way about the shooting, he felt like telling her to shut up but he didn't. At the house he managed to unload the trunk and put it by the front door, he told Rosa to stay and watch it. "I'll take the rig back to Manuel."

As he drove into the stable Manuel met him. "How much do I owe you?"

"Nada."

"I'm more than willing to pay." Sam tried to insist.

Manuel shook his head and repeated, "Nada."

"Okay."

He walked back up the hill to the house. Rosa was sitting on the trunk.

"What do you have in this thing?" she asked. "It's too heavy for me to move."

Two Mexican boys appeared with Dolores. "They will help you take it to your room."

Sam helped and they got it to his room, Sam tried to pay them.

Dolores said, "No! I use them all the time. I will give them something to eat, they like that the best." She herded them into the kitchen.

He unlocked and started to remove his belongings from the

trunk. Rosa stood watching and wanted to help.

"I'll do it!" Sam insisted.

From it he took a heavy coat, shirts, colored and white, a black suit with a vest, several pair of boots, several pairs of long johns and lots of miscellaneous clothing. He laid it all on the bed. He removed a twelve gauge sawed off shot gun wrapped in oil cloth, a Winchester rifle in a leather saddle scabbard, two double barrel derringers, a Smith and Wesson Schofield 44 pistol with a gun belt, many boxes of 44 cartridges, boxes of buckshot and more clothing.

Rosa tried to help. Sam pushed her away. He took a leather fringed shirt from the trunk. Rosa asked to feel it. He handed it to her. She rubbed it against her cheek saying how good it felt. "It's so smooth, where did you get it?" she asked.

Sam took it away, folded it and put it in a drawer. Next came a pair of beaded moccasins.

"They're beautiful." Rosa was impressed. "Where did these things come from?" she asked again.

"A young woman made them for me a long time ago, you weren't even born yet," Sam replied.

"Was she as pretty as me?" Rosa asked.

"Yes, she was very pretty." Sam turned away and said again in a low tone, "She was very pretty."

When he turned back, Rosa could see tears in his eyes. He said to her, "Get yourself outa here, I'll finish this up, I need to take a nap, okay?"

Rosa smiled and left, shutting the door easy.

Sam called after her, "Call me when supper is ready."

He finished and lay down and slept until he heard Rosa knocking on the door and calling, "Supper's ready."

After supper Dolores had coffee on the patio. Sam sat and smoked his pipe. The boarders asked many questions. Rosa was telling about the shooting at the depot. Sam shushed her.

"I'm not proud of the things I have to do."

He passed most of the questions off and asked about the town. He didn't get much information about the town. The people sat very quiet. They all watched the moon rise over the patio wall and spread its silver light onto their faces. Soon he asked to be excused, went into his room, washed up and went to bed, soon fast asleep.

Saturday morning when he opened his eyes the bright sun was streaming into his room over the back wall. He got out of bed, went to the dresser and looked at his watch, it read six thirty. He quickly washed his face and hands, dressed and opened the double doors and went onto the patio.

He stretched and as he looked around he saw Louise in a tub chair with her feet on another, sound asleep wrapped in a colorful sarape. She looked so beautiful, her long auburn hair laying over her right shoulder and down to her waist. He went closer. She opened her eyes, looked at Sam and said, "You need a shave."

"Today Louise, sorry I woke you."

"It was so hot in my room I came out here about midnight. I've been awake off and on all night, I don't work today so it doesn't matter, please help me up?"

He pulled her to him and said softly, "What you need is a good morning kiss."

"I know but not by you." She turned away, saying, "I'm hungry, let's go eat breakfast."

They entered the eating room, Rosa was setting food on the table. "Good morning you two," she said with a smile. "I'm so happy we're going dancing tonight." She played like she was dancing and danced into the kitchen.

Louise remarked, "I wish I had her energy."

"She's quite a girl." Sam was smiling.

Louise asked, "What are you doin today?"

Sam answered, "Shave and a hair cut." He laughed. "Gotta look good if I go to that dance tonight, how about you?"

"I'm resting all day, the dance you know," Louise said with a smile.

Sam said, "I better get on my way." He picked her hand up and kissed the back of it. "See you later." He took his leave.

Louise said to Dolores, "That man thinks he's a real lady killer."

"He looks good to me," Dolores said with a big grin.

As Sam left the house a train whistle sounded, he checked his watch, Eight fifteen. "She's right on time," he said to himself. "I wonder how the trains manage to run on time most of the time?"

He walked on up Meyer Street across Broadway to Congress and turned east to go up town. He walked on past Stone, past Scott St. The people he met were all friendly and smiling. He saw the barber pole a few stores ahead, he could read the sign above the door, Shave fifteen cents, hair cut twenty-five cents, shampoo twenty- five cents, hot bath with soap, fifty-cents.

A man in a white apron leaned against the door and said looking at the Badge on Sam's vest, "You must be the new U.S. Marshal. Everyone in town is talking about you."

Sam shook his head yes.

"Come on in, shave or hair cut?"

Sam pointed to the sign, "I want it all."

The barber laughed and said, "My business is picking up, my name is Bob White, also know as the barber man of the Old Pueblo.

Sam hung his hat on a coat rack and sat in the chair. He pulled the Schofield and laid it on his lap.

As Bob put on the barbers sheet, he was looking at the pistol and remarked, "You don't take chances I see."

177

"Force of habit."

"You want a bath too?"

"Sure do."

Bob went to a curtain in the back and told someone to fill a tub. He came back and laid Sam back in the chair and put a hot wet towel on his face and started mixing soap in a mug. "How you like our town Marshal?"

Sam hesitated.

"You can tell me, I've lived here for years, nothing you can say will offend me."

"Well," Sam said slowly, "too much horse shit in the streets, they ought to pick them dead dogs and burros up once in a while, makes the whole damn place smell awful bad."

"Where you come from they do better?"

"San Antonio, they have an old fella pushes a cart and picks up the shit and all the trash in the morning and evening. He works at it all the time, makes it smell a little better."

Bob took off and put another hot towel and started mixing the soap again.

Sam could hear two men come in and sit down. He sat up a little to get a view of them. There were howdies all around. Bob was strapping his razor and talking at the same time. "Got the new marshal in the chair here, he'll want to meet you boys."

He took the towel off and shaved Sam's face, toweled his face off and patted some good smelling wet stuff on his face. Then started to cut his hair with scissors. With the scissors, he pointed to the man in a grey suit. A well built older man with a well groomed moustache. "This is Mr. Ronstadt, he owns a buggy and wagon factory around the corner. The other handsome gentlemen is Mr. Steinfield, he owns a dry goods store up the street, both on the city council."

Steinfield a smaller man had a well groomed grey beard

178

and a ready smile. Both men got up and shook Sam's hand. "We're sure glad to have you here, we need one good law man in Tucson."

Mr. Ronstadt showed his enthusiasm to have a new marshal in town.

Bob said, "Maybe not, he says our town smells like horse shit." He told them what Sam said about San Antonio.

Steinfield said, "We better call a council meeting, we want to try to make this man happy."

Sam laughed saying, "Since you feel that way, do you reckon I could get a white shirt and some under drawers from you Mr. Steinfield?"

"Please call me Al, all my friends call me Al."

Sam asked again. Al walked to the door and called to a young Mexican boy playing in the street. Talked to him for several minutes in Spanish and came back, sat down and said, "Shirt and drawers coming up."

Bob took the sheet off of Sam and he stood up, he returned the Schofield to its scabbard. "Maybe the shampoo should wait, these men may be in a hurry?"

Both men shook their heads no and both said they were not in any hurry.

"These men are regulars, I hope you will be too Marshal."

"I sure will."

Bob started the shampoo. The conversation turned to horses. Sam told them he had horses coming by rail. Bob asked what they were. Sam told them he had an old gelding and a black stallion.

"I used to race the stallion in Texas."

"Good, we need more horses to match, we race on the other side of the Santa Cruz river just below Centennial Peak every Sunday in the winter time. Getting too hot now, we'll only have a few more races before we quit for the summer." Proudly he said, "I'm the starter."

"I'm sure I'll see you there, nothing I like better than a good horse race."

Bob finished and rinsed Sam's head. Sam seeing the dirty water said, "Damn that water's dirty."

Bob said, "Traveling by train everybody gets dirty." Then he told Sam, "Your bath is ready."

He led Sam to a room in the back. There a wooden tub three feet deep and four foot across was filled with steaming hot water. He showed Sam where soap and a towel was on a shelf. "You can put your clothes on them hooks," pointing to the wall. "I'll send the shirt and drawers soon as they come."

He pulled the curtain and left. Sam sat in a chair, pulled his boots off and undressed as fast as he could and climbed into the tub and sat on the bottom.

It was wonderful. He stood up, soaped all over and sat back down. He set there quite awhile enjoying his bath. Bob pushed a package thru the curtain, it dropped to the floor. Sam got out of the tub and dried off. He dressed and went into the shop and asked Al how much he owed him.

"Seventy cents, how do they fit?"

"Great." He fished a silver dollar from his pocket and gave it to Al.

Al returned the dollar, saying, "This one's on me."

Sam tried to give the dollar to Bob. He put his hands up said, "The first one's on me."

Sam shook his is head and said, "You boys sure know how to make a man feel at home. I thank you all."

He told Bob to toss his old shirt and drawers away. With that he bid them all good bye. He walked out and went west on Congress Street and crossed Stone Street and stopped at Alameda Street. Looking north he could see a Marshals star on a sign hanging from a building, farther on he could see the county court house.

He walked to the Marshals Office and entered. No one there. Laying on a desk was a paper. The heading read, SHOOTING REPORT. It had yesterday's date, with a space, that read shooting at Rail Road Depot. There were blanks to fill in, Sam filled them in. He put the paper back on the desk and walked out.

He walked on down to the court house and entered the Sheriff's Office. A young gent in his early twenties sat with his feet on the desk, his hat pulled down over his face. Without moving he said, "What-da want?"

"I want to see the Sheriff."

Without moving again the man asked, "I'm his deputy, right now I'M in charge. What the hell you want?"

Sam not saying a word reached and with a mighty jerk pulled his dirty boots off the desk, spinning him around in the swivel chair. The young man sat up startled. Looking at Sam, he saw the badge and got up. "You the new Marshal?"

"Yeah, where's the sheriff?"

"He, he, he'll be around shortly, can I help ya?"

"Just wanted to know if I can use the jail?"

"Are ya gonna bring someone in?" he asked all excited.

Sam shook his head, "No, just wanted to know if I can use the jail if I need to." Then he turned to leave.

The young gent in a sharp voice said, "My name is Clinton, Clint for short." Then he really smarted off saying, "You the bad shot that shot the SOB Greek? I'd kill the little bastard if it was me."

Sam looked at the six-shooter on his hip. An 1851 re-chambered colt Navy and said nothing. He walked out the door.

The deputy followed him out onto the side walk and called loud and clear, almost yelling as Sam walked away, "I'm the best fu—g shot in town, I'd killed the fu—g bastard, damned old fu—g men like you shouldn't be allowed to be a law man."

Sam shrugged his shoulders said nothing in return and walked on up the street. The deputy was still yelling something as Sam reached the next cross street. He walked on up to Congress Street.

Seeing the telegraph office, he crossed over and went in. The man at the keys didn't look up. "What you want?" he said in a very unfriendly way.

"I need to send a telegraph."

Without looking the man tossed a pad on the counter. "Write it up." He went back to his keys.

Sam started to write. The man finished with the keys and turned his attention to Sam. Seeing the badge, he said, "You the new U.S. marshal?"

"Yeah, that's right."

"You Sam Duncan?"

"Yeah."

"Got a telegraph for you, just came over the wire a few minutes ago."

He handed an envelope to Sam. He opened it, it read, "Shipped horses. Stop. Should be there sixth of May. Stop. Good luck Sam. Stop. Signed Tom."

Sam asked, "When is the sixth?"

"Monday."

"Send this wire."

The man looked at Sam in a harsh tone said, "Write it up."

Sam didn't like the tone in his voice. "Hell, you can send it now, your key is open." Sam pointed to the key, anger was in his words.

"OK, ok, what's the message?" This little man wanted no trouble with a marshal.

Sam told him, "To Tom Gilman. Care of the Texas

Rangers. San Antonio Texas. Many thanks for your help. Stop. Be waiting for horses. Stop. Come see me some time. Stop. Sign it Your old pardner, Sam." He told the operator, "Send it! I'm in no mood to screw with you." Sam's face showed he was a little mad at this man.

The operator set to working the keys, not saying another word. Sam tossed a quarter of a dollar on the counter. He walked out of the office and said to himself, "I sure don't like to get mad. Makes me feel bad but that deputy and asshole telegraph man sure pissed me off! My belly is telling me it's empty, I need something to eat." He looked at his watch, it read a little past twelve noon. He headed to the Shu- Fly Café on Broadway. This was the first Saturday in May 1880.

Walking toward the Shu-Fly, he stopped at the corner of Alameda and Congress Street. There he could look four ways. All the buildings were built of adobe with false wood fronts except the court house. It was made of red brick and native stone. A lot like some of the buildings in San Antonio.

Hunger was now on his mind. He hurried on to the Shu-Fly and entered the café. He saw plank tables with white oil cloth covers on them, benches lined both sides. He went to a table in the back of the room and sat down in a chair with his back to the wall. The walls were white washed adobe with muslin cloth covering the ceiling. Young Mexican boys in white jackets with fly swatters were swatting at and killing the flies as much as they could.

Sam ordered a jerked beef stew, a buttered flour tortilla and black coffee. Before the food came he saw Stein enter the front door. He called and motioned for him to come over. Stein said, "Sam I didn't expect to see you here. I eat here often, it's not far from the bank, but this is Saturday and it's my religious day. I don't work on Saturdays."

Sam asked, "You don't go to church on Sunday?"

"No," Stein replied, "I'm Jewish, our Temple day is from Friday sun down to Saturday sun down, I just came from my Synagogue. I want to tell someone, I'm going to ask a girl to be my wife to night at the dance."

"That's wonderful Stein, is she Jewish too?"

"Oh yes Sam. She's the most beautiful girl in the whole wide world."

"What's your chances?"

"I think she'll say yes, oh my Lord help her to say yes." Stein seemed to be talking to himself.

"I don't want you to think I'm dumb but I don't know what a Jew is. Don't reckon I ever met one before. You don't look no different than any body else."

"Sam do you read the Bible?"

"No," replied Sam, "My Ma did read it to us, my Pa, brother and me when I was a young boy."

"Do you remember her reading about Hebrews?"

"I think I do, that's a long time ago."

Stein started telling him about Jews. "We're the oldest religion know to man."

Sam interrupted, "Are there many Jews here in Tucson?"

"About one hundred families."

They finished their meals at the same time. After paying they walked out on the wood sidewalk, Sam looked at his watch. "It's almost two o'clock, I Think I'll go home and take a nap, I'm sleepy all the time since I've come here."

"I was the same way when I first came to Tucson, it's the heat I guess."

Sam told him, "Good luck with your girl." They parted ways.

At home Sam went straight to his room. No one was around. He took off his clothes and boots, lay down and was soon fast asleep. He slept for a couple hours. When he woke up he dressed and went to the kitchen for a cup of coffee. Rosa was there.

"Sam how handsome you are with a shave and hair cut."

"Had a bath too and I smell good, the barber slopped some kind of good smelling water on me."

She leaned over, put her head on his chest and sniffed. "You do smell good to me."

He pushed her away. "I need some coffee, is there some in the pot?"

"Yes, it's hot." She poured a cup. He took it.

"I'll go drink on the patio." He went there and sat in his favorite tub chair. Rosa followed and pulled a chair in front of him. She set down and kicked off her huaraches. She put her feet in his lap and asked, "Rub my feet, they feel so tired, will you Sam? Please?"

Sam remembered his Fawn used to ask him the same thing. Rosa snapped him back by pulling her skirt up over her knees to the middle of her legs. Sam looked away, tried to pay no attention, she pulled her skirt higher and asked, "Do I have pretty legs Sam?"

He let out a silent whistle and replied, "Yes, your legs are very pretty."

Just then Dolores called, "Rosa where are you?"

Rosa called back, "I'm here on the patio with Sam."

"Come, I want you to go to the market, it's getting late, we must fix supper."

Dolores had anger in her voice. Rosa pulled on her huaraches and started to leave. Sam laughed at her. She stuck her tongue out at him and disappeared into the hall.

He sat a few minutes more. Then went to get another cup of coffee in the kitchen. Rosa was going out the front door. He whistled at her. Again she stuck her tongue out at him. He repeated his whistle and laughed. She shut the door hard.

Laughing he asked Dolores for another cup of coffee and told her, "That's some girl you have."

"Sam I have been wanting to talk to you."

"What about Dolores?"

"My Rosa and Louise."

"Louise, Rosa?" he was puzzled.

"Yes, Sam you know Louise is not well. She's much better than when she first came here, she coughed all the time."

"You think she has TB?"

"No she would have to live out in the tent town if she had that. I've come to love her Sam. I don't want her hurt."

"I won't hurt her Dolores. Not if I can help it."

"Good. I knew I could count on you. Now about my Rosa. She really has taken a like-n to you. I know when that girl falls in love with a man it will be forever. I don't want her hurt either."

"Dolores, she's just a young girl." Sam was perplexed by her talk of Rosa.

"You know Sam, there are older men who have their eyes on her, they ask about her all the time, how old are you Sam?"

"I'll be fifty next December, some days I feel like a hundred," Sam laughed.

"I'm older than you Sam."

He tried to kid her. "You don't look very old at all to me Dolores. I'll tell you, I would never hurt Rosa. At least not on purpose. I promise you that."

Dolores came and hugged him and said, "I know you couldn't, I know you're a good man. You know, there are men that have asked for Rosa. Mexican men like younger women, one man in his late seventies, he has daughters older than Rosa. There are several more who have offered mucho dinero for my Rosa."

Sam shook his head. "That's like selling her as a slave, you couldn't do that to her."

"No, No I wouldn't, I chased those son-of-a-guns from my house. Sam. I must ask, do you have any feelings for my Rosa?"

"I like her but not that way, she's just a young girl, I like older women, like you Dolores." They both laughed.

Sam asked as gentle as he could, "I would like to ask you, where is Rosa's papa?"

Dolores shaking her head said, "That son of a gun ran off with a young Senorita. He went to Mexico, Rosa was just a baby."

"That's too bad." Sam felt sympathy for her. "You're doin a good job of raising her."

"It's not too bad. I have this house, it was his papa's. I get thirty five American dollars from you boarders each month. Rosa and I live good on that."

Rosa came thru the door saying, "We must hurry Momma, or we won't get a good table at the dance."

Dolores said to her, "Call the people supper is ready."

The little group of boarders after supper walked together on the way to the dance. They walked to Congress Street then turned west. Sam was wearing his blue suit, white shirt, black string tie, a matching vest with the U.S. Marshal badge pinned on it, a black hat cocked on his head, he was carrying his coat over his left arm, the trusty Schofield hung at his right side. Louise and Rosa walked in the front, Louise in a blue skirt, a white high necked blouse, she carried a white silk wrap. Her hair was done up in the latest style. Rosa wore a white silk blouse ,a full red skirt, black patent leather shoes, her long shiny black hair was covering her shoulders and down to her waist. Both women were a beautiful sight to behold, Sam was impressed with their good looks. The other women were dressed typical of the day with their long dresses down to their shoes. Leon , the big one, was smoking a long black cigar, he walked beside Mrs. Martinez, Hilda and Sam followed along, Stein was not with the party.

They crossed the Rio Santa Cruz river on a rickety wooden bridge. The Pavilion was just south of Congress street on the bank of the river. Sam could see a large wooden dance floor, a foot or so off the ground, smoothed from thousands of dancing feet. A man was tossing corn starch on the floor as they walked on to the platform. At the far south end was a raised platform where musicians, both Mexican and American were tuning their instruments. Tables with benches lined both east and west sides. Tall posts along the sides of the dance floor held ropes that were strung post to post and across the floor. Colorful lanterns hung from the ropes. There must have been several dozen. The north end was open. A lake doglegged around the south and west side of the pavilion. The only table left was at the far north end, the group sat at it. Hilda, Louise and Dolores sat on the far side, the men took the bench next to the dance floor.

Rosa, all the time complaining, she wished they had come sooner to get a better table, no one else complained. Old Sol was setting over the west mountains. Men started to light the lanterns as darkness set in, the music started.

The dancers took the floor, what a colorful sight. The dancers in their colorful dress, the Arizona sunset streaming over their heads, with all the colors of the rainbow, no one could have painted a more magnificent picture.

The men talked of the women dancers, the women of the men dancers. All the people were having a good time.

Manuel and his family sat at a table across the way, his little girls dressed in colorful Mexican dresses were on the floor trying to do all the dances.

Rosa danced every dance, most of the time with different

partners, only stopping to get her breath, then she'd be back on the floor dancing.

"She's a great dancer," Louise remarked, everyone agreed with her.

Several men came to talk with Sam and the men. One was Doctor Fenn, the town doctor. He thanked Sam for the business he had made for him. He was taking care of the Greek Sam had shot. Sam asked how the little fella was doing and how sorry he was to have had to shoot him.

He asked how the Doctor was gonna get paid? The Doctor told him, "When the Sheriff cleaned out his room, he found over one thousand dollars in gold coin and green backs." The man asked the Doctor to tell Sam, he was grateful that Sam had not killed him. The Doctor said the Sheriff was sending him to Los Angeles to rid Tucson of him. "See you boys later." He returned to his table and his wife. She waved and smiled at the Mrs. Martinez group.

At the intermission Rosa came to Sam and asked him to dance the next dance with her.

Louise said, "Go Sam, dance with her."

"I can't dance these dances," he flatly refused.

The music started again and Rosa was back on the floor dancing with a handsome young Mexican boy.

Sam saw the deputy Clint come up and lean against one of the light poles, a hand rolled cigarette dangling from his lips, he looked unsteady on his feet, a slough hat sat back on his head. He was wearing the same dirty white shirt and boots he had on this morning.

As Rosa came back to the table, he stepped over and grabbed her by an arm saying in a loud voice, "Dance with me bitch."

She tried to pull away but couldn't. "I don't dance with drunks," she said as she pulled harder.

"You dance with them greasers, I'm as good as them." He pulled her to him, she tried to pull away again, he held her tight. She was struggling to get away.

Sam rose, his jaw was set, his fists clinched. Louise grabbed his arm. "He's armed," she said as she pointed to Clint's pistol.

Sam had early taken his pistol belt off and laid it on the table. Sam could see the old colt hanging from Clint's belt. He pulled away from Louise and stepped to the deputy. "LET HER GO," he said in a demanding voice.

Clint spoke back, "Get away old man, this is none of your affair."

Sam asked again. Clint stepped back and reached for the colt with his right hand. A crashing right fist landed square on the Deputy's left jaw, making a bone breaking sound, he hit the floor like a rock, out cold.

Two men who worked at the pavilion came and dragged him by his feet toward the river and pushed him off the bank. As they returned to the pavilion, smiles beamed all over their faces, one gave Sam a salute.

The music started again. Dolores said, "It's the last Mexican dance, It's always the Mexican hat dance."

Rosa and her partner were so good the other dancers drew back to watch. When they finished the crowd clapped and cheered so hard the lanterns almost came down.

The last dance by the American musicians was a waltz. Memories flooded back into Sam's mind, he and Little Fawn watched from the porch, thru the windows at Ft Laramie. The officers and their ladies glided around the dance floor, waltzing. Sam and Fawn were trying to do the same with much difficulty. The Captain's wife Sue, saw them thru a window and came out and asked Fawn if she would like to learn the white mans dances. She shook her head violently, yes, yes.

Sue told them, "Come to our quarters, bring Sam, I'll teach you both."

They went many times and danced to her music box. The band was playing the same music now.

Louise came, she stood in front of Sam and asked, "Dance with me Sam, it's a waltz, they're playing the Blue Danube. Please Sam, dance with me," she begged.

He stood and took her in his arms and in the best manner of a dancer, waltzed and whirled her around the floor so smoothly the other dancers stopped, stood back to watch. Around and around they danced and when the music finished the applause was so deafening, the cheers and bravos could be heard uptown.

The dance was over. As the group walked home, Louise was so out of breath, Sam and Rosa had to half carry her. They stopped several times to let her get her breath. She was so happy, she smiled all the time.

At home they all said good night. Dolores put Louise to bed. Sam went to his room and to bed, one tired dancer.

On Sunday morning he rose from a sound sleep, sat up on the side of the bed and wiped the sleep from his eyes. Went to the wash pan, poured water from the pitcher and washed his face and hands, he wiped his face with his hand, and said to himself, "I need a shave."

Looking at his watch, it read seven am. Someone must be in the kitchen by now. Pulling on his pants he retrieved his moccasins from the dresser, slipped them on and headed for the kitchen, while putting on a shirt.

In the kitchen, Dolores was preparing breakfast. She turned and welcomed him with a smile. "What a Saturday night, I can't remember having a better time. Sam, I'm sure you made an enemy of Deputy Clint, watch out for him he's been known to shoot from the back."

"I've known men like him, I'm sure we'll meet again. How's the coffee?"

"Hot and ready." She poured a cup. "How do you like your eggs?"

"Scrambled."

She broke two eggs into a fry pan. She told Sam to get a plate and get the bacon from the stove. "Breakfast is ready."

As he sat down, Stein came in showing a long face. Sam asked, "Where were you last night? We were all looking for you."

"Got tied up, my girl's folks. They questioned me all evening, you know the usual things. How I plan to take care of her and a whole lot more."

"Did you ask her?" Sam asked.

"I did. She never gave me an answer."

Dolores chimed in, "Don't give up, keep asking."

"I will." He sat down at the table looking dejected.

Sam asked Dolores if he could have some hot water as he needed to shave.

"I'll heat some." She put a pan on the stove filled with water. Sam and Stein sat talking while the water was heating.

Just as they finished eating, Rosa entered the kitchen wearing a white lace rebozo (shawl) over her head and shoulders. It really turned Sam's head. "Rosa, you are very beautiful this morn-n."

He stopped short and bit his upper lip. Dolores gave him a dirty look. He put his head in his hand and shook his head. Said to himself, "I shouldn't have said that."

Rosa looked to him and just smiled. To Dolores she said, "Momma we must hurry, we've missed first mass. We will be late for the next, hurry Momma, hurry Momma."

Dolores went to their room and returned wearing a black shawl over her head. The two left by the back gate. Stein started to leave. Sam told him to not get down on himself. "It'll work out, go easy, I know sometimes these things take time."

Stein turned to leave and said, "My first name is Benjamin, I like my friends to call me Ben, they call everyone at the bank by their last name. Please call me Ben, will you Sam?"

"You're Ben to me, from now on."

Ben turned to leave again and said, "I'm gonna take a long walk by the river." He departed, his head hanging like a hound dogs, losing a good scent.

Sam returned to his room with the hot water. Taking a mug, a razor and a strap from the dresser, a mirror from his carpet bag, he shaved his face.

On the way to the outhouse, he dumped the shave water. Back in his room he sat in the rocker to relax. Louise knocked and opened the door. She was wearing a white dress, a flowered hat with lace on the edges. She asked Sam if he would like to go to church with her.

"No," he said firmly.

As she left she said, "I must hurry my ride is due any time." She went out the front door.

Sam still setting in the rocker, took out, filled and lit his pipe. He was content to rock and smoke for a while.

Putting on his brown boots he decided to walk down to Manuel's corrals. When he entered the barn, he saw Manuel was busing himself in the harness room. He greeted Sam with. "Buenos dias Marshal."

Sam asked him, "Please call me Sam if we're going to be friends."

"You are my friend Sam," he replied in a most friendly fashion. "What a night we had, eh! My woman has talked of nothing else but the dance. How you and the pretty Senorita danced, my woman says that one is falling in love with you. She kept saying, you see the way she looks at him. She told me if she was younger she herself would be in love with you too."

Sam smiled and said, "I saw your little ones, they liked dancing, they were trying all the dances, you have a nice family Manuel."

"Si" was his only reply.

The two men talked and walked thru the corrals. They looked over Manuel's horses. Manuel told Sam he bought most of the horses in Mexico. Sam was impressed with them, he told Manuel he had a fine bunch. He asked if there would be a place where he could keep his. He had two coming on the eight-ten in the morning.

"Si, no problemo, plenty room."

The two walked and talked a while longer mostly of horses. Sam bid him adios and walked back up to the house.

On approaching the house he saw a magnificent matched pair of grey horses pulling a black surrey coming toward him. He stepped back to watch them go by. They stopped in front of the door, Louise stepped from the rear seat saying, "I'm so glad you're here, I want you to meet my friends, Professor Adolf Hamsteen and his wife Christine."

Sam could see the man was in his sixties, of medium build, with a well manicured beard, wearing a beautiful tailored grey suit. The woman looked on the plump side, very well dressed, graying hair with a friendly smile.

She said, "We are so pleased to meet you, Louise has talked of nothing else all morning, I hope we can call you Sam."

" I'd be darn mad if you don't." Sam wanted to get to know them and thought he might like these folks.

Louise interrupted his thinking saying, "The professor is an anthropologist."

Sam asked, "Anntro –what?"

Louise said, "He's here at the university studying early

man."

"Early man?" Sam asked with some doubt in his voice.

"Yes Sam, Early man, did you know that Tucson is the oldest city in all the United States Territory, men lived here many centuries ago."

"Is this true professor?" Sam was curious.

"Yes," he answered. "He lived on this very spot, hundreds of years ago, we have proof of it."

Louise broke in, "We're going on a picnic, won't you come Sam? We have fried chicken and Christine has baked a fruit pie, won't you come, please Sam! We're going out to see the San Xavier del Bac Mission, the oldest church in this country."

"Yes I'd like to come, the food sounds too good for me to pass up, I'll have to change my boots first."

Louise told him, "We'll wait right here."

When Sam returned all three were seated in the surrey. Sam stepped up and into the rear seat with Louise. The professor clucked to the team and they were off in a trot. They drove south on Meyer Street to the road along the Rio Santa Cruz river, Christine had turned in her seat talking to Louise.

As they drove along the two women talked of the Sunday service, Christine asked Louise if she had planned to go and hear Susan B. Anthony the next Sunday. Louise said she wouldn't ever miss hearing her. Sam asked who she was and what she's talking about.

"She's the foremost woman pushing women's suffrage in these United States." Louise seemed excited about seeing and hearing this woman.

Sam asked, "What's she suffer-n about?"

The three laughed so hard the professor had to take a hard hold of the horses to keep them from running.

"No Sam, she's trying to get the right for women to vote."

"I've never met a man I'd vote for, well maybe a couple,

never voted, don't guess I ever will."

Louise could see this was going nowhere. She changed the subject. "Sam, the professor and Christine come from Austria, Vienna, Austria away across the sea."

"Are these horses from there too?" asked Sam.

"Yes they are," the professor said with pride in his voice. "We shipped them by boat then by rail to Arizona."

"They're a fine looking pair, I've never seen better." Sam was impressed with them.

Louise said, "Look there's the Mission." She pointed to a large white building across the river. "That's where we're going."

The professor broke in, "We must find a spot to eat first, it's pasted noon."

They stopped in a shaded spot under a big mesquite tree. Spring grass covered the ground. They spread blankets and had their picnic. Afterwards they forded the river and went on to the church. A friendly Padre greeted them as they entered the building. He told of the wonders of this ancient building. The women were so pleased to see and hear about it. Sam asked why the one tower wasn't finished.

The Padre explained, "A worker fell and was killed falling from there, the Indians were so superstitious they refused to work on it more."

"Yes," Sam said, "I know how they are."

The two couples returned to town as the sun set in a spectacular sundown, spreading yellow, orange, blue and green colors across the western sky. Sam told Louise that it was the most beautiful setting he had ever seen. She squeezed his hand and said in a low voice, "I like you Sam Duncan."

Sam and Louise were dropped off at the Martinez house. They thanked the professor and his wife for such a nice afternoon. Dolores saw them enter the house and asked if they were hungry. Both said no, but Sam asked if there was any coffee. Rosa heard him from the kitchen and called, "I'll bring some to the patio."

Louise told the two women all about their picnic and seeing the church. They talked several hours. Finally Sam said, "I have to go to bed, all this talking is making me tired and sleepy."

They all bid each other good night and went to their rooms.

This May morning Sam was up early, he was dressed and in the kitchen making coffee. Dolores came in and said, "I see you have fired the stove and are making coffee. Please go set down and let me have my kitchen."

Sam obliged. Then she asked, "What would you like for breakfast?"

"Anything you want to fix."

"I have fresh chorizo." As she uncovered a pan, she put the contents in a fry pan and set it on the stove.

"I hope it's not too hot." He grimaced as he said the words. "They make it too hot for me in Texas."

She laughed. "You gringos need a little heat in your belly." He laughed too.

Rosa came into the kitchen. Seeing Sam she asked, "Are you ready for your horses to come?"

"I hope they'll be on time and be okay," he replied.

"Can I come to the depot with you?"

He looked to her mother for her approval. She told them as she set a steaming plate of chorizo on the table before Sam, "It's okay, Rosa you must eat something first."

"No, no, Momma, I'm too excited to see Sam's horses," she said frowning and making a face like a little girl.

"Drink some milk. You can eat when you come back." Dolores poured her a glass of goat's milk.

She took the glass. "I must go change my clothes," she said

as she left drinking the milk on the way.

Dolores asked Sam, "That girl, what do I do with her?"

He shrugged his shoulders. "Don't ask me. I've never raised a kid."

In a few minutes, Rosa returned wearing a white shirt, black pants, black shiny boots and a red bandana tied on her head. It held her long black hair back. Her hair fell down in the back to her waist. As they walked out the front door and down the street, her hair flipped at the ends and her hips swung from side to side.

She reminded him of Fawn the way she used to walk. "A more beautiful sight I've not seen in a long time," he said to himself.

She turned to him and said, "We can cut across the desert here." A path led toward the station.

"Fine."

Looking down at the shirt she wore, the top three buttons were undone. He asked her to fix them, she ignored him. They walked thru grease wood and small paloverde trees were blooming on both sides of the path, a warm gentle breeze from the west blew into their faces.

Approaching the station from the east, he could see the stock pens a little distance south of the depot. As they approached the depot, a train whistle sounded announcing the train's eight o'clock morning arrival. He looked at his watch and said to Rosa, "Eight o'clock, she's right on time."

Rosa and Sam stopped by the pens as the engine huffed by squealing its brakes. A great puff of white smoke and steam was expelled from the engine making a loud hissing sound. The engineer leaning from the cab watched the flag man drop from the caboose waving his flag. He stopped a stock car in front of a chute extending a few feet from the door of the car.

Sam could see his two horses thru the slats of the car, the

horses were moving around in great anticipation. The flag man slid the door open. The black first, jumped from the car onto the chute and on down into the pen. The Dunn followed. They went running jumping and bucking around the pen. Rosa climbing on the pen's rails called to him, "They're beautiful! They're beautiful!"

Sam saw his canvas sack being tossed on the depot platform. A man started to drag it into the baggage room. "That's my sack," he yelled as he climbed the platform steps.

"You need to get the paper work done," the man called back.

"Where?"

"In that office," the man was pointing to the baggage room.

Sam went in, paid, picked up the sack and went back to the pens. Opening the gate, he went in and dropped the sack on the ground. He opened the draw string, dumped the contents out. By then the two horses had settled down.

From the sacks came a stock saddle, saddle blankets, two halters with leads, two bridles, a coiled rope, saddle bags, a rifle scabbard and a small bag of tools.

He approached the black, talking in a low soothing tone. He slipped a halter on his head, throwing the lead rope over his neck, he patted and talked to him. "That's my good boy, Old fella, I been miss-n you."

Rosa called, "He's the most beautiful horse I've ever seen." She started smooching to him. He trotted over to her. "He likes me Sam."

"Careful Rosa, he's a stallion, he might nip you."

"Not me, he likes me." She was patting him on the head.

"He likes all beautiful females." He could have bitten his tongue saying that.

"Can I ride him Sam, can I ride him?" She was rubbing the horse's neck as she asked.

"He's well broke, can you ride a horse?" He had doubt in his voice.

"Oh, yes I ride all the time."

"We'll ask your mama."

He bridled, then saddled the Dunn and hung the canvas sack on the saddle horn.

He called, "Come here Rosa."

She jumped from the fence and strolled to him. He picked her up and set her on the back of the black stallion and told her, "Hold on to his mane."

He mounted the Dunn, reached the black's lead rope, moved to the rear gate of the pen, reached down, shoved the latch back and opened the gate.

As they rode thru the desert he told the girl, "It's good to be horse back again."

Rosa started chatting away. He didn't listen to her. He was watching how the horses traveled after their long ride in the stock car.

He told to her, "They seemed to take the trip ok." They rode on down to Manuel's stable.

Entering the barn, Sam stepped off and started unsaddling the Dunn. Rosa slid off the stallion's back. He remarked, looking at the horse's hoofs, "They're both in need of new shoes."

She reached down to pick up a hoof, as to have a look. As she did her shirt gapped open and exposed her full round beautiful breasts. Sam pulled her up and buttoned the three top ones. She said not a word, just smiled. He shook his head. "Girl, you are something else."

Manuel saw them enter and came from the rear of the barn. "I see your horses are here, a fine looking pair they are, I have prepared a pen for them." He took the black's lead and led him to a pen just outside the barn. Sam followed with the Dunn.

Both horses were turned loose in the pen, the horses responded, running, bucking and chasing each other. Sam, Rosa and Manuel watched.

Sam told them, "It must be good to be out of the stock car, it's a shame to have to coop horses up that way." Rosa and Manuel agreed.

Manuel told them he would put the two in a stall after a while, after they settled down. Sam asked if he could get a farrier to come and shoe the two. "They both need to be shod."

"I'll have one come manana."

Rosa and Sam walked up to the house. All the way she begged him to let her ride the black stallion. "The trails along the river bank are soft and good to ride. Manuel has a saddle I can use."

"We'll ask your Mama."

As soon as they entered the kitchen, Rosa went to begging Dolores to let her ride the black horse. Dolores said it would be ok if Sam said it was safe. He told her the horse was safe for anyone to ride. Dolores told Rosa she would have to do her chores first. Rosa agreed, it was all set.

Sam looked at his watch and remarked, "It's almost noon, I'm going to see Louise at her office."

He went to his room, changed his clothes and boots. On the way he stopped and had a meal at the Shoo-fly.

At her office he saw she was eating a bean burro. She told him Dolores packed a lunch almost every day for her. Just as she spoke a commotion in the street below could be heard. Sam rushed to and opened a window and yelled to a man in the street, "What's goin' on?"

The man hollered back, "The owner of the Red Bird Casino, Ace Cole, needs you to come, there's trouble there."

Sam rushed down the stairs and out into the street. He told the man, "Go, I'll follow."

He was led to Ochoa street, to the Casino. Stopping to get his breath, he looked over the swinging doors. What he saw he could not believe, the town Marshal Henry was on his knees on the floor between the bar and gambling tables being beaten by three men, blood covered his face and head, a pool of blood was on the floor in front of him.

Sam with the Schofield in his right hand stepped thru the swinging doors and demanded in a loud voice for them to stop. The three swung around to meet their challenger. Seeing the big pistol and the man behind it, they backed off.

"What in the hell is going on here?" he asked in his most demanding voice.

A bystander gave him the word. "These men are cheaters, Ace sent for Marshal Henry, they knocked him down and jumped on him when he came in and started beat-n him."

Sam cocked the Schofield and told the three, "Hands on the bar. Now!"

The two closest obeyed, the one in the rear started to back away. A short ugly little man, reached for the pistol in his belt.

"It's a good day to die, mister." Sam meant business.

The little man rushed to the bar and put both his hands down on the bar. "Don't shoot, I ain't fight-n," he cried.

Sheriff Bell and his deputy came busting thru the swinging doors. Someone had gone for him too. The Sheriff asked, "What's going on here?"

Sam told him. "These men are trying to kill the town Marshal."

Doc Fenn came rushing in, he started to administer to the Marshal right away.

Sam motioned to Deputy Clint with his pistol, "Get their guns, boy."

Clint circled behind Sam and did as he was told. He was glaring at Sam all the time.

Sam turned to the sheriff, "These men are yours." He holstered his pistol, pushed out thru the crowd on the board sidewalk and calmly walked home.

As he passed the kitchen Dolores called, "Supper's ready, wash up Sam."

He did and came back to the eating room. Every one was there but Stein. He slid into a chair next to Louise.

"What was that all about?"

"Not much, a little commotion at one of the casinos." He changed the subject and asked her how her day went.

After supper as usual, Dolores announced coffee on the patio. They all went there and sat down in the tub chairs. Sam by now had a favorite spot. Rosa came in with a tray with cups and coffee. They talked well into the evening hours, darkness surrounded them and the evening coolness set in. Around ten o'clock Sam stood, stretched and told them, "I'm tired, gonna hit the hay, I'm really tired." Everyone said good night and went to their rooms.

He was up early, dressed and in the kitchen looking for coffee. Dolores had just put the pot on, she was still stoking the fire.

Sam asked, "What smells so good?"

"It's a surprise for supper, it's Louise's birthday, we'll have a party tonight, I want it to be a surprise. Sam she's such a sweet woman, I want every thing to be good for her, she was so pleased with the dance Saturday night. Sam I think she's falling for you, don't hurt her," Dolores said with compassion in her voice.

"I don't want to hurt her or anyone else, and where's that Rosa this morning?"

"She was up before sunrise and did her chores, and went to Manuel's to ride that horse of yours. She's so excited to ride the horse I couldn't hardly get her to sleep last night."

In the days that followed Rosa and the black became fast friends as the two walked, trotted, loped and galloped the trails along the banks of the Santa Cruz. Most days they didn't return to the barn until well in the afternoon. A tired girl and horse. Anyone who saw the two would see love in bloom by both parties.

Sam ate a hearty breakfast, went to his room to sort the papers he had been given to serve.

Louise knocked, "Can I come in?"

"Door's open."

"Are you gonna serve summons today?"

"I'm gonna take the oldest ones first."

"Sam," she said, "there's an arrest warrant, did you see it?"

"Yes, it's for a Mexican cowboy for stealing army horses, it's getting old."

"You better take some help when you go, I've heard there's bad blood between the army and these people." Louise had a tense sound in her voice.

"There won't be any trouble," Sam assured her.

"Please Sam, be careful."

"Have you had breakfast?" he asked.

"I don't want any, I must get to the office, I'm late."

"Hold on I'll walk with you." He took her by an arm.

"Good, I have something for you at the office."

As the two of them went out the front door Sam said, "Look," as he pointed to the south-west at a cloud of dust. "Must be Rosa and my horse."

"That's the nicest thing you could have done for that girl. Why do you have to have that gun all the time?" She pointed to the Schofield. "You had it at the dance and on our picnic."

"Just think of it as a tool, some men have saws, some have hammers, I have old Schofield." He patted his pistol. "It's been my pardner and helper a long time, I'd be nak-..." he stopped short. "Know what I mean?" She shook her head yes.

At the office Louise gave Sam a leather valise with a shoulder strap. Sam asked where she got it.

"From the judge, he has several, I don't think he'll mind."

Sam put the papers in the case. "I have four to serve, I'll make all of eight dollars if I can find them all." He laughed. "I'll see you later."

After a lot of walking, and asking directions, he found all the people and served all the papers. On the way back he passed the Steinfeld store and went in. Albert met him with a smile and a hand shake, saying, "Welcome to our store, can we help you, Marshal?"

"You sure can, I need something for a lady for her birthday."

A lady clerk hearing, came over and said, "We have just the thing, a comb and brush set from Spain, all the ladies want them."

"Good, I'll take a set."

"We can gift wrap it, if you wish?" the clerk said.

"Please do."

Albert and Sam talked awhile. When he got his package he thanked him for his help said goodbye and walked home hoping to beat Louise.

At home he was greeted by Rosa. She asked what the package was.

"A gift for Louise, is she home yet?"

"No, what did you get her. Rosa was feeling the package.

"Not much, just a hair brush."

"That's nice, we got her a silver comb for her hair," Rosa offered. "Momma has invited Manuel and his family, the professor and his wife. We're going to have a party on the patio. Come see, I've put candles and lanterns up." She took his hand and half pulled him onto the patio.

"What a nice job you've done."

"We're going to eat out here, I'm setting the table now," Rosa said proudly. "I hope she'll like it."

"I'm sure she will." Sam was impressed that a young girl like Rosa would be so handy and he told her so.

"Some day I'll be a good wife, maybe to you Sam." He could not reply to that.

Dolores came in carrying a lot of food. She told Rosa to go get the rest and bring it from the kitchen.

"Louise and everyone else are here, we should eat, before the guests arrive." What a meal they had, baked quail, a baked potato with butter, corn on the cob, brown gravy, white bread and sliced peaches. All had plenty and told Dolores how much they enjoyed it.

As the shadows grew long on the patio, the guests began arriving. Manuel brought his guitar, played and sang Mexican love songs. Louise was overjoyed as she cut the cake Dolores had baked. The tears flowed. Christine and Hilda comforted her and asked her to open the gifts. She did and the tears flowed again. She was so happy. She had to kiss everyone. When she came to Sam, she pulled his head down, kissed him full on the lips. They all clapped except Rosa, she turned and ran into the house.

The guests said goodnight. The boarders went to their rooms. Louise stayed and asked Sam if he was going to serve the warrant on the cowboy. "Yes in the morning. I'll go early."

She put her head on his chest, hugged him and said, "Be careful Sam I don't want to lose you." She turned and ran into the hall and to her room.

Sam was a little choked up, he went to his room, undressed, washed up and went to bed.

Chapter 14

Apaches - Horse Race - Mexican Cowboy

Wednesday morning Sam entered Manuel's stable just as the sun peeked over the mountains to the east. He was carrying a saddle ring Winchester carbine, a canteen, saddle bags and the leather valise.

He had finished saddling the Dunn and started to slip his rifle into the scabbard, when Hector came in the rear of the barn. "Marshal Sam," he called. "You ride-n this morning? We haven't fed the horses yet."

"That's all right he won't starve," Sam answered. He mounted and rode up on Meyer Street then to Congress. He turned east thru town, out on the wagon road. In a mile he saw a sign that read, Fort Lowell six and one half miles.

It was a pleasant May morning, the smell of grease wood was strong in the air, a slight breeze blew from the south, cooling the morning air, in all a good day for a ride he thought.

He rode past a small adobe ranch house. A lady waved from the yard, he waved back. On farther another small house came in view, he rode into the yard. A young Mexican woman and two small children came out to greet him.

"Good morning, Senora," Sam said as he tipped his hat.

The lady replied, "Buenos dias Senor."

"Can I water my horse?"

She told him a horse trough was over at the barn, by the

wind mill, he could help himself, he did and the Dunn drank some. They both listened to the cranky wind mill's song. Afterwards he called to her, "Muchas gracias, Senora." She and the children waved to him as he rode off.

It was midmorning when he could see the Fort ahead. Riding thru the front gate, he rode straight to a building with a sign that read - Commanding Officer, Fort Lowell, Arizona Territory.

He reined up at the porch. A Captain came out of the office door and stood on the porch, a man in his late fifties, sporting a full handle bar moustache on a suntanned face, he was short and stout in stature. He greeted Sam, "I see by the badge you must be the new U.S. Marshal from Tucson." He continued, "Maybe the law has come at last to the Old Pueblo."

Sam smiled and asked, "Can you tell me where the Silva ranch is? I'm told it's nearby this Fort."

"Just keep going north on this road up in the hills. You can't miss it, are you after the Mexican horse thief?"

"I have a summons for Jose Badilla at the Silva ranch, how far is it to the ranch?"

"Several miles after you cross the wash, You'll see it before you get there, watch yourself you might hit a beehive up there." The Captain seemed concerned. Sam bid him goodbye and thanked him for the information. He rode out the gate and onto the road, he reined his mount north.

As he rode past a hay field where soldiers were cutting hay, a Sergeant on horse back blocked his way. He asked, seeing the badge on Sam's vest, "You the lawman after the Mexican horse thief?"

"That's right, I have a summons for a cowboy up this way."

"Wa'll I'm a gonna tell ya," he spit a long stream of tobacco juice at a lizard that ran across the road under his horse. He wiped his mouth with the back of his right hand. "I ken't see that fella doin the deed, ya see some of our boys kinda sweet on his gal. They shore like to see him out-a the way, whole dam thing looks funny to me, you's can take my words for what they're worth."

"Thanks, I'll keep your words in mind."

Sam rode on, soon he had to cross a small clear stream. He stopped to give the Dunn a drink. He had to spur him up a steep bank on the other side and on to the road. It took the most part of an hour, up one hill then up another, climbing higher in the hills. Javelina, white tail deer, quail and jack rabbits watched and scurried away as he rode past.

On top of a rise he stopped to view a large white hacienda in the valley below. Mesquite in full leaf and paloverde trees in bloom surrounded the hacienda. Green grass was abundant. The road led right to the gate of the hacienda. Sam urged the Dunn on.

Riding thru an arched gateway into a brick court yard, he saw a vaquero sitting on a horse to his right just inside the gate, a Winchester rifle lay across the pommel of his saddle. He gave Sam a hard, hard look but didn't speak.

What Sam saw and smelled stunned him, the patio had orange, lemon and grapefruit trees on both sides, all in bloom ,the aroma filled the patio. A veranda stretched the full length of the house, colorful flowering vines grew up the porch posts, six steps led to a big carved door. A tall older Mexican man with graying hair, smoking a long black cigar, came thru the door to greet him.

"Mi Vaquero told me you were coming up our Camino." He spoke very broken English. "What can I do for you Senor?"

"I'm Sam Duncan, the Deputy U. S. Marshal of this district, I have a summons for a cowboy named Jose Badilla, I understand he works on this ranch."

Si he does, is this about his stealing army horses?"

"Yes, I must see this boy."

"Are you going to take him to the cercal?" asked the Senor.

"No, I am here to talk to him and give him a summons, not to take him in. Can I see him today?"

"He's working cattle up on the mountain with my vaqueros. I'll send for him." He called to the waiting rider in Spanish. "Andale, Andale, go bring Jose."

The rider reined his horse out thru the gate, dug his spurs into his mount and galloped north up the road from the Hacienda.

Senor Silva asked if Sam was hungry and thirsty. Sam told him he was thirsty. Silva pointed to a holla with a dipper hanging from a porch beam and said, "Help yourself, Senor."

He got down, climbed the stairs and drank two dippers full of cool sweet water from the holla.

"Come set with me and tell me about yourself." The Senor seemed to be friendly.

Sam sat in a leather tub chair, Silva did the same, a small table between them. Silva called to a young boy to come and take the Marshal's horse and let him graze the green grass outside the walls. A boy came and took the horse, he led him out the big gate.

Silva asked if Sam would like some thing to eat. Sam said, "I haven't had a thing to eat all day."

Silva went to the door and called for food to be brought, soon a good looking Senorita appeared with plates of frijoles, meat, tortillas and coffee. As she set the food on the table, she looked Sam over closely. Silva swatted her on the butt and in Spanish told her to get back in the house, she gave Sam a big smile and winked as she departed.

Silva said, "That one likes all good looking men." Sam just smiled.

The conversation turned to his vaquero. "This boy, Jose, is no thief, I say the soldiers no like him. He was having a drink with his sweetheart down at the Cantina near the Fort where she works, a soldier came in, he say he wanted her, Jose say no. The soldier hit Jose, Jose gave him a good beating. Next day soldiers say Jose take horses, we find them running in hills just below this hacienda, we take them back to Fort but soldiers never report them back, Jose, he is no thief."

When Sam and the Senor finished eating, the Senor offered Sam a cigar. Sam thanked him, "I'll smoke this." He took out his pipe, filled and lit it.

They talked for most of an hour about horses, cattle and Indians. Silva said he hadn't had trouble with Indians in years.

Soon horses could be heard approaching the hacienda, two riders came thru the big gate, the young man dismounted and asked, "You send for me Senor Silva?"

"Jose this is the United States Marshal from Tucson, he has a paper for you."

He spoke to the boy in Spanish. Silva told Sam, "He doesn't speak too much Ingles."

Jose backed up and put his right hand on the butt of his pistol. Silva jumped to his feet. "No, no Jose!" All the time shaking his hands at him. "He's not here to take you to cercel, just to give a paper."

Silva took the paper from Sam and handed it to the boy.

"Tell him he must come in, in the fall or I will come for him."

When Silva told the words to the boy, he again right handed his pistol, and shook his head no. Silva said to Sam, "I promise he will come when you ask."

Sam asked for his horse, Silva called to the boy to bring Sam's horse. He mounted, said, "Adios," and rode out the gate and on down to Fort Lowell.

As Sam entered the gate at the fort a lot of excitement was going on. Reining up at the commander's office, the Captain came out on the porch and told Sam two soldiers had been killed by Apaches who had left the reservation, he pointed to the end of the porch where four booted feet could be seen protruding from blankets covering the bodies.

"Come look," the Captain urged.

Sam dismounted and went to look. He saw a Lieutenant that had been shot in the chest, a Corporal cut and badly hacked up.

The Captain told Sam the story. "The Lieutenant was to be here for a Court Martial this morning, they were coming from Fort Bowie, the Lieutenant and Corporal Black were in a buckboard. They had an escort of eight troopers. Driving the buckboard they got far ahead of the escort, passing a canyon the Apaches attacked and killed Lieutenant Davidson outright, Corporal Black ran for the hills. They caught him, tied him to a tree, they shot over fifty arrows into his body, hacked and cut him to pieces. The escort came up and ran them off. Marshal, we need a scout bad. I know you were an army scout in the north, will you help us? Our scout is Mickey Free, he's up on the reservation to see his woman. I'm sending a patrol to put these bucks back on the San Carlos reservation. One of the privates on the escort will be with the patrol, will you help us?"

Sam asked, "Who'll command the patrol?"

The Captain called a Lieutenant Ellis to come out and meet Sam. A tall, blonde haired, blue eyed young man in his early twenties came out and stood on the porch. He just looked at Sam, not saying a word.

The Captain asked, "Can I count on you to go?"

"I'll go, just one thing, when I give advice he has to take it, will he agree?"

Sam had seen young Lieutenants like this one before.

"Damn right he will," the Captain said in a positive manner. The Lieutenant turned on his heels and went back in the office without uttering a word.

The Captain said he would have the patrol in the saddle within the hour. "What do you need to go Sam?"

"I have to go to Tucson, where can I meet the Troop?"

"They'll take the wagon road east to the rail road and camp at the Vail Station, it's a water and wood stop, a material storage yard for the rail road, you can meet them there."

"I'll be there some time before first light in the morning," Sam said as he reined the Dunn around and went out the gate and on the road to Tucson.

Sam pushed the Dunn hard. He rode into Manuel's just at dark, and asked if he could use a fresh mount. "It's government business, you'll be well paid."

"For you Sam, you can have my best horse any time."

Sam asked Manuel to put his saddle on the horse. "I'll be right back."

He took the valise and saddle bags with him and hurried up to the house. Dolores was in the kitchen. "Can you put some food in my bags? I have to make a trip tonight."

"What's your hurry Sam?"

"I have to go, I have to go now." He called back to her as he hurried to his room. He rolled a serape off the bed, got his heavy coat and a box of 44 cartridges, returned to the kitchen, Dolores had his saddle bags ready, he thanked her and hurried out the door.

Rosa was coming home as he passed her, she asked, "Where you going Sam?"

"Government business, I have to go now."

She begged, "Let me go with you Sam."

She had a hold of his arm, he pulled away saying, "You

can't go, I have to go alone."

As he left he heard her cry, "Let me go, let me go with you Sam."

At the barn Manuel had a big blue roan gelding saddled and waiting. As Sam tied the saddle bags, serape and coat on the saddle, he asked Manuel, "How's the best way to Vail Station?"

Manuel told him he could cut east across the desert or follow the tracks.

"Which will get me there the fastest?"

"Across the desert," Manuel said. "If you get lost, just head south you'll hit the tracks, follow them they'll take you there."

"I'll go the fastest way." He bid him "Adios."

Sam headed the roan east at a long trot, he rode in total darkness, the moon hadn't come up, he rode thru sand washes, sage bush, mesquite, paloverde trees and grease wood there was lots of pad and barrel cacti. He had to rely on his mount to keep the direction. Once he came out of a wash, they had to fight their way thru catclaw bushes that tore at both rider and horse, Sam cussed under his breath, "God must love cactus and thorns he made so much in this country."

The moon came up, he could see the wild life using the darkness to hunt, a bobcat crossed in front of him after a jack rabbit, several times he heard the rattle of a snake, a pack of coyotes howled in the distance, they sang a familiar tune.

On a rise he stood up in the stirrups and saw camp fires off to his right. A train whistle sounded from that direction, he reined his mount that way. Nearing the camp he called for permission to come in. A Trooper called back, "Come on in."

The Sergeant he had met on the road at the hay field, greeted him. "Come in, we've been waiting for you Marshal, thought you mighta got lost, coffee on the fire, get down, I'll get ya some." Sam could use some black coffee bad.

By the fire light, he could see horses on a picket line, Troopers standing, sitting and having the usual soldier talk, staying close by the fires, the Lieutenant lay in blankets sound asleep, his head propped on a long telegraph pole. He never made a move as Sam squatted down to drink his coffee by the fire. The Sergeant ordered a trooper, "Put the Marshal's horse on the picket line, hang a nose bag on him." Sam asked the trooper to loosen the cinch.

"Have you had some eats?" the Sergeant asked. "We have some beans and bread if you want some"

"I could eat some." Sam was hungry, a trooper heard and brought a plate of beans and bread.

As Sam was eating, he and the Sergeant talked. Sam asked where he was from. "Macon, Georgia," the Sergeant told him. He had been a reb during the war, just a youngster, he had married before he went off to the war, got captured at Shiloh, was in a Yankee prison the rest of the war. When he finally got home, found he had a baby girl, but never found his wife or her. He drifted west and joined the Yankee army. Been a trooper ever since.

Sam asked him, "You like the army?"

"Ain't so bad, it's them damn shave tails gets ya' all in trouble."

He pointed to the sleeping Lieutenant. Sam agreed. They talked awhile longer, the Sergeant had to change guards. Sam looked for and found a spot to sleep. Wrapped up in the serape, lay down and went to sleep.

He was up before the sunrise, he shook the sand and cactus from the serape, rolled and tied it on his saddle. As he stretched his arms, he felt sore all over. "I'm get-n too damn old for this shit, I should be live-n in a fine hotel somewhere, not sleeping out here in the desert."

Hunger had got to him, he looked to his saddle bags for the

food Dolores had sent him. He found a baked potato, some dried meat and a flour tortilla in the bags. He walked over where some troopers had made a fire. He asked if they were going to make coffee.

"It's on the way," a young trooper told him. "Be ready in a minute."

The Sergeant came out of his blankets, giving orders for the troopers to get the horses saddled and be ready to move as soon as the Lieutenant gave the order. Hearing the commotion the Lieutenant came storming out of his blankets half asleep wanting to know what was going on.

"Not a thing Lieutenant, Sir," the Sergeant reported. "We're ready to move as soon as ya'll give the order."

"Fine, is our scout here?"

"Yes sir, been here since late last night, he's over drinking coffee with the men."

"Hey Scout," the Lieutenant called. Anyone could tell he was in a bad mood. "Get over here I want words with you."

Sam walked over. "What's on your mind Lieutenant?"

"I want you to know, I'm in command here, you got that, Scout?"

Sam smiled, said nothing. turned his back side and went back to his coffee.

After breakfast the Lieutenant told the troopers, "We're going south maybe we can cut their trail."

"No. No," Sam said. "We'd best go to where the men were killed, we'll have a better chance to pick up a trail, might miss it goin' south. We can find out a lot by study-n sign around the kill site, that's where I's go-n." The Lieutenant never said another word.

Sam tightened the cinch on his saddle, stepped on and headed east on the wagon road. Within the hour the troop caught up. The Sergeant came alongside and said, "Ya'll sure made him mad as hell Marshal, he'll be tough to live with now."

"Haw, he's young, he'll get over it. That's a pretty fancy Springfield he's carrying, can he shoot it?"

"Don't know ain't ever saw him shoot. They call that rifle, officer's model, they just started makin' em. It's same caliber as ours, 45-70 special made for Officers."

The road followed the Railroad tracks. They rode several hours, the road turned north away from the tracks for a mile, then east again, within another mile, the trooper who was with the escort came up and told Sam, "We should be where the kill-n took place any time now."

Soon an overturned buckboard was found just off the road. Sam dismounted to have a look. The Lieutenant and Sergeant came to look also.

"They cut the harness to get the mules, two bucks took the mules with them, followed the others up that ridge," Sam said pointing up a high ridge to the south.

The escort trooper said, "We found Corporal Black tied to a dead tree about a mile along on that ridge."

"Let's go take a look."

Sam mounted and spurred his horse up the ridge, the Lieutenant and the troop followed. They found the tree just as the trooper said.

"Keep your men back," Sam told the Lieutenant. "I gotta take a look around." He dismounted and surveyed the ground.

"What do you see?" asked the Lieutenant.

Sam studied the ground a while longer. "There's six of 'em, they're headed west, they're in no hurry, took the mules with' em."

Sam took the Lieutenant aside. "I'm gonna follow their trail, you bring the troop up slow, I have a feel-n you're gonna need your horses fresh before we get done."

"What if we lose the trail?" the Lieutenant was concerned.

"Hell, a one-eyed blind man could follow their trail, they're not afraid of us, soon they'll stop and butcher one of them mules soon's they get hungry. Send one of your troopers with me, I'll send him back if I can find them before dark."

Sam mounted and rode west, it was a little after noon. The sun was high overhead, a young trooper rode up beside him. "I'm supposed to stay with you, sir," said the trooper. He looked young, about eighteen.

"What's yer name boy?" Sam wanted to know.

"Trooper Roberts, sir, do you think we'll catch up with em today, sir?"

"For God's sake, don't be call-n me sir, okay?" Sam showed he was annoyed.

"Yes sir."

"Where you from?"

"Indiana....Elkhart."

Sam told him, "If we run into the Indians, I want you to hightail it back to the troop, you understand, bring 'em up fast, you got it?"

"Got it," the trooper replied.

They rode several hours, over ridges, thru sand washes, a lot of mesquite trees, paloverde trees, grease wood bushes and all kinds of cactus.

On a rise they stopped. A flat desert lay in front of them, not far away a small ranch house could be seen. The tracks of the Indian riders led straight to the ranch. Sam sat studying the situation then he turned to the trooper. "Roberts, go get the troops, tell' em to come easy, our renegades might be there, that's where I'll be." The trooper not saying a word turned his mount and spurred away East at a gallop.

Sam approached the house slow with his Winchester at the ready. As he got close he called as loud as he could, "HO THE

HOUSE!" A door opened a crack, he could see a rifle barrel protruding out the door.

"Who call-n?" a man's voice came back.

"U.S. Marshal from Tucson."

The door opened, out stepped a white man with a Winchester rifle, two young boys, ten or twelve years old and a women followed, all of them had some kind of fire arm.

"We hoped them red devils were gone," the man said. "They was here and camped most of the night. Drove off all our livestock, they never tried to get in the house, we gave 'em a few shots. They didn't shoot back, guess they must a seen we had lots a guns. I better take a look at my barn, gotta see what they stole."

Sam dismounted and followed the man to his barn. Once inside the man looked around, poking here and there. "Dag gum it!" he said. "Them sons-a-guns red skins found my four bottles of tequila, I hid em out here from my woman, she don't take kindly to my drink-n hard liquor, looks like I'm gonna be dry awhile."

They returned to the house. Sam asked if he could water and feed his horse and put him in the barn.

"Shore," the man said. "We ain't got nothing to feed no how any more."

"There's a troop of soldiers a-come-n," Sam told him. "After I take care of my horse, I'll just set here in this chair and wait."

"My woman will fix us some food and coffee while you wait. My name is George Thurber, how they call you?"

"Sam Duncan. Glad to meet you George. I wish it was in better circumstances."

"Me too." George was a friendly person.

After supper the two men sat and talked. The boys took in every word. Sam smoked his pipe, he told George he had a nice place. "Hope to have one myself one day, would like to raise horses."

"The army will buy all the horses you can raise," George said. "If you got good ones."

It was almost dark when the troop came in, full of questions. Sam told them, "We'll stay here tonight, give them bucks a chance to hole up somewhere, they'll be drinking this man's Tequila, without a care in the world."

Sam found a spot in George's barn, rolled up in the serape, and fell fast a sleep.

Sam was up before the sun, cleaned his pistol and Winchester. From his saddle bags, he took his breakfast of jerked beef, a floor tortilla and a big red apple. Said to himself, "That Dolores knows how to keep a man in eats."

The Sergeant came in the barn. "That damn Lieutenant, grumpy as hell this Morning."

The Lieutenant came in bitching. "Sergeant, the troop won't pay any attention to me at all. Go get em' move-n."

"Yes sir," the Sergeant saluted and left.

Sam told the Lieutenant, "I'll go on ahead and Scout, you come up slow, they won't be far."

"Take Trooper Roberts with you, he can come get us if need be."

Sam agreed. The two rode west, it was almost noon when the tracks led up a canyon into the mountains on the south. Sam and Roberts followed the tracks. Soon Sam could smell smoke, he turned back and told Roberts to go for the troop.

"I'll be at the entrance of this canyon, tell' em, come up slow, no noise." Roberts turned and at a gallop went for the troop.

Sam moved back to the entrance of the canyon and tied his horse in a mesquite thicket and sat down to wait. It was over an hour before the troop came up. Sam laid it out to the

Lieutenant.

"You keep the troop here, I'll climb that ridge and see if I can spot em."

"No! The Sergeant and I will go with you, lead the way."

Sam took off his spurs, hung 'em on the saddle horn. The Sergeant put the troop into the mesquite thicket and told them to stay put. The Lieutenant stopped Sam and told him, "We should form up and charge up the canyon like I've been taught."

"No! You want to get a lot of your troopers killed? Them bucks will take to the rocks and we'll have a hell of a time get-n to' em, we'll do it my way, you follow me."

The three men climbed the off side of the ridge until Sam figured where the Indians would be. He sat the two down and crawled to the top of the ridge and peeked over. There he saw the Apaches just where he thought they might be.

A butchered mule lay the other side of a small dry wash. Empty tequila bottles lay strung about, three bucks lay in the wash, an older buck was fishing mule meat out of the fire, two younger bucks were playing some kind of game, up the wash a few yards or more.

Sam returned to the Sergeant and Lieutenant. He told them to crawl up to the top. "Don't be seen, we got 'em all, I'll go over a little farther and go to the top where I can get a better shot. Don't do any shoot-n til I do, got it?"

The two troopers could see he meant business and shook their heads, yes. Sam moved on up the ridge to a better spot. There he could see the two soldiers move into position as he studied the layout. "I'll take the one by the fire first, he's the most danger to us, his rifle is close. Then go for the three in the wash," he said to himself. "The Lieutenant and Sergeant can take the two young ones."

He took aim at the Apache at the fire, sighted the

Winchester over his head a little and fired. The Apache never knew what hit him, he pitched forward into the fire. Next came the farthest one laying in the wash, he rose a little and fell backward. The other two started to run wildly up the canyon, past Sam. He took the one in the rear, down he went, as did the next one. Sam could hear the Lieutenant and Sergeant open fire. He saw the two young ones taking a lot of hits around them, one tried to get up. "That 45-70 hits like a cannon," he said to himself. "His leg must be broken?"

The Apache fell back and took several more rounds in his body. The other one had not been hit, he jumped and ran a few yards down the canyon, stopped and raised his rifle over his head in surrender fashion.

Sam half slid, half ran down to the bottom of the canyon. Out of the corner of his eye he could see the Sergeant and Lieutenant reach the bottom too. He checked the ones he had hit, both were gone, he started for the young ones.

He saw the Lieutenant reach the one with his rifle over his head. What he saw next he couldn't believe, the Lieutenant put the mussel of his rifle to the Indian's head and pulled the trigger.

Sam was too late. He ran yelling. "No! No!" When he reached the Lieutenant he was cussing for all his worth. He lay his rifle down, grabbed the Lieutenant's rife and began breaking it over a big rock, again and again he drove it into the rock, it flew apart, he threw the remainder as far as he could over the wash. Turning on the officer he said, "That was cold blooded murder you dirty low down no account bastard."

He picked up his rifle and headed to his horse. As he left, he heard the Sergeant say, "I think you made that man mad Lieutenant."

Sam reached the horse, mounted and rode for Manuel's stable, he rode in just after midnight. Unsaddled the horse, watered and fed, then he walked up to the house. Dolores let him in, after some heavy knocking.

"We've been worried, Sam."

"Let me go to bed, I'm dead tired." Sam could hardly hold his head up, he didn't wash, just kicked off his boots, lay down and went sound asleep.

Fighting sleep he finally became aware his room was filled with sun light. He was sweating heavily, the air in the room was stale and hot. He got up and opened the door to the patio, still in his clothes, trying to shake sleep off, he looked at his watch, one pm, his back hurt, his left shoulder sore.

"I can't take days like that in the saddle any more," he said to himself. "That was a bad time," he felt total remorse. "Why do men have to kill each other? Will it ever end?"

As always he did his best to forget, rubbed his face. "I need a shave and a bath. I better go see Bob."

He wrapped some clean clothes in paper, pulled on his boots, his hat on his head, pistol belt over his shoulder and went out in the hall.

As he passed the kitchen, Dolores called to him, "Sam, we wondered when you would come alive. Everyone looked in on you, you were dead to the world. You must have really been tired."

"Can I have a cup of coffee?"

"It's already poured."

She handed him a cup, as he drank it he told her, "I've gotta go get a shave and bath, see you later." He headed for the barber shop.

Walking in the shop Bob greeted him with, "Here's our Apache fighter."

He put up both hands. "I don't want to talk about it," Sam pleaded.

"Hell, it's all over town, the soldiers have been in town

telling all about it. I guess there's one Lieutenant got a lesson, huh Sam?"

"I don't want to talk about it, not now or never, I'm not proud of killing. I need a shave and bath, okay with you Bob?"

Bob could see Sam was in no mood to be trifled with. He dusted off his chair and said, "Set Marshal." He called to a boy in the back room to get a hot bath ready. As he shaved Sam he made small talk, he told him the last match races will be run this Sunday. "You know I'm the starter," Bob said proudly. "You should try to come."

"I will come, I'd like to see some good horse races."

"You will, there's gonna be some good ones, there always is the last few race days. We start nine in the morning and go till there's none left."

"I'll come for sure."

Bob gave him a sack for his dirty clothes. He took his bath, paid Bob, and told him, "I'll see you at the races."

As he walked home, ladies gave him smiles, men stepped off the walk to let him pass, some tried to shake his hand. He pushed them away and said to himself, "I can't understand people making such a fuss over killing, even if they're Indians."

Reaching the house he went to his room, took off his boots, lay on the bed, went fast asleep.

Right away he dreamed he was back on the plains with the three Indian braves he had killed on the trail near the Mormon train. They rode at him screaming their war cry, he dreamed and remembered the way the painted warrior looked when the bullet hit him in the chest. The most surprised look on a person he had ever seen, just a young boy, he fell right at his horse's feet. It was the first time he killed. As he rode away he had the most sickening feeling he ever had, he felt like throwing up.

Sam sat up in bed. He had the same sick feeling. The only

thing that kept him from tossing, was a knock on the door. "Who is it?" he called.

"It's Louise," she spoke loud enough that he could hear her. "Can I come in?"

"The door's open."

She slowly opened the door. "Are you OK Sam? We heard you calling."

"I had a bad dream. I'm okay."

"You look terrible." She sat on the bed and took his hand in hers. "Are you sure you're feel-n alright?"

"I'm fine, just need some food, let's go eat."

She pulled him up and put her arm around his waist. They walked to the eating room and as they entered the room, the folks stood and started clapping.

Sam told them, "Please, I'm not proud of what I do. Please, let it pass."

Louise could see he was hurting. "Everyone, let's eat and let Sam eat he's very hungry." She pleaded with them.

After supper Dolores served coffee on the patio. Sam sat and smoked his pipe, it was the quietest group. No one spoke, a blind man could see Sam was hurting. Darkness had taken over the patio when Sam stood and said, "I must go to bed. I'm real tired."

Both Louise and Rosa came to hug him. Sam thanked them all for understanding. He went into his room, undressed, washed and went to bed.

He was up before sunrise, too hot to sleep, he opened the door to the patio, saw people were sleeping on cots. He hurried back in, got dressed, returned to the patio and sat in the tub chair waiting for the sunrise. A cool breeze came over the back wall making it pleasant to be there.

As the sun peeked over the wall, the people began to stir. Louise was the first to see him sitting there, she called in a hushed voice, "Come here Sam, I want to see you."

He moved to her cot, kneeled down, looking her in the eyes he said, "Did you know you're very pretty in the morning? Your long hair reminds me of my mother's. Only she had light colored hair."

Louise pulled him close saying, "Any man who compares another woman to his mother must be after something or in love, which is it Sam?"

"I mean it Louise, you are a very pretty woman, would you give me a morning kiss?"

She pulled his face close with both hands, kissed him on the lips. "I wish it were love Sam."

He returned her words with a smile and said, "Thank you for the kiss, you're a great kisser, did you know that? What are you doin today?"

"Noth-n, I'm gonna lay around and do noth-n. How about you, Sam?"

"I'm going for a ride by the river, I have to keep these old bones loose, maybe we could take a buggy ride this evening?"

"Let's do, now you get and let me go to my room to dress."

"Can I come and watch?" he asked laughing.

"Sam, you never ask a woman that."

As he walked away, he said, "Louise I've never even seen your ankle let alone a leg."

She threw the cover off and pulled her night gown up over her knee. "Now you have."

He laughed and went down to the kitchen looking for a cup of coffee, Dolores had coffee and breakfast ready. She told Sam to go set, she'd bring it now. As she set the food on the table Sam asked, "Where's that girl Rosa, this morning?"

"She's up and gone to ride, before sun up, Sam. She's in love with your horse."

"If I hurry, maybe I can see her ride my horse." He finished

226

eating and hurried to Manuel's. He saddled and rode the Dunn along the trail by the Rio Santa Cruz looking for the girl and horse.

Sam rode several miles south along the river bank, he stopped to rest. Looking across the river and some distance to the south he saw the girl and horse emerge from a group of mesquite trees farther down the trail. They followed the trail some distance and turned into another group of trees. He urged the Dunn into a lope. Looking for a way to cross over, he had to go quite a ways to find a spot, he jumped the horse down a small bank and splashed across and up the other bank, he rode north up the trail.

His black horse and Rosa soon appeared on the trail ahead. She saw him and rode hard and stopped beside him horses head to tail.

"You look-n for me Sam?"

"I wanted to see if my horse still had four legs?"

She reined back and around, pushed the horse up beside him saying. "He's the most wonderful horse I've ever ridden, he does anything I ask and he's so fast my eyes water when we run, Sam, I love this horse."

"We must go back to the barn, it's past noon."

As they rode Rosa asked many questions about the horse, Sam told her the story of how he got him.

"Have you ever been in love with a woman?" Rosa wanted to know.

"Yes, it was a long time ago."

"Was she the one who made the leather things you have?"

"Yes." That's all he would say.

"Where is she now?"

"She died a long time ago."

"Was she pretty?"

"Very pretty."

They rode awhile longer. She had to ask, "Can you love a woman again, Sam?"

"A man can love many times and many things, Rosa." When she heard his answer, she spurred her horse into a lope, he followed, they crossed the river and into the barn.

Riding in Manuel remarked, "See you found the girl and horse, is she doin okay, Sam?"

"Much better than I could ever of hoped for." His answer was very positive. Rosa lit up with the biggest smile she could make.

Manuel asked, "Will you go to the races with us tomorrow? I'm taking a wagon, we have plenty of room."

"What time Manuel?"

"Around eight in the morning."

"Can I come too?" asked Rosa.

"Sure ,why not?" Sam told her, he liked the idea of Rosa coming along.

"See you then Manuel." Sam and Rosa walked up the hill home.

Entering the house Dolores, came out of the kitchen and said, "Go in and set, I'll bring some food."

In the eating room Louise was finishing her lunch. Sam asked, "Still doin noth-n, Louise?"

Dolores brought their food, Sam told her she was going to go broke feeding us all the time.

"I like to see my boarders eat well, when you all finish go to the patio, I have iced tea today, we will have ice delivery two times a week now that the railroad is bringing it from El Paso."

"That's wonderful!" Louise was excited about the ice.

Everyone went to the patio, sat in chairs, Dolores came with the tea, everyone said how great it is to have ice. A lazy afternoon was enjoyed by all. Louise told Sam she had a letter from Washington D.C. for him, she had it in her room.

"I just forgot to give it to you yesterday, I'll go get it!" She hurried to her room and returned, handing it to Sam she said, "I'm sorry I forgot to give it to you."

"I'll make you pay." Laughing, he opened the envelope saying, "I don't get many letters." Sam read with some concern on his face.

"What is it?" They all wanted to know.

"Seems I must go to the town of Tombstone and find and commission a Deputy Marshal, they have named several men who are acceptable."

"May I see the letter?" Louise asked.

He handed it to her, she read it and said, "This is dated two weeks ago, he will be under the same authority as you, Judge Henricks, they want you to go right away and telegraph the confirmation as soon as you can, I know they have a lot of trouble there, you should go right away."

"I'll plan to go early next week." She asked not to go for a buggy ride as it was getting late. She wanted to help Dolores fix supper.

"Some other time Louise."

All three women went to the kitchen and soon called to come and eat. Afterward Dolores asked everyone to go to the patio for coffee. The talk was about tomorrow, it would be Sunday.

Louise told them, "Miss Anthony will talk in the afternoon, would anyone like to go?" Dolores and Hilda both said they would like to go.

Rosa said, "I want to go to the races with Sam, Momma, we must go to early mass so I can go."

As darkness came to the patio, Ben came in with his girl, she had accepted his proposal of marriage. A happier man could not be found in all of Arizona Territory that evening.

"When is the happy day?" Sam asked.

"As soon as we can," the girl just beamed. "I love him so."

Ben grinned and hugged her so hard she had to ask him to stop. He said, "Everyone is invited to the wedding." All the people agreed to be there.

Sam said, "I want to kiss the bride, I wouldn't miss it." He winked at Louise.

Ben told him, "Why wait?"

Sam moved over and kissed her on the forehead, she looked disappointed. They all talked awhile longer, Rosa announced she was going to bed.

Dolores asked Sam if he needed a cot?

"No. Ma'am."

Everyone said good night and went to their rooms.

As Sam turned in, he said to himself, "One of the better days I've ever had!"

Sam woke Sunday morning, Checked his watch, six a.m, voices from the patio could be heard. He hurried to the open doors, looking out he could see Dolores and Rosa were engaged in a heated conversation. They were late for six o'clock Mass, Rosa wanted to go on to church, Dolores wanted to wait for the next, Rosa won, they went on out thru the back gate.

Louise saw Sam from her cot and called, "Sam come here."

He walked over and asked, "Are you ready for a morning kiss?"

She raised both arms as to say, yes, he fell in and kissed her hard on the lips. He told her, "You're very pretty in the mornings."

"Go back to your room and let me get dressed and I'll fix your breakfast."

"Best deal I've had this morning." He said laughing and returned to his room, he pulled on his boots, put on his vest and carried the gun belt with him to the kitchen, he stoked the stove and started to make coffee.

Louise entered the kitchen. "Sit down and let me make your breakfast."

"Don't let me stop you."

As she prepared the meal they talked. She told him she was the new Sunday school teacher for the children in her church.

"That's good, I've never been very religious, I don't think God cares much about me."

"Sam," she said very curtly. "God cares for everyone. Do you ever talk to him?"

"No! Louise, I've cussed him several times for the things he's done to me." He was trying to constrain his real feelings.

"Have you ever read the bible?"

"My Ma read to us when I was small, I never have."

"You never asked God for anything?" She tried to be as gentle as she could.

"Only once, when my Pa and Ma died. I asked him to save them, he didn't help. From then on I always figured I can take care of myself." He started to say more, but Dolores and Rosa entered the kitchen.

Dolores asked, "How are you two doing?"

"Fine, this lady fixes a great meal."

Louise started to go saying, "I have to get dressed, my ride will be here soon." She turned to Sam, "We have a lot to talk about, you can't be as bad as you put on." She shook a finger at him.

Rosa chimed in, "I have to change, we're going to see the races." She left the kitchen to change her clothes.

Dolores said, "I have a lot of cleaning to do."

"Don't you know yer supposed to rest on the Sabbath?" Sam said.

"Look who's talk-n." Saying that, Louise went out of the

kitchen and to her room.

Rosa came back dressed in brown pants, white shirt, black boots and red bandana holding back her long black shiny hair. The way she was dressed made her look a lot older than she was. "Is it time for Manuel to come, Sam?" she asked.

He looked at his watch. "Any time now, lets go out and wait."

They had just stepped out of the front door when Manuel pulled up with his wagon and family. The two climbed on board, off they went, down to Congress St, left across the tracks then across the wooden bridge, past the pavilion to the foot of the pointed mountain.

The crowd was already gathering, town people, Cowboys, Mexican Vaquero's, ranchers, the Casino people and a group of Yaqui Indians. All had brought their horses to race. Bob, Dr. Fenn, Sheriff Bell, gamblers and the women of the night, were all there, ready to bet and watch the races.

The first match had been made, Dr. Fenn's job was to hold the purses, Bob the starter was explaining the rules.

"Take your horses down to the pole across the track and get side by side, try to hold that position, wait for the flag to drop. If you cheat you'll forfeit the race, the winner is the first to break the string across the track, No if ands or buts, do you all understand?" he yelled.

No one objected. The first match was on the way!

A cowboy won the first, the screaming and hollering was deafening, great fun for the spectators. Rosa was jumping and yelling at the top of her voice, "I love it, I love it."

Sam had to get hold of her afraid she might fall out of the wagon, anyone watching could see she was really enjoying the races!

Sheriff Bell came to talk to Sam, "Clint my deputy has been bad mouth-n you, Sam. I can't control that boy, I'm look-n for someone to replace him and will soon as I can find someone."

Sam asked about the City Marshal Henry. Sheriff Bell told him he'll be back on the job soon, so Doc Fenn says. The race horse matches continued.

Most of the people had brought food. Manuel's wife had a nice lunch for them, while they ate, they watched and enjoyed the races, the horses and the people.

The last race was over and all the money paid.

A tall Mexican, standing in a French Carriage called to the crowd, he was saying in Spanish, he was willing to match anyone for one thousand American dollars to his horse, EL ROJO FUEGO.

Manuel told Sam about this man. "He's a rich rancher in Mexico, he takes this horse all over Mexico and California, matches him all the time, he's never been beaten. See the Senorita with him? She's French, stayed when the French left, she's very rich also."

Sam remarked, "What a beauty she is."

Manuel poked him, "You like, huh?"

"No, she's not my type."

Rosa grabbed Sam's arm saying, "Match him with our black one, Sam."

"No Rosa I don't have a rider and besides he isn't ready yet."

"I'll ride," she was almost begging. "I know he can win, I know I can ride him and win, he will do anything I ask of him, do you have a thousand dollars to bet?"

Manuel said, "They look good Sam, I believe Rosa and the black can beat him if anyone can."

Looking at Rosa and Manuel Sam shook his head, "NO." But their demeanor was so positive, he gave it a second though. "Oh, okay, let's give it a try."

Rosa was jumping up and down saying loudly, "He can win, he can win, I know he can win."

"Calm down Rosa." He asked Manuel to come. "Tell me what to say."

They walked on the track and told Bob, "We'll give it a go, tell the Senor to come on."

The word was relayed to the Mexican. The man stepped from the carriage and onto the track, with his hand extended to Sam saying in Spanish, "I am Don Diego Romero Reyes of Santa Cruz, Mexico. I have the fastest horse in all the land, maybe in all the world."

Sam shook his hand and told Manuel, "Tell him to stop the small talk, let's get down to business, tell him we must go get my horse and money, will he wait?"

Manuel relayed the words to the Senor. He would wait, saying with a big smile, "Plenty time, I have for you Senor."

Sam, Rosa and Manuel drove the wagon back to the house, Sam dropped off to get his money. Manuel and Rosa went for the horse and saddle. They returned and picked up Sam. He and Rosa sat on the tail gate leading the black horse, he jogged along behind.

Rosa had misgivings. "I'm sorry I got you into this, maybe I'm not a good enough rider, maybe he's not ready, maybe we..."

Sam stopped her short. "Maybe, maybe, maybe... Damn it girl, we're in it now don't let me down, I know you can do it."

He put an arm around her, looked her in the eyes and told her, "You can do anything you want, if you try." He reached over and kissed her gently on the cheek. "Let's give it a good try, Okay?"

"Okay Sam." She had tears in her eyes. "I'll do my best."

By then they were back at the track, the Senor had his horse and rider on the track waiting. As Manuel and Sam saddled the black horse, Sam told the two of them, "We have the advantage, that horse has been standing in the shade all day, our horse has been warmed up coming over, looks to me like he's ready."

Rosa watched and said, "We will win, I know he will win."

Sam went to Bob, gave him the money. Bob asked the Senor for his and turned it over to Dr. Fenn, the race was on!

Rosa mounted and rode the black stallion onto the track, both girl and horse had the look of a winner. Both horses danced and pranced, the Mexican rider rode close and told Rosa, "No baby girl gonna beat me."

The red horse looked magnificent, shiny, stout, big and muscular. The young Mexican rider had his cap on backwards, riding a light race saddle. Bob told them to get to the post. Both horses trotted down the track, Rosa and the black led the way.

Bob cried to the crowd, "Get your bets made, we're about to start!"

The two reached the post and turned to face the finish line and the crowd. The people moved on to the track to get a better look at the two racers, Bob demanded all the people to get back. "Lets have a fair and good race, now get back all of you," he shouted. Bob was showing his anger, he was out on the track waving his arms making the people move back.

Both horses knew their job by now, both danced and plunged at the bit and reared both front feet off the ground, both ready to run, ready to give it their all.

The riders' jaws were set, Rosa had an impish smile on her face as she watched the other rider. Both had their bodies leaning over on to the neck of their horse, both were ready for the start.

Bob held the flag high, waved, then dropped the flag. The black had turned slightly to the right, he was beaten at the start by a good length, the red one driving away had an easy lead. The girl's horse dove into the bit, ears pinned, nostrils flaring, driving his hooves into the ground with every jump. She was leaning over the neck, driving with both hands, screaming in his ear "go-go- go."

Down the track they came, both riders urging their mounts to give every thing they had. Both horses, muscles straining, responded to their riders. Down the track they flew, dust swirled at their feet.

The crowd was going crazy, such noise that mountain had never heard, the wildlife came alive. Deer pricked their ears looking in that direction, a big cat came to attention, turned his nose up to get a better smell. Ground squirrels scrambled for cover, rattler mommies pushed their babies farther under the rocks. A huge sound resonated throughout the mountain. Down on the streets in town, people stopped to listen.

At the track the race went on, both horses and riders giving their all. The black came head to hip, then head to shoulder, head to neck, on they came. Both riders driving their mounts hard, leg to leg, then head to head.

The boy went to the whip, driving it hard into his horse's flank. The girl using her body and hands, in motion with the horse, screaming in his ear all the time, "GO- GO- GO." He responded with all he had, he gave a mighty surge. The finish loomed ahead, the black horse and girl a clear winner.

Both horses took awhile to slow to a stop, the red first, he turned back to the crowd. Rosa and the black stopped and turned back. Slowly they trotted to Sam and Manuel. A loud cheer came from the crowd for both riders and their steeds.

Her look told all. Sam told her, "You were just magnificent, I never doubted you for a minute."

Rosa collapsed off the horse into his arms, she was a spent little girl. Sam carried her to the wagon tail gate, gently set her down, praising her as he did. He returned to Bob, Dr. Fenn and the Senor.

"A very good race," the Senor said in Spanish. "We must match again soon."

Sam thanked everyone, he saw the French woman, standing in the carriage, smiling and she waved to him as he collected his winnings.

All the way home people waved and cheered. Rosa sat on the tail gate, proud, knowing she had made Sam happy.

At the house Sam carried Rosa in. Dolores asked, "Is she hurt?"

"No," Sam told her, "just one tired, spent little girl, a bath and food is all she needs."

He set her in a chair and returned to Manuel and the wagon. At the barn the horse got a bucket bath and a full bucket of oats, Sam gave Manuel one hundred dollars, shook his hand and thanked him for all his help.

All the time the races were going, Louise spent the afternoon with the professor and Christine. She confided in them, she had fallen in love with Sam. "What should I do?" She didn't know, her health was not good enough to be a good wife. "What should I do?" she asked again.

"Take life as it comes, if you love him, tell him, let him make the decision. Many people have your sickness and live full lives, don't be afraid to tell him. If he loves you what difference does it make? Tell him Louise." They both agreed she should.

They drove her home, supper was on the table. The talk was of nothing but the afternoon horse race. The evening was spent on the patio, Sam drinking coffee, smoking his pipe. Rosa told the race over and over. Dolores finally told her, "We all have heard, please talk of something else."

Rosa said, "I am so happy to have helped Sam, I don't want

to stop telling about it, but I will." She pulled a chair over next to Sam, Louise had been sitting on the other side of him. Sam told Rosa how much he appreciated her for what she had done and took her hand in his.

"I'm going to give you some of the winning money. You earned it."

He turned to Louise and asked about her day. She told him she had a lovely day talking to the professor and Christine.

"What about?" he asked.

"I'll tell you when we are alone."

He announced he was going to bed. The group broke up and they all said good night!

The sun was well over the back wall when Sam got up from a good nights sleep. A cool breeze came thru the big doors. He dressed, then hurried to the kitchen. Dolores had breakfast waiting. Louise was finishing hers.

"Another Monday," she said.

"Are you feeling alright?" asked Sam.

"Why do you ask?" She turned to face him. "Do I look that bad?"

"No, no. You look good to me, but your eyes are red."

"I didn't sleep very well last night, I rolled and tumbled all night."

Dolores asked, "Are you feeling sick?"

"Oh no, I just have a lot on my mind. It's all your fault Sam Duncan." Louise looked hard at Sam as she spoke.

Sam hardly knew what to say. "If I did anything to make you unhappy, tell me, I'll do my best to fix it." Sam was almost pleading.

"We will talk another time, I have to go to work now, people will be waiting."

She turned to leave, he took her by the arm saying. "Hold on I'll get my things and walk with you."

They took their time walking to the court house. At the office she reminded him of the letter telling him he must go to Tombstone. "I'll go get a ticket and go down in the morning, I'm looking forward to meeting some of the folks in Tombstone. Some of these men are real famous lawmen."

Sam seemed to her to be interested in the men in Tombstone. Louise told him she would send someone to get his ticket. "You must go see Sheriff Bell, he can tell you all about the people in Tombstone. You have several summons to serve, I have them ready for you." She handed him the papers.

"I'll get right to it." He left to do his work, he had to walk to serve the summons.

On the way he stopped to get a shave and jaw with the barber shop boys. He asked about the folks down in Tombstone, most had little to say. Bob told him to see Sheriff Bell. "He knows everyone there." Sam said he would take his advice.

He walked west on Congress St. As he approached the Saloon, Cowboys Hangout, Deputy Clint and two young men were struggling with a young Mexican girl on the board sidewalk, they had pulled her out of the swinging doors. Two of them had her by each arm. Clint was behind her and had his arms around her, he had her picked up, she was kicking, cussing and screaming at them in Spanish.

Sam hurried to confront the three men and asked, "What the hell's goin' on here?"

A few people had gathered to see what the commotion was about. A bystander told Sam, "This gal done nothing, these old boys just want to take her down to the jail so they can rape her, I done see'd them do it to gals before."

Sam in a loud voice told Clint to let her go, Clint and the two boys turned to face Sam. The three let her go, she dashed back in the saloon.

Facing Sam, Clint said, "You old bastard, you've interfered with me for the last time."

Sam could see he had a new colt 45 on his hip. "I've seen men like you before." Sam was visibly mad. "None of your kind is worth two dead flies. If you're gonna make a play, do it now." He held his right hand out just touching the Schofield with his fingers, ready to take it in hand.

One boy backed- off yelling, "I ain't armed." He faded into the crowd.

The other one had a pistol stuck in his belt, he put up his hands saying, "This ain't my fight Clint, leave me out." He backed into the crowd, turned and ran as fast as he could down the side walk.

Sam moved to within arm's length of Clint saying, "It's your play boy, do it now or hightail it."

He could see the fear in this boy's eyes. He had seen this many times in better men than Clint, he was giving him a way out.

Clint began to shake uncontrollably, Sam motioned with his hand to leave. Clint backed off, turned and sprinted west down the side walk. Someone in the crowd yelled, "You yellow coward, come back and fight."

Sam turned and with fire in his words spoke to the crowd, "Who said that?"

The big mouth was silent. Sam told them, "Go on about your business, there's noth-n here fer ya to see." He gave them a hard look, turned away and headed for Sheriff Bell's office.

At the Sheriff's office, Bell was sitting with his feet on a desk. "Come on in. How the hell are ya? Come set, let's talk, I ain't seen nobody all day."

Sam sat down and asked, "Tell me what you know about the folks in Tombstone, I have to go there on government business."

"I heard you did, you're a mighty brave man to go down there, the whole damn place is a firecracker. It's gonna blow any time, don't get in the middle. There's them Earps, they have a lot of friends on their side. Then there's them cowboys, they have a bunch on their side. Where the law is, I kin't tell ya. There's a few loose cannons who won't take sides with nobody. Sam, be careful, its gonna get hot down there, get in and out as fast as you can, that's my advice to you. I'll tell you who to see, John Clum. He has the newspaper, the Tombstone Epitaph. He knows everybody and everyone, he's the best man to see, I can telegraph him if you want, to let him know you're coming."

"That would be fine, I hoped you would do that for me." Sam was glad to have his help and thanked him. He asked about Deputy Clint, had he been there?

The sheriff told him, "Clint ain't been around all day." Bell asked why he was asking.

Sam told him he might have to get a new deputy. "This boy has had it, you'll hear soon enough." He thanked him for the information, he'd see him when he got back.

He walked on over to the Shu-Fly to get something to eat.

At the Shu-Fly Ben was there eating. "Come set with me," he called to Sam.

"Have you ever seen a happier man than me? I'm getting married the first of June, I'm so happy I can't hardly do my work."

Sam told him, "Ben, you take care of that girl, don't let no one stand in the way, I've never seen any one more in love than you two, God Bless you both, that's something I've never told anyone before." He admired Ben. Ben thanked him. They finished their meal and went on their different ways.

At the house Sam took a long nap. Got up just in time for supper. Spent the evening with Louise, Rosa, Dolores and

Hilda on the patio drinking coffee and smoking his pipe. He listened to the women talk about their day. Just after dark he said good night. Went to his room, packed a bag for the trip to Tombstone. He washed up and went to bed.

Chapter 15

Tombstone

Sam woke up early, washed, dressed and went down to the eating room. Louise was there in a beautiful pink dress, all dolled up.

"My, my," Sam said. "How can you look so good in the mornings?"

Dolores with a big smile said, "I think she does just for you Sam."

"I doubt that Dolores."

Louise said nothing, she finished eating, excused herself and left the room. Sam finished and told Dolores, "I've got to hurry, gonna catch the nine o'clock east bound to Benson."

He hurried to his room and returned fully dressed and carrying a carpet bag. "Tell Rosa I'll see her when I get back, I left some money on my dresser for her." He went out the front door.

There was Louise, with a bag, smiling saying, "I'm going with you, you may need me, okay Sam?"

Sam was delighted to have her come along, he took her bag and said, "I never will figure you out, that's what makes you so damn interesting." She just smiled.

On the train it was so crowded they had to sit apart. At Benson they took a stage to Tombstone, the stage was packed. Again they could do very little talking. Arriving in Tombstone,

John Clum was there to meet them. He introduced himself and seeing Louise said, "Didn't know you were bringing a lady friend, does she need a room too?"

"Yes," Sam said. "Can we get her one?"

"O yeah, Tombstone will never be the same with this beautiful lady here, she may need a bodyguard."

Sam put his arm around her and said, "That's my job." Louise gave a big smile.

"This fair lady is Judge Henrick's secretary, Miss Louise Talmidge. A New Yorker by birth, an Arizonan by choice. She's here to help me if needed. I'm told you're a news paper man."

Mr. Clum replied, "Not only a newsman, I'm the Post Master too. I have rooms for you at the Cosmopolitan Hotel just up the street. I know you would like to clean up after your trip. I would like to treat you two to dinner, if you like."

"Sounds good to us, you can give me some low down on these people live-n here."

"Come with me, I'll take you to the hotel." He told them on the way, with some pride. "We have the finest hotels and restaurants west of the Mississippi."

Entering the lobby, one could see it was indeed a beautiful place, thick flowered carpet covered the floor, plush settees and chairs were plentiful. The walls were covered with beautiful flowered paper and pictures of fancy ladies hung around the room. A man was lighting gas burner lights as it was getting dark. John Clum told them all the rooms, restaurants and stores have gas burners.

"The town has put in gas burners in the streets, it's very well lighted at night."

He turned them over to the desk man. They registered and went to their separate rooms. They cleaned up and both returned to the lobby at the same time. They sat in the lobby to wait for John Clum. Louise and Sam talked for a few minutes. She was asking Sam if he could fall in love again. Before he could answer, John came and took them into the Maison Doree restaurant. John said it was the best in all of Arizona. While waiting for their food, John started telling them about the people in town.

"The Earp brothers and Doc Holiday have had big trouble with some of the cowboy element, the people here began taking sides."

"Who are the cowboys?" Sam asked.

John named names. "Curly Bill Brouis, he seems to be the main trouble. Wyatt Earp and Curly Bill got into it right away, Bill was drunk and accidently killed Deputy City Marshal White. Wyatt laid a pistol barrel on Bill's head. He had to spend some time in the Tucson jail while the whole thing was sorted out. Bill didn't take kindly to getting his head busted, Bill is just a big old kid, wears two guns and can use either with both hands, he's a dead shot. He can be nice as hell and then mean as hell. He'll take no bullshit from anyone, excuse my French ma'am." He looked at Louise.

She frowned and shook her head.

He continued. "Then there's old man Clanton and his sons Ike and Billy, they're in strong with Frank and Tom McLawery. Those boys are mostly cow and horse thieves. John Ringo, Pete Spencer and his sidekick Frank Stillwell, all can handle a six-shooter. Joe Hill fits some where with all these people. Sheriff of Cochise County, John Behan and his deputy Bill Breakenridge try to stay out of the way. Seems they're on one side then the other, I never know which."

After finishing supper, Louise told them she was tired and wanted to go to bed. Both John and Sam excused her, she went up to her room. John and Sam decided to take a walk to observe Tombstone night life.

John told him, "Dance hall girls have come to Tombstone from every part of the country, just name it and there's one that's been there or comes from there. Girls of the night have flooded the market, I believe there must be several hundred, most of them work pretty cheap. Allen Street goes day and night, the saloons never close."

They walked the south side of Allen to the Birdcage Theater, crossed over, walked the north side, past the saloons and dance halls. Music and laughter drifted out thru the swinging doors. At one saloon a young woman came bursting out of the swinging doors, a cowboy hot on her heels. He caught her, picked her up and headed back into the saloon, all the time they were both laughing their heads off. The walks were so crowded with miners and cowboys, they had to push their way thru.

"This looks like Saturday night in Dodge City," Sam remarked.

They stopped at the Oriental Saloon and went inside and stepped to the bar. John talked in low tones. "See the man dealing Faro? That's Wyatt, he's a good gambler, he owns the table, all the Earps hang out here."

The bar keep came and asked what they would have? "Two beers."

John ordered for them, he went on, "See the man at the last table? That's Doc Holiday. The woman hanging on him is Mary Haroney, she's known as big nose Kate, some say he can't make a move without her, he has TB bad, he plays poker here every day and all night, day in and day out, nobody dares cross him. He don't give a damn if he lives or dies, is he on your list?" John asked.

"No the three Earps and Luke Short are the ones I have to choose from."

"Short's not here, the other Earps are probably in the back

room playing pool, do you want to meet them now?"

"Not tonight, I'm gonna turn in."

"Hells bells, they all know what you're here for, fact is the whole damn town knows, how they found out I can't tell you, I sure as hell told no one." John had apology in his voice.

"These things leak out, I don't give a shit how they know, I'll do my job and go on back to Tucson."

John and Sam walked to the hotel. Sam thanked him and bid him good night. Sam went up to his room to go to bed, his room was on the street side, it was a hot night, he had to raise the window. The noise was so bad it was impossible to sleep, he sat and watched the goings on and thought to himself, "glad I'm not the law in this town." Around midnight he lay down and fell asleep.

Sam opened his eyes, someone was knocking on his door.

"Who is it?" he hollered.

"Sam, it's Louise, you gonna sleep all day, it's nine o'clock, I've had breakfast. Are you awake?"

"Hold on Louise, let me put my pants on." He slipped out of bed and pulled his pants on and opened the door.

"Louise how can you look so good this morning. Come on in."

"O, no," she said. "I'll wait in the lobby, I've never watched a man dress, John is waiting in the lobby for you to come down. Hurry up!" She turned and went down the hall.

Sam was in the lobby in ten minutes. "Sorry to keep you two waiting, I really passed out this morning, I can't ever remember sleeping this late, must be getting old." Sam shook his head as he spoke.

John chimed in, "I just got here a few minutes ago, let's go get some breakfast, if this pretty lady will join us."

Louise excused herself, she wanted to do some shopping. "There are such beautiful things here, much more than in

Tucson, I just have to go look."

The two men went on to breakfast. Afterwards Sam told John he had to get a shave. They entered the hotel barber shop and both men had a morning shave.

After being shaved, John took Sam to meet the Sheriff of Cochise county, John Beham was at his office. Beham was very friendly, greeting Sam with, "I've been looking forward to meet-n you, I understand you'll be commissioning a new Deputy U.S. Marshal for this district and Tombstone, have you made a choice yet?"

"I haven't met any prospects yet, just got to town yesterday, it'll take some time, do you have any suggestions?"

He was goading Beham to see his reaction. Beham started giving a list of several plus himself. Sam put up his hands saying, "I have plenty of names, I just have to talk to them, I'd like to get this done today or tomorrow, thanks just the same."

Sam and John bid the sheriff good by and walked up Tuffnut street, on to third down to Allen street. On the way John asked why Marshal Drake hadn't come down from Prescott for this job. Sam told him he didn't know.

"Maybe he didn't want to come this far, it's a long trip from Prescott, I kinda wish he had, I don't like this kind of job and I don't get a dime to do it, trouble is it's hell if you do and hell if you don't." Sam talked like he could cash the whole damn thing and get on back to Tucson.

"I want to talk to you plain Sam, this Earp bunch really stick together, if one don't like you the whole bunch won't, but if they like you, they'll all back your play."

"I don't give a big rat's ass one way or the other, let's go meet these people, I'll do my best to keep you out of the mix."

Walking into the Oriental Saloon John and Sam approached Wyatt Earp. He stood drinking at the bar. He was talking with several other men. When he saw the two men he greeted them with, "Well if it ain't the man about town John Clum. Is this the Marshal we've been hearing about?" John shook his head yes.

"Meet Deputy U.S. Marshal Sam Duncan."

Sam sized Earp up, big man six feet tall with heavy dark hair and a heavy handle bar moustache, well built, can handle himself.

Earp put his hand out saying, "Glad to meet you Sam."

"Same here, I've been told you're a good law man."

"Have an eye opener," Earp said handing Sam a shot glass.

"No thanks, I'm not much of a drinker, I thank you kindly just the same."

"That's Okay," Earp said, "I'll have one for ya. Come set at my table, I want you to meet my brothers." He turned to the bartender and told him, "Go get Morg and Virg, bring Old Doc. too."

Earp made some small talk as they sat down. "See you carry a Scohfield, I've carried one for several years myself." He patted his coat pocket. "Had a special leather lined pocket in my coat made just for her, don't ever carry a holster."

Sam motioned with his hand to the pistol at his side, "She's never let me down."

Two men approached the table, Wyatt made the introductions. "This is my older brother, Virgil, one of the finest pistol shots you'll ever meet, an all round good guy. This other handsome devil is my brother Morgan, a real lady killer."

They all laughed at the remark. Virgil had the look of a gun man, Morgan looked like a lady killer should. Both men shook Sam's hand.

"Set boys, let's talk."

Anyone could see Wyatt was their leader. Only a few words were spoken when a tall thin man approached the table. Wyatt got to his feet and rushed to steady the man saying,

"This here man is my good buddy Doc Holiday, he always has too much to drink."

Sam could see this man had cold steel for eyes that looked right thru ya. Sam put out his hand, Holiday pulled his hand away saying, "I ain't meeting no son-of-a-bitch this morning, unless he wants to play poker."

Sam could see this man was drunk on his feet. Wyatt told Doc in a kind way for him to go on to bed as he had been up all night, drinking and playing poker. "Hell yes," Doc replied. "Where the hell is my old woman, I ain't seen her all night." He almost fell, Wyatt grabbed him and pushed him into a chair.

Wyatt reached in and pulled a pearl handled colt pistol from his shoulder holster saying, "You're too damn drunk to have this, some hick gonna shoot your ass off. Set there and wait for Kate to come get ya."

He motioned for the bartender to get going. Holiday slumped in the chair, dropped his head and fell fast asleep. Only a few words were said when a well dressed woman came thru the doors with the bartender. She was very attractive and went straight to Holiday. She shook him awake saying, "Come on Doc, let's get you to bed."

She looked to the men saying, "I don't know what to do for this man, he drinks way too much, I wish you could help him Wyatt."

"Hell Kate, he feels no pain when he's drinking, I can't stop him, wouldn't if I could, he's trying to get the most out of life, at least what he has left." Wyatt asked the bartender to help Kate take Doc to his room.

As they left, a tall well built man in a buckskin coat came thru the door and looked over at the men at the table. He went to the bar, pounding it with his fist, demanding whiskey. Wyatt told Sam in a low voice, "That's Buckskin Frank Leslie, he's one hell of a woman beater. I'm gonna clean his plow one of these days, just because he needs it."

The other men all agreed. Leslie downed his drink and left the saloon, adjusting his gun belt as he went, looking over his shoulder and smiling at the men at the table.

Wyatt suggested to Sam, "Why don't we all have supper at the hotel this evening? My woman'd like to meet ya, I understand you brought a fine look-n lady with you, I'd like to meet her too."

The other Earps shook their heads in agreement. "I'm sure all the girls would like to meet her."

Sam agreed to the dinner, John told them it was a good idea. He'd bring his wife and would arrange for a private room. All agreed to meet at seven this evening.

Sam and John bid them goodbye and walked to the hotel. They met Louise and had lunch, John went on to his office.

Louise wanted Sam to go shopping with her. He declined saying he didn't feel too good, he wanted to take a nap. He told her John had made a dinner date for them this evening at seven, with the Earps and their women. She went on to shop, he went to his room, lay down and napped.

Again Louise had to wake him. "It's six o'clock, if we're a-goin to meet these people at seven, you best hurry, I'll wait in my room."

In a few minutes Sam was knocking on her door. She opened it, told him he could come in. He took her in his arms and kissed her on the lips hard, she pulled away saying, "You're messing my hair and make up."

He pulled her back again and kissed her even harder. Letting her go, he said to her, "You're the best look-n woman in all of Tombstone, I ain't seen none better."

She pulled away and said he was just a flatterer.

"Well I haven't seen any better, that's the honest truth."

"Let's go eat," She said. "Kiss me again Sam, I like it." He did and they went on down to the Café.

Waiting there was the Earp brothers and their women. John Clum and his wife came in behind Sam and Louise. The room was well lighted and the table set and ready for the meal, Doc Holiday and his Kate were the last to enter, John sat at the head of the table with the Earps and their women to his right, his wife, Sam and Louise to his left, with Doc and Kate on down the table. Doc looked as if he had just got out of bed. Kate was pampering him like a small child. He kept telling her to let him be, he slumped in his chair, pulled a pint out and took a big swig. Wyatt sitting across from Sam told Doc to try to make this a nice party, Doc never said a word.

The conversation turned to questioning Sam about his commission, had he made a choice for the Deputy. He shook his head, no and he asked Wyatt if he was going to run for the county sheriff's office. Wyatt with his elbows on the table, hands under his chin looked straight at Sam and in a demanding voice asked, "Where did you hear that from? Who started that rumor?"

"We visited Sheriff Behan and he hinted the same."

"I got no intention to run for sheriff." He asked Sam how he became a U.S. Marshal.

Sam told them all he had been a deputy at Ft. Smith and had been recommended by some people he had met and worked for.

Doc in a loud voice said, "Tell us who these top people are who made you a Marshal."

Sam with his hands and arms folded on the table, looked down at Doc and said, "President Cleveland, General Grant, the commander of the Texas Rangers and a few others."

Doc dropped his head, slumped back in his chair and didn't say anything else.

John Clum took over the conversation. Talking mostly to the ladies, about their times in Tombstone and if they liked the town.

The meal was served, it was roast beef, chicken, fish, gravy, steamed vegetables, hot baked bread and hot apple pie for dessert. As they were finishing the pie, Sheriff Behan came in with a very attractive lady on his arm. He introduced her as Josephine Marcus. Not one in the Earp party turned toward them except Wyatt. He rose and said, "We don't need the sheriff of Cochise at this party!"

"No offense intended, just wanted to tell you Johnny Ringo is in town, he's looking pretty mean. He's drinking and talking about gun play, I'll say no more."

He turned and pulled the lady with him. She smiled at Wyatt and gave him a come hither look. He smiled back and shook his head yes. Sam caught the looks that went between the two of them.

The party broke up about ten pm. They all said good night and left the dining room.

Sam told Louise on the way to their rooms, "There's trouble brewing in this town and it ain't cowboys doing the brewing."

Louise said, "I'm not follow-n you, Sam, what are you talk-n about?"

"Looks to me as if Wyatt has something goin with the sheriff's lady friend."

"Oh, I think you're just looking for trouble." Louise seemed perplexed at Sam's words.

He told her, "We're leave-n in the morning, the stage leaves for Bisbee at eight, be ready, it's time for us to leave." He couldn't have made it more plain.

"I have something to ask you, I'll get to it on the stage."

He escorted her to her room, at her door he pulled her close and kissed her hard on the lips. He opened the door and said, "Good night my beautiful, lovely lady." He turned and hurried away.

Next morning Sam was up early and headed to the Earp boy's saloon, where he found Wyatt, Virgil and Morgan. Sam asked Virgil to come with him. In a small room off the bar, Sam asked if he would be a Deputy Marshal. Virgil was agreeable and Sam swore in the new Marshal, Virgil Earp. Sam pinned the badge on his vest and handed him his signed commission papers. They returned to the main bar, seeing the badge, there were hurrahs all over the place. Sam shook hands with the Earps and said, "Nice to meet you boys."

He hurried back to the hotel. John Clum was waiting in the lobby.

"Got it done Sam?" he asked.

"Yep! The new Deputy is Virgil Earp."

John told him it was as good a choice as he could make. Sam told John how much he and Louise appreciated his friendship and help. "When you come to Tucson be sure to look us up. You would be more than welcome. We're take-n the stage to Bisbee this morn-n, I just have to see the town for myself."

Louise was in the lobby with their bags. She had sent a boy to fetch John to tell him they were leaving. John said he would see them both soon. "I have enjoyed meet-n you both, I love good looking women." He smiled at Louise as he spoke.

The stage clattered to a halt outside the hotel. Sam and Louise bid John goodbye and seated themselves inside. The stage pulled out for Bisbee, with two other passengers, on their way from Tombstone to Bisbee in the Arizona Territory.

Chapter 16

Louise-Rosa-Sam

As the stage rumbled down the hill toward the San Pedro River, Sam pulled Louise close and whispered in her ear, "I'm glad to leave that town, never have I felt like an explosion was about to happen as I did in that town. Mark my word there's gonna be lots of trouble in a short time."

Louise replied, "I didn't feel it at all, I liked all those people."

"Couldn't you feel the tension in the air at supper last night, when the Sheriff came in?"

"No Sam, I think you are just looking for trouble. Let's drop the whole thing, I thought you had something to ask me?"

"I will ask when we're alone."

Sam nodded to the other people. "Okay we'll talk some other time."

The older man passenger spoke at this time. "My name is Ezek Bronski, from St Louis, I sell hardware." He was distinguished looking, a short gent with a long grey beard wearing a black derby.

Sam told him, "I know the town well, I spent a few years there."

The lady spoke up and said, "I'm on my way to marry an old beau, I haven't seen him in ten years, he lives in Bisbee."

Louise said, "That's wonderful, you have got to tell us

about it. It's a great story don't you think so Sam?"

"You bet I just can't wait." Sam winked at the man.

Louise said, "Tell us please."

"Well," said the lady, "My name is Lois Applegate, I'm from Pennsylvania. My man is Douglas Walker. He's a mining engineer. He came west to find his fortune. He wrote and said he has and sent for me. It's been ten years since I've seen him. In just a few hours we will be together again."

Louise said, "How great it will be for you to see him again."

Louise then motioned for the man to move so she could sit next to Lois. He moved to the seat by Sam. He pulled a pint from his pocket and offered a sip to Sam, Sam shook his head no. The man took a swig and lay back and went to sleep. Sam did the same.

In a few hours the stage stopped at the Hereford way station to change horses and let the passengers stretch and get a quick meal. The people there had a lunch of frijoles, dried meat, a flour tortilla and coffee for the passengers.

Back on the road everyone tried to sleep. After the meal and the rocking of the coach, it was hard not to. When Sam woke Louise had her head on his chest. He asked if she was awake. She shook her head yes and said, "Un huh."

Sam said in a low voice, "How about you and me get-n hitched in Bisbee?"

She sat up, looked Sam in the eye and with eyes tearing up, "I never thought you were gonna ask. I was about to ask the same thing. Sam, you know I'm not real well. If you really want me, I'm ready."

Sam told her he didn't see any thing wrong with her. "Louise, I love you and I'll take you just as you are, okay?"

Louise asked, "When are we going to do it?"

"As soon as we get to Bisbee."

"Fine with me."

Louise pulled Sam to her and kissed him over and over, tears ran freely down her cheeks.

Sam said, "Give me some air lady, save some for later."

When the stage pulled into Bisbee, darkness was falling in the Copper Canyon. The stage stopped in front of the Copper Queen Hotel. The passengers asked the clerk for a room. The other two got a key and went to their rooms. Sam asked if the clerk knew where they could get a parson as he and his lady wanted to get married. The clerk said a church was just up the canyon.

"I'll send a boy to see if the preacher would do the job this time of day."

Sam signed in for a room, the boy returned and told them the preacher was waiting. Sam and Louise walked up the hill and entered the church. The minster, a Mr. John Babbitt introduced himself and his wife. He said they must wait as another witness must be there. A lady friend was on her way. He then told them they must have an Arizona marriage license. Louise opened her hand bag and handed him a paper.

"This will do fine," the preacher said.

Sam took the paper and read it. Both their names were written on the license. "When did you do this?"

"The day before we came down here, I hoped it would be needed," Louise said with a big smile on her face. Sam shook his head and laughed.

"Louise you are full of surprises, that's why I love you, on top of being so pretty."

In the next few minutes they became man and wife. Sam gave the minster a twenty dollar gold piece, thanked them all, the newlyweds walked down the hill to the hotel.

The manager greeted them as "Marshal and Mrs. Duncan."

"We have a supper ready for you in our dining room, I have

changed your room to our very best in this hotel, follow me to the dining room."

The manager led them to a candle lit table. A supper of baked ham and turkey with all the trimmings waited their pleasure. Louise was delighted. A fine red California wine was served. Sam said he had never had such treatment before. The manager asked if they had any thing else they would wish. Louise asked if she could have a bath. The manager told them he would have two hot tubs in their room by the time they were finished. He left to see to the job.

Sam and Louise were alone at last. Louise told Sam she had never been with a man before, would he be patient with her?

"When two people love each other the loving comes easy," Sam told her. "No reason to be worried."

After the meal they were shown to their rooms. Two steaming hot tubs of water waited with soap and bath towels. Sam being very playful said to her, "Last one in's a piker."

After their baths, Sam stood with a towel wrapped around him as did Louise, the night passed in pure wedded bliss.

Next morning, they had breakfast in their room. The couple stayed in Bisbee for several more days taking in the sights around this mining town.

They had to take the stage to the rail road town of Wilcox to get the train to Tucson. The stage traveled up the Sulphur Springs Valley to the mining town of Pearce for an overnight stay. Arriving in Wilcox late the next day they stayed in a hotel near the tracks. Louise sent Dolores a telegraph to tell everyone she and Sam had gotten married.

They caught the early morning train to Tucson. On arrival in the Old Pueblo a crowd of well wishers awaited them. A celebration had been planned at the Martinez house. All their friends were there except Rosa. Sam missed her at once and asked Dolores where she was.

"When we got Louise's telegraph she decided to go to Mexico City and visit my brother and his family. She left on the early morning stage for Nogales. Sam, that girl loves you! She told me to tell you and Louise she was happy for the two of you. I think her heart is broken, she cried all last night."

"Dolores, I never encouraged her in any way. I love her as a father or brother would, I'll always love her." He wiped a tear away as he spoke. "I hope she can find a man she can love, she'll be a wonderful wife to some lucky man."

Dolores thanked him and said, "I miss her already." She started to cry. "Sam, that girl has a mind of her own, she'll never find a man like you, I'm afraid she'll never marry."

Sam tried to console her. "I'm sure she will, she's so young, she has her whole life ahead of her."

The fall of 1880 came to the Old Pueblo cold and rainy. The judge returned from San Diego. He and Sam became good friends. The Mexican cowboy was found innocent. Ben Got married and later he became the bank manger and owner.

Sam and Louise lived at the Martinez house for two more years. They purchased a ranch type home on the north side of town. It had a stable and a patio. Louise loved the house, it was much like the Martinez house.

Sam was becoming more discontented as time grew on. Louise could see it. She knew he had something on his mind as he seemed preoccupied when they were together. She confronted him and asked, "What's up Sam? You're not very talkative this morning, some thing wrong? What's on your mind?"

Sam answered, "I'm tired of law work, I'm fifty three and not as good as I should be, when you get a step slow you should hang it up and quit, don't you think?"

"What do you want to do if you stop being a Marshal?"

Louise tried to be understanding.

"Let's take a ride Sunday afternoon, I'll show you what I want to do." Sam watched her intently to see her reaction to his suggestion. She was more than ready to go.

"I know what you're up to," She mused.

Sunday afternoon found them in their buggy and on the road west along the Santa Cruz River. Several miles out of town, they turned and drove onto a road a mile north, a small adobe ranch house loomed before them in a patch of mesquite trees. An older man came out to greet them. Sam introduced him to Louise.

"This is Clyde Reed, he wants to sell this place and move to town. Says he's get-n too old to chase cows. I offered him a thousand dollars for this place, he's gonna give us an answer today."

"Sam, I have to have more than that." Clyde watched to see how they were gonna take his answer.

Before Sam could reply, Louise spoke, "What's your price? If Sam wants it we will pay any thing you want."

Clyde smiled and said, "Could you make it fifteen hundred?"

Louise spoke right up, "Let's make it two thousand, okay with you Clyde?"

Clyde nodded yes as he shook both their hands and said he would sell his cattle the coming week and Sam could have the place after that.

Back on the river road, Sam stopped the buggy and walked over to look in the river. Louise followed pulling her skirt up to walk thru the weeds. "What's the matter Sam?"

Sam turned to her with tears in his eyes and told her he was a lucky man to have married a lady like her. He took her in his arms, hugged her so hard she cried, "Don't break my ribs. Why didn't you tell me long ago what you wanted? We have money to buy any thing you want"

Sam kissed her lips and repeated how lucky he was to have married her.

In the following weeks Sam resigned his marshal job and Louise quit hers. The judge was understanding. The little ranch was pretty run down. Sam spent a lot of time there building new pens and a new barn of adobe. With Manuel's help he purchased a few mares and turned the black stallion out with the mares, he had his horse ranch up and going.

On a trip to Sonora, Mexico, Manuel and Sam found a rancher with many good mares who wanted to sell, he purchased thirty on this trip. They herded the horses up the trail toward the states. It was getting toward dark. Manuel was in the lead, Sam was bringing up the drag. Mesquite trees closed in the trail ahead. Sam heard a loud Mexican voice, demanding them, "ALTO." Sam rode the left side of the herd and stopped a few feet from a Mexican horseman blocking their way, another Mexican with a large sombrero, a Winchester across his saddle, blocked Manuel's way. Sam asked what they wanted.

Manuel told him, "They want five horses to let us pass."

"The hell they do!"

Sam spurred his mount into the horse and rider to his front knocking them down. At the same time he shot the Mexican to his right with the Schofield, the bullet hit him square in the chest, he was dead before he hit the ground, the other rider was scurrying away into the mesquite thicket, Sam threw a shot after him, the bandit's horse went down and struggled to get up, a broken front leg stopped him. Sam ended his pain with one shot from the Schofield.

He yelled to Manuel, "MOVE-EM OUT!"

Up the trail they went at a lope. In a few hours they crossed into Arizona. On to Pete Kitchen's ranch and into a corral. Pete had his boys feed the herd and invited the two horsemen inside to eat. The kitchen was warm and friendly, Pete's woman had a big meal of beans, meat, flour tortillas and coffee.

After the meal the men sat before the fire place and talked. Manuel told Pete of the trouble they had on the trail. Pete said this had been going on for some time.

"These men are banditos who rob anyone on the trail, the Federales have been trying to get them for some time with no luck."

"Who are they?" asked Sam.

"They're led by a man whose name is Pancho Villa, he's a real big man among the people. If you go again, ask the feds for help, they'll sent a troop with you."

Sam and Manuel got the herd to his little ranch two days later. They did return to Sonora several times the coming year. Sam took Pete's advice and asked for help, but he had to pay for it in cold hard cash.

The ranch started to pay well and Sam stayed there a lot of the time. He was building a new house for Louise and himself. It was in the fall when a rider on a well lathered horse rode in telling him that he was needed at home. He saddled and rode hard for home.

He put the horse in the stable and entered the house. Dolores and their house keeper Maria were waiting. Dolores told him Louise was sick and in bed. "It don't look good Sam," she said. "Doc Fenn is in the room with her, you better go in."

Louise smiled a weak smile as Sam came to her bed side.

"Here girl we can't have you sick."

"Come close, I must tell you what I want. I'm so tired, I want you to promise me something I want you to do for me if I die."

The tears swelled up in her eyes as she spoke. He kneeled by her bed.

"No!" Sam almost yelled as he spoke. "You can't leave me now, I won't let you go."

She in her usual quiet way, pushed his hair back. "Sam if I go, I want you to take me home and put me beside my mother and father. Promise me, Sam, promise you will Sam."

"I'll do any thing you want Louise."

She told him she wanted to sleep and closed her eyes.

Doc Fenn and Sam went into the living room. There the Doctor told him Louise's heart was failing. "It's very weak and you must be ready when she goes, it won't be long."

Sam told him, "It must be my fault she's so weak."

"No," the Doctor said. "She's been fail-n a long time, I told you when you married her she won't have a long life. Remember what I said? You made her happy. She's had a good time of it with you, so face up to it and be gentle with her now." He could see Sam was in pain. He said goodbye and told Dolores to watch Sam, as he was not taking this very well. She said she would. She told Sam she would go sit with Louise.

"Go on to bed," she urged him. "There's nothing you can do now."

Sam built a fire in the fire place, walked the floor, went out and talked to the horses and asked God to help Louise. He made a pot of coffee and smoked his pipe. Maria came and sat with him awhile, then he lay down and fell asleep.

Just after midnight the Angels came for Louise. Sam was asleep on the couch in the living room. Dolores sent Maria for Manuel.

"Tell him to bring some strong boys." She didn't know how Sam was going to be after learning of her passing. They came just at sun up.

Dolores woke Sam and told him. He went into her room and locked the door. Manuel tried to talk him out to no avail. Dolores had them break in, Sam was in the process of cutting his arms as the Indians do on the death of someone you love. Manuel and the boys overpowered him and tied him to his rocker. Doctor Fenn had come by then and gave Sam something to make him sleep, he slept all day and all night. When he was awake the doctor talked to him almost all day, along with Dolores. A service would be held the next day at her church, would he go?

"No! I'll never enter a church again, never again," Sam said loud and clear.

Dolores scolded him badly as did Doc Fenn. Doc Fenn reminded him he had made a promise to Louise. He told him he was having a box made for her coffin for the shipping, was he going to take her home? Sam said he would.

The judge came to talk to Sam, as Louise had instructed him.

"You're a wealthy man Sam," he said. "Louise made a will before she quit her job. Her father gave his daughters an endowment of several thousand dollars a year. She had quite a bit of cash, all was given to you, here's a letter she left for you."

Sam opened and read it, it told how much she had loved him and how she had enjoyed her time with him. At that Sam wept unashamed.

Sam and Louise caught the evening train east two days later. Sam rode the baggage cars all the way to Albany New York, at each change, Sam was there to see she was handled easy and with care. The station people could see not to anger this man, he was firm but gentle. He had strength in his words.

"This is my sweetheart handle her with care," he told them and they did.

As they set the box off at her home station, a light snow was falling. Sam asked to have her put inside the station, the men refused saying, "We don't put coffins in our station."

Sam opened his coat exposing the Schofield, he fingered it with his right hand. "You will this day," he told them. Sam meant business, the men got the idea in a hurry and started to move her into the station.

Two women came up the platform and introduced themselves, they were Louise's sisters, they would take charge now.

"Come stay at our house." A service would be held for Louise the next day.

The church was full and people stood out in the snow, as did Sam. The preacher told of Louise's child hood and how kind and gentle she was, how little children always loved her, how the whole community missed her when she had to go to Arizona and all the great things she had done for this community.

She was laid to rest next to her Mother and Father as requested. The sisters wanted Sam to stay awhile. They told him he was part of their family, Louise had written so much about him. He told them he had to go home, he couldn't be away any longer.

The trip took five long days on the train. He spoke to people only when he was spoken to. When he got back to Arizona he sold the house in town. The ranch house was finished enough that he could live in it.

He sat on the porch and rocked the days away smoking a pipe and gazing into space. Manuel came and tried several times to talk to him, he just rocked and mumbled and looked away. People who saw him began to say he had lost his mind, Sam Duncan has gone crazy they said.

He had two Mexican cowboys working the horse ranch. Sam paid little mind of the goings on around him. None of his friends or neighbors came to see him. There was more talk of him losing his mind. Dolores had heard of the talk about Sam, talk she couldn't understand about her friend.

She decided to pay him a visit, Manuel drove her out to the ranch on a Sunday afternoon. As they approached the house she could see him sitting on the porch in his rocker. When she got out of the buggy, she lit into him and left nothing unsaid, she jumped on him with all the power of the words she commanded.

"What kind of man are you?" He could see she was boiling mad. "You think you're the only man who has lost some one you love? You look like some kind of a tired old man sitting here and looking crazy, get off your dead butt and do something." She had no mercy. "The world don't stop for you or any one, we all lose some one we love."

She shook his shoulders and took him by the arm she forced him to stand.

"Come out in the yard," she demanded. "Come with me."

Sam slowly followed her into the yard. "Look," she said, "look at those mountains." She was pointing to the majestic Catalinas. "The Papago Indians tell that a God lives up there on that mountain, take yourself, go up there and try to make peace with your maker, or so help me I may do something I will be sorry for."

He was looking at her wide eyed. He could see this woman he so admired was mad as hell at him. Of all the people in the world, he wanted her to like and respect him. Tears started to run down his face. She put her arms around him and hugged him. She was sobbing as she told him he was loved.

"Don't give up, Sam. Please don't give up, you're too good to give in like this for me, for all of us, don't give up, please do as I ask."

"I will, I'll go to the mountain, I'll go tomorrow."

The next morning he took a saddle and a pack horse. He rode high into the mountain, in the pines he found a cool mountain spring and made camp nearby. It was quiet and peaceful, only the sounds of the birds and the whistling of the wind thru the trees could be heard. Not far from camp he could walk to a large rock. He would sit and look into the valley below. He had to cook his meals and take care of the horses, that way his mind stayed somewhat busy. He spent many hours sitting on the rock and watching the clouds pass thru the sky, he would set and watch the colorful sun sets, reminded him of being with Louise.

At last he began to feel a little better. "Maybe there's a meaning to my life yet." He began to think what a lucky man he had been to have had Fawn and Louise for his wives.

One sunny, cloudless afternoon a bald eagle began to circle in the clear blue sky above him, he could not keep his eyes off the bird. The eagle circled lower and lower and landed on a dead tree branch near him. The bird's piercing eyes stared into his. "Are you a God? Were you sent by God?"

The eagle ruffled his feathers and pushed his wings forward. Sam in a begging voice asked, "Give me a sign, tell me what I should do."

The Eagle with all his power lifted his wings and raised himself into the air, almost hanging stationary for a minute, the bird slowly turned and glided away disappearing into the valley below.

Sam said to himself, "If I were an Indian, I would have my sign, I now know I have been wrong about God all along, I'll try to be better, I will be different." He made a promise to God.

That night he rested and had the best sleep he could remember, no dreams, no nightmares.

The sun was high in the sky when he rose and started a fire to make coffee and breakfast. He heard the sounds of a horse coming his way in the distance. His horses had their ears pricked and pointed in that direction and made a muffled whiney. He tried to quiet them, he grabbed his Winchester rifle and kneeled behind a pine tree, his attention was fully on the horse moving toward him.

"Maybe it's the Apache kid," he thought. "He's been known to have been in these mountains."

He levered a round into the chamber and waited. Soon the horse and rider came into view, the rider was a woman with long black shiny hair. Sam rubbed his eyes in disbelief, as he stepped from his hiding place he called, "Is that you Rosa?" He didn't have to call a second time.

She spurred her mount to him and flew off and almost knocked him down, she had her arms around him crying. "I knew I could find you."

Sam stood there stunned. "Why have you come up here, Rosa?"

"Momma said I should come for you and tell you how much I care, can't you understand how I feel, Sam?" Tears were streaming down her beautiful face. "I love you Sam, I have since the first day you came to our house, I will always love you." She was begging now. "Can't you love me just a little?"

Sam was trying to push her away. "Rosa I'm fifty-five, way too old for a young girl like you, you should love a young man." Sam was doing his best to reject her. "What does your Momma say about this feeling of yours?"

"I'm twenty now and I know what I want and need, Momma said I should tell you, she says if I want you it's fine with her, If you don't want me, say so now, I'll leave and never bother you again."

Sam was overwhelmed. He dropped to the ground on his knees his hands covering his face so she couldn't see his tears. "I have to be the luckiest man on the face of this earth to have three wonderful women love me, God is surely in this mountain, I can't turn you away."

Sam and Rosa spent the rest of that day and all night talking. She told him of her time in Mexico. What a beautiful country it is and how much she liked Mexico City. She had many suitors, some were very rich and handsome. She always measured them to him, none could take him from her mind. She had met Benito Juarez, the president and said how he had made the country better since the French Emperor Maximilian had been shot. "You would like it there, we must go sometime."

Sam and Rosa returned to Tucson and with Dolores's blessing they were married within a week. A big celebration was held at the Martinez house on Meyer Street.

The ranch house was finished, many rooms were added thru the years. Rosa gave Sam a child every year for the next seven, five boys and two girls.

A happy and contented family lived on the horse ranch. Their horses were prized by all who knew of them and sold as soon as they were old enough.

It was early on a spring morning, Rosa and two of the younger children had gone to visit her mother in town. Sam decided to take a ride and saddled a young green horse, he rode the river road west. An hour or so later the horse returned to the barn with an empty saddle. Two of his cowboys rode to look for him. They found him laying just off the road, they could see the horse had spooked and thrown him, the fall had broken his neck, he had died instantly. They took him home and one rode to tell Rosa and the children.

Rosa told everyone that Sam had always said he wanted to die with his boots on.

A well attended service was held were he was placed to rest under the shade trees in a cemetery just off Oracle road. After the funeral Rosa told a small gathering, "Sam is happy, now he was with his Fawn and Louise and some day I will join them in paradise."

From this union of Rosa and Sam came many solid American citizens, men and women who served God and country well.

The year Sam died the Arizona Territory became the 48th State in the Union of United States of America. It was the year 1912. Sam would have been 83 come December.

Rosa Duncan lived to be one hundred and one year's old. She lost two sons in the war to end all wars. She lost a Grandson in the Marine Corps fighting in the South Pacific, two other Grandsons and a Granddaughter were laid to rest in France serving their country during the second world war.

About the Author

Francis M. {Frank} Worden was born in Oklahoma in 1930. He migrated to Tucson, Arizona, as a youngster with his family for the health of his mother.

Growing up he became an avid student of the history of Arizona and America, especially the Civil War and the Western movement.

He served seventeen and a half years in the National Guard of Arizona and Army Reserve, honorably discharged as a Captain.

Frank has a deep admiration and love for his ancestors and the people who through courage, resourcefulness and hard work settled and developed this great nation.

He lives in Tucson with his wife Beverly, is the father of five sons, a daughter, twelve grandchildren, and two great-grandchildren.

He owns a small business, race horses, is an outdoors-man and gun collector.